Highlander Spurned

Rebellious Highland Hearts
Book Three

JAYNE CASTEL

Highlander Spurned, by Jayne Castel

Published by Winter Mist Press

ISBN: 978-1-7385901-8-6

Edited by Tim Burton
Cover design by Winter Mist Press
Cover photography images courtesy of www.shutterstock.com and www.depositphotos.com
Rose image generated by MidJourney

Visit Jayne's website: www.jaynecastel.com

Pride keeps them apart, yet fate brings them together. A farmer's daughter struggling to save her family from destitution spurns the man she blames for all her problems—but when her life crumbles around her, she must turn to *him* for help.

Kerr Mackay burns for the one woman he cannot have. He leads his brother's guard and is dedicated to keeping order and peace, but not everyone appreciates his efforts. The daughter of a local farmer who's caused Kerr no end of trouble blames him for her family's ruin.

She spurned his advances once—pride prevents him from ever trying again.

Thanks to the Mackays, Rose MacAlister's father is now a cripple, and her family is struggling to make ends meet. Fighting to keep the bailiff from seizing their land, she rages against the injustice of it all.

However, when tragedy strikes, Rose finds herself an outcast, persecuted by those she once trusted.

And the only person who can help her is the man she'd sworn to hate forever.

Rebellious Highland Hearts is a four-book series following Iver Mackay of Dun Ugadale and his three brothers—Lennox, Kerr, and Brodie—as they meet women who will change their lives forever.

Historical Romances by Jayne Castel

DARK AGES BRITAIN

The Kingdom of the East Angles series
Night Shadows (prequel novella)
Dark Under the Cover of Night (Book One)
Nightfall till Daybreak (Book Two)
The Deepening Night (Book Three)
The Kingdom of the East Angles: The Complete Series

The Kingdom of Mercia series
The Breaking Dawn (Book One)
Darkest before Dawn (Book Two)
Dawn of Wolves (Book Three)
The Kingdom of Mercia: The Complete Series

The Kingdom of Northumbria series
The Whispering Wind (Book One)
Wind Song (Book Two)
Lord of the North Wind (Book Three)
The Kingdom of Northumbria: The Complete Series

DARK AGES SCOTLAND

The Warrior Brothers of Skye series
Blood Feud (Book One)
Barbarian Slave (Book Two)
Battle Eagle (Book Three)
The Warrior Brothers of Skye: The Complete Series

The Pict Wars series
Warrior's Heart (Book One)
Warrior's Secret (Book Two)
Warrior's Wrath (Book Three)
The Pict Wars: The Complete Series

On the Empire's Edge Duology
Taming the Eagle
Ensnaring the Dove

Novellas
Winter's Promise

MEDIEVAL SCOTLAND

The Brides of Skye series
The Beast's Bride (Book One)
The Outlaw's Bride (Book Two)
The Rogue's Bride (Book Three)
The Brides of Skye: The Complete Series

The Sisters of Kilbride series
Unforgotten (Book One)
Awoken (Book Two)
Fallen (Book Three)
Claimed (Epilogue novella)
The Sisters of Kilbride: The Complete Series

The Immortal Highland Centurions series
Maximus (Book One)
Cassian (Book Two)
Draco (Book Three)
The Laird's Return (Epilogue festive novella)
The Immortal Highland Centurions: The Complete Series

Guardians of Alba series
Nessa's Seduction (Book One)
Fyfa's Sacrifice (Book Two)
Breanna's Surrender (Book Three)
Guardians of Alba: The Complete Series

Stolen Highland Hearts series
Highlander Deceived (Book One)
Highlander Entangled (Book Two)
Highlander Forbidden (Book Three)

Highlander Pledged (Book Four)

Courageous Highland Hearts series
Highlander Defied (Book One)
Highlander Tempted (Book Two)
Highlander Healed (Book Three)
Highlander Sworn (Book Four)

Rebellious Highland Hearts series
Highlander Seduced (Book One)
Highlander Honored (Book Two)
Highlander Spurned (Book Three)

Epic Romantic Fantasy by Jayne Castel

Light and Darkness series
Ruled by Shadows (Book One)
The Lost Swallow (Book Two)
Path of the Dark (Book Three)
Light and Darkness: The Complete Series

***

To Kathy T, for giving me inspiration for Hazel the eagle
owl!

***

"Nobody has ever measured, even poets, how much a heart can hold."
—**Zelda Fitzgerald**

1: IT HAS TO BE NOW

Dun Ugadale,
Kintyre Peninsula, Scotland

Samhuinn—October 31, 1453

HE COULDN'T TAKE his eyes off her.

The saints be damned, he tried. He'd told himself he would eat, drink, and dance around the Samhuinn bonfire like everyone else. He wouldn't look for her, wouldn't wrestle with his desire to talk to her. Instead, he'd pretend she didn't exist.

But as soon as he climbed the hill a few furlongs from his brother's broch, Kerr's gaze had searched for Rose MacAlister, and then, when it had seized upon her, there was no letting go.

She walked through the crowd, a basket of soul cakes in her arms, bestowing delicious treats baked with honey and currants on the revelers. Dressed as one of the Sidhe this eve, a fae maid with pointed ears and ivy wreathed through her hair, Rose was even lovelier than usual.

Kerr took every detail in. The way her kirtle hugged the lush curves of that strong, magnificent body as she moved, the bloom to her soft cheeks, and the gleam of her long walnut tresses in the glow of the fire. He noted the way her pine-green eyes gleamed with good humor as she bestowed smiles too, on the elderly folk and bairns.

But she had no smile for him. No warmth.

Earlier, when she'd brought her basket before his family, her expression had cooled. She wasn't fond of the Mackays, that much was evident. After all, the laird had struck off her father's hand in the summer, after Graham MacAlister had been caught thieving cattle—yet again.

Aye, she disliked Iver for the punishment he'd dealt her father, yet she'd kept her ire in check as the chieftain helped himself to a soul cake. He was her laird, after all.

Nonetheless, she didn't bother hiding her disdain for Kerr. After his brothers had taken cakes, Kerr had reached out to help himself, but Rose deliberately turned away and walked off.

His cheeks still burned from the humiliation of it.

Standing on the edge of the revelry, he downed his second cup of wassail and gathered his courage.

He was done yearning for this woman. He needed to stop staring at Rose like some love-struck fool and approach her.

The air needed to be cleared between them—this evening.

Rose had just emptied her basket of cakes and was standing alone for the moment, hands wrapped around a cup of mulled cider, as she watched the dancing flames of the bonfire.

Kerr's stomach clenched.

It has to be now.

Casting his own empty cup aside, he strode through the crowd, past where Iver and his wife, Bonnie, were laughing together, and past where his brother Lennox was locked in a passionate embrace with his wife, Davina. A few yards away, the youngest of his brothers, Brodie, was watching the dancing around the fire, his face shrouded by a ram's skull. The guise was unnerving, and the black cloak that hung from his shoulders made his brother look like one of Lucifer's messengers.

A couple of lasses nearby were whispering together and darting Brodie flirtatious glances. Clearly, his grim guise didn't put either of them off. Brodie never seemed to make any effort to attract women, yet they clustered around him nonetheless, like wasps to honey.

But Kerr's attention didn't remain on any of his three brothers. Instead, it fixed upon the comely woman standing just a few feet away.

She hadn't seen his approach, and he needed to reach her side before she did.

"Rose."

A man's voice roused Rose from her introspection.

After emptying her basket of cakes, she was enjoying watching the flames and listening to the laughter of revelers holding hands as they danced around the fire. However, someone had just intruded upon her peace.

Turning, her gaze alighted upon a tall man clad in close-fitting seal-skin breeches and vest, a cloak of the same material hanging from his shoulders.

Kerr Mackay, Captain of the Dun Ugadale Guard, had dressed as a selkie for Samhuinn this year.

And although she couldn't stand the man—the sight of him made her stomach curdle—she had to admit the guise was a striking one that highlighted his tall, muscular body and proud bone structure. Piercing blue eyes settled upon her, and the firelight shone on pale-blond hair that fell in shaggy waves around his face, brushing his shoulders.

Rose took a smart step backward, her heart lurching into her throat. What the devil was Captain Mackay doing approaching her? He knew she despised him.

But before she could flee, he moved closer, a hand closing over her forearm. His grip was gentle, yet firm, and for a moment she stilled, shocked that he'd dare touch her.

"Please, Rose," he said, his voice roughening. "I must speak to ye."

Her gaze narrowed. "I have nothing to say to ye," she said, her voice clipped.

A nerve ticked in his cheek, yet he didn't release her. "Why?" he challenged. "I have done nothing to ye."

"What?" she choked. "My father has been humiliated, crippled, because of *ye*."

The captain's throat bobbed. "That was his doing, lass, not mine."

A red veil descended, heat flushing across Rose's chest. "Ye have persecuted my family, Captain. Ye seek to make an example of us."

It was true, the Dun Ugadale Guard had tangled with her father and brothers a few times over the last couple of years. Rose wasn't a fool. She knew the men of her family could be difficult, and the souring of relations between them and the MacDonalds who lived locally had worsened things. Yet Kerr Mackay had taken to visiting their farm regularly, to questioning her father and brothers over every crime that occurred in the area.

It was Kerr who'd arrested her father that fateful day, who'd dragged him before the laird so that he could strike off his right hand.

"That isn't the truth," he growled, his grip on her arm tightening just a fraction. "I'm simply trying to keep the peace. Yer father and brothers are constantly stirring up trouble. Why don't ye keep a leash on them?"

Her heart started to pound in her ears. "What do ye expect me to do?" she bit out, glaring at him. She was tall and barely had to lift her chin to hold his gaze. "I'm one woman in a household of men." Since her mother had died, a couple of winters earlier, Rose toiled twice as hard to look after her father and two elder brothers.

His nostrils flared, and he took a step closer.

She inhaled the scent of clove and leather, mixed with the warm, masculine smell of his skin. It was pleasant, although when she realized she was dragging it into her lungs, her spine snapped straight, fire igniting in her belly.

Curse him, he was standing too near. "Let me go," she ordered between gritted teeth.

The anger in his eyes banked. "I don't want to argue with ye, Rose," he said, his voice hoarse now. "That's not why I approached ye."

"Why then?" she demanded, her gaze fusing with his.

He stared down at her before clearing his throat. "I don't want us to be enemies, lass. For a long while, I have admired ye ... have wanted to woo ye. Can we not put all this unpleasantness behind us and start again?"

Rose's lips parted, her breath rushing out of her.

Had she heard correctly? Surely not. The heat smoldering in her belly blazed high, catching fire in her veins.

The arrogance of the man.

Teeth clenched, she stepped back and twisted her arm so that he released her. He let her go easily though, his gaze never leaving her face. His expression was solemn, his gaze expectant. He actually thought she might consider such a proposal.

Anger beat like a hunting drum in her chest. Thanks to Captain Mackay, her father couldn't work the fields like he used to; instead, he drank away the last of their coin, his mood bleak. His despair had made her brothers wilder and more argumentative than usual. Her family was on the brink of destitution. They'd barely made their last rent to the laird and would likely forfeit the next. The man before her was a thorn in her family's side. How dare he pursue her?

"Goats shall sprout wings and fly before I'd let ye anywhere near me," she said, her voice low and fierce. He flinched, yet she didn't care. "Go to the devil, Mackay."

Trembling from the force of her rage, she turned then and stalked off into the crowd without a backward glance.

2: SPEAKING UP

One month later ...

WEEPING CARRIED THROUGH the dank, chill air. The folk of Dun Ugadale huddled together in the kirkyard, their faces crumpled in grief.

It was hard to believe the priest was gone.

Standing with his brothers, head bowed, Kerr Mackay felt the weight of their sorrow—a sorrow he shared.

"Father Ross of the Mackays" —a man's reed-thin voice pierced the hush— "we have committed yer body to the ground, earth to earth, ashes to ashes, dust to dust—in sure and certain hope of the Resurrection to eternal life."

Raising his chin, Kerr's gaze settled upon Father Macum, the priest from the nearby port town of Ceann Locha. Father Macum was getting on in years, at least two decades older than the man he was burying, yet his dark eyes were still bright, his body still spry.

Kerr's attention shifted then to the mound of fresh earth, scattered with what flowers the local women could find this time of year.

It didn't seem right. Father Ross was the picture of health the last time Kerr had seen him. However, Kerr's sister-by-marriage Davina had found the priest dead on the kirk floor the morning before.

One of the village women started sobbing in earnest then. Maisie MacDonald covered her face with her hands in an effort to stifle the noise, yet her weeping carried high above the mourners. Gazes swiveled to her. Everyone knew the widow had been fond of Father Ross. There had even been whisperings that she'd taken to visiting him some evenings.

Murmuring something to the older woman, Rose stepped close and placed an arm around her shoulders. Her voice was low and soothing, yet such was Maisie's grief, she barely seemed to notice.

Kerr did though.

Curse him, he couldn't take his eyes off Rose. He hadn't seen her since that fateful night, a month earlier, when she'd spurned his attentions and made it clear he'd never have a chance with her. Kerr had kept his distance from the lass ever since; however, the funeral had brought them together once more.

Over the past weeks, Kerr had given himself a strict talking-to. Rose didn't want him. He had to stop pining like a lovesick halfwit. Over the past few days, he'd even started telling himself he no longer cared what Rose MacAlister thought of him.

But seeing her now was a punch to the gut.

The truth was, he did care—just as much as he ever had. This cursed affliction still had him within its grasp.

"Receive the Lord's blessing," Father Macum concluded, his thin voice cracking as he strained to be heard over Maisie's noisy weeping. "The Lord bless ye and watch over ye. In the Name of the Father, and of the Son, and of the Holy Spirit."

"Amen." A chorus of soft voices followed the priest's words.

Silence lay heavily in the moments afterward, interrupted by the harsh caws of a crow sitting upon a nearby yew tree. The beady-eyed bird watched the mourners as, one by one, they drifted away.

However, the laird of Dun Ugadale, Iver Mackay, remained. As did his kin and Father Macum.

And so did Maisie, for she was still sobbing helplessly, cradled against Rose's chest.

Forcing himself not to stare at the woman he couldn't seem to forget, Kerr glanced over at the eldest of his three brothers. Iver's face was unusually austere this afternoon, while next to him, his wife, Bonnie's face was wet with tears. Likewise, Davina was silently weeping as she stood with Lennox. As usual, the youngest of the four brothers, Brodie, waited a little apart from the rest of his kin. Shrouded in a black cloak, his face shuttered, Brodie's gaze remained fixed on Father Ross's grave.

All the Mackay brothers had grown up under the priest's gentle guidance. He was their second cousin—a good, caring man who'd done much for the people here.

Kerr's throat constricted. Lord, he'd miss him.

Father Macum cleared his throat then, approaching the laird. "This is a great loss to Dun Ugadale, indeed," he muttered. "Without a man of God to lead them, folk can lose their way."

Iver nodded, his mouth tightening sightly. "Father Ross was *kin*," he reminded the priest. "His loss is also a personal one."

"Of course," Father Macum replied hurriedly, wringing his hands. "However, despite the gulf his passing has left ... his role must be filled. Shall I see to it?"

"Aye," Iver replied with a brusque nod. "If ye must."

Bowing his head, the priest gathered his robes about him and hurried off. His garron was tied to the fence encircling the kirkyard, and now the burial was done, Father Macum was eager to be on his way.

Iver let him go without another word.

Meanwhile, nearby, Maisie lifted her tear-streaked face and rubbed at her eyes, clearly trying to pull herself together. She then glanced up at Rose, stiffening when she realized who'd been comforting her.

Jaw clenched, she twisted out of Rose's hold.

The woman's reaction didn't surprise Kerr. Many of the MacAlisters and the MacDonalds who lived on the lands around the broch didn't get on. It was a pity though that Maisie couldn't put it aside on a day like this.

Rose too seemed to think the same, for hurt flickered across her features, her green eyes clouding in confusion.

Drawing herself up as she stepped away from one of the hated MacAlisters, Maisie glanced at the laird. "This is the devil's work, Mackay," she croaked. "It can't be a natural death … to be struck down so, in the prime of life."

"The healer said it was his heart, Maisie," Iver replied, his tone softening a little. "As tragic as his loss is to us all, none of us know when our time will come."

Maisie's eyes filled with tears once more, and she nodded. Her shoulders sagged then as sorrow barreled into her.

"I can walk ye home, if ye like, Maisie?" Rose offered gently.

The older woman cut her a sharp look before shaking her head. "I can manage." She paused then, her gaze narrowing. "If the likes of yer criminal father and yer heathen aunt followed Christ's teachings, evil would never have crept into this village. Neither of them was here to pay Father Ross respect, I note."

Rose flinched at these harsh words, her lips parting as a soft gasp escaped.

"That's enough, Maisie," Kerr cut in, speaking without thinking. "We all grieve Father Ross … but that's no excuse to lose yer manners."

Maisie stiffened at the reprimand—while Rose looked his way, focusing on Kerr for the first time since they'd all gathered at the graveside.

Their gazes held for a heartbeat before she dropped her attention to the ground, high spots of color appearing on her cheeks. Then, without acknowledging anyone, Rose turned and walked away, threading a path through the gravestones toward the gate.

Kerr watched her go, an ache rising in his chest.

By the time Rose reached her family's cottage, the heat in her face had finally ebbed. At the graveside, her cheeks had burned like hot embers. It had been humiliating to be insulted like that in front of the laird and his family—but worse still was when Kerr had come to her defense.

He was the last person she wanted to speak up for her.

Heat washed over Rose once more as she recalled the concerned looks on Bonnie and Davina's faces. Rose liked the two women. The wives of Iver and Lennox Mackay had been good to her over the past months, dropping off loaves of bread and even a few wedges of cheese after they'd learned she and her kin were weathering tough times.

Approaching the cottage up a narrow path, between fallow fields, Rose's gaze went to the stacked-stone chimney upon the turf roof. She then frowned. Usually, dark peat smoke drifted into the air at this hour. Her father or brothers should have been at home by now to tend the fire; she hoped they hadn't let it go out.

Rose's jaw tensed. She'd wanted to slap Maisie MacDonald for insulting her kin so, yet the woman's words had cut deep all the same, for they held a grain of truth. Despite that they'd often visited the kirk on a Sunday, and had enjoyed Father Ross's sermons, the rest of her family hadn't attended his burial—and Lord knew where any of them were at present.

However, Rose hadn't expected her aunt to come to the burial. Kenna had never been pious and barely knew Father Ross.

Completing the final few steps to the front door, Rose let herself into the cottage. She then removed her cloak and crossed the hard-packed dirt floor to the stone hearth.

As she'd suspected, it was cold.

Cursing under her breath, Rose grabbed a flint and tinder.

An odd cooing sound interrupted her, and she turned to it, her gaze alighting upon a pair of dark-golden eyes peering up at her from inside a basket nestled in the corner next to the hearth.

"Sorry, Hazel," she muttered. "I'm not in the best of moods this afternoon ... don't mind me."

In response, the eagle owl, its mottled buff-brown feathers blending in with the straw and wood shavings in the basket, cocked its head. Its ear tufts gave it a quizzical look, and Rose found herself smiling.

Putting aside her flint and tinder, she approached the basket and crouched down before it. "How's that wing faring today?"

Hazel merely gazed up at her, amber eyes unblinking.

Rose extended her hand, stroking the owl's soft feathers. She'd rescued the female owl a fortnight earlier, having found it hopping around the field outside with a broken wing. Her father and brothers had thought her foolish to bother with the bird, yet she'd ignored their jeers.

The owl was injured, and she'd not let it die.

Instead, she'd brought the owl inside, splinted the broken wing, and done her best to care for it. After a day or two, she named the bird Hazel. She regularly went out and checked traps she'd set, bringing it dead rats and mice.

Hazel was surprisingly tame these days, and Rose wasn't nervous about putting her hand anywhere near that wickedly sharp, hooked beak.

Stroking the owl now, a little of the tension knotting her belly eased. Her smile lingered. Hazel brought her solace this afternoon.

"Ye'll be getting hungry," she announced with a sigh, rising to her feet and moving back to the hearth. "But if ye wait just a wee bit, I'll get ye something tasty." Kneeling, she picked up the flint and tinder once more. "First though, I need to get this fire relit."

It wasn't an easy task, as there wasn't a breath of wind this afternoon to create a much-needed draft. By the time Rose had coaxed a tender flame to life, her knees hurt from kneeling on the floor and her back ached from being hunched over the lump of peat she'd been trying to light.

Once the fire was burning, Rose also lit a lantern. She'd have preferred to have at least three alight, for the interior of the cottage was dark and gloomy with just one. However, they were getting low on candles, and she had to conserve them.

Rubbing her back, she glanced over at the bench, where the turnip and onions she planned to cook up for supper waited. She'd start on that soon, right after she fed Hazel.

Ducking outdoors, she noted the wind had picked up. It snagged at her clothing and blew icy needles of rain in her face. Autumn was sliding into winter, and the air held winter's bite. The light was fading now, for the gloaming was upon them. As they began the last few weeks up to Yuletide, the days grew increasingly short.

Rose bent her head against the wind and hurried to the edge of the garden that surrounded the cottage. To her relief, she found a dead rat in her trap. It was a big one too—Hazel would be pleased.

Grabbing the rodent by the tail, she carried it back indoors and deposited it into Hazel's basket.

The owl attacked the rat with zeal while Rose made her way over to the bench and began deftly chopping vegetables for pottage.

She was running very late today. Unsurprisingly, the funeral had thrown her routine into chaos.

Rose's days were always busy. In the mornings, after she finished her chores at home, she often walked into the village and helped her friend Eara brew ale for a few hours. Ever since she'd been widowed, the alewife needed assistance—and Rose was happy to give it. Eara appreciated Rose's help, while her father and brothers took everything she did for them as their right. However, they were pleased about her job—for Eara paid Rose in ale.

After a full morning, Rose would return home to prepare the noon meal. Her afternoons were then passed tending the garden where she grew most of their vegetables.

However, Rose found it difficult to focus on her chores this evening. In truth, Maisie MacDonald's harsh words had both angered and unsettled her.

The gall of the woman.

Rose's jaw tightened as she tossed chopped turnips into a large iron pot.

Her father liked supper on the table at a certain hour—but he'd be having it late today. She'd just begun to fry the vegetables off, in a tiny portion of pork fat, when the door to the cottage flew open. Graham MacAlister stumbled in, followed by his sons, Knox and Clyde.

Tall and broad with ruddy faces, chestnut-brown hair, and green eyes, all three men appeared cast from the same mold.

Rose turned from where she was stirring the vegetables in the pot before the fire. "There ye are," she greeted them, trying to keep the irritation out of her voice. "Where have ye all been?"

"None of yer business, lass," her father slurred. Rose's heart sank. *God's bones, not again.* He'd been drinking. Where had he gotten the coin? "Why isn't supper on the table yet?"

3: THE WEIGHT OF RESPONSIBILITY

ROSE TURNED BACK to the pot, stirring carefully to prevent the vegetables from burning. "I was late starting my chores in the afternoon," she replied. "After *Father Ross's* burial."

Her tone was pointed, a veiled criticism against them all. But her father merely snorted before heaving himself down on a pile of sheepskins near the fire. "A pity that ... Father Ross was a good man."

"Aye," Rose murmured, her throat constricting. "He was."

"What's for supper then?" Clyde asked, his tone surly. Clearly, the priest's passing wasn't of interest to him.

Rose reached for a ewer of water, which she then added to the frying turnip and onion. "Pottage." She glanced over her shoulder to see that the youngest of her two brothers was scowling. He'd never enjoyed pottage.

"No bannock with it, I suppose?" Knox asked hopefully.

Rose shook her head. "Ye ate it all this morning."

Ignoring disgruntled looks from all three of them now, she added a handful of herbs—parsley, sage, and thyme from the garden—to the pottage. They'd run out of salt the day before, and the vegetable stew would be even blander than usual as a result.

Irritation speared her, even as she tried to stifle it. She wanted to point out the three of them ate like plow horses, and that if they wanted bannock for their supper, they needed to restrain themselves in the morning. Their reserves of flour and oats were dwindling, and they hadn't yet entered the winter.

But after the sorrowful day, she couldn't summon the energy to bicker with them.

Silence fell in the cottage, broken only by the bubbling of the stew.

Eventually, Rose went to retrieve wooden bowls and spoons. As she did so, she caught Knox's eye. "I thought to find ye working the fields this afternoon," she said lightly, hoping that he might reveal where they'd been.

He shrugged, pushing a shaggy fringe out of his eyes. Knox was the one she often addressed, rather than her father or Clyde. He was generally the least surly of the three and the most approachable. "The sheep needed moving."

Rose tensed yet bit back a reply. They'd moved the small flock of sheep they tended to lower pasture just three days earlier. Knox must have read her face for he added. "They're nearer to home now."

"Aye," their father snapped. "I'm not having one of those whoreson MacDonalds stealing from us ... like they did last winter."

Rose sighed and began ladling out pottage into the bowls. "Ye have no proof it was them, Da."

"*Five* of our black-faced sheep went missing," he spluttered, glaring at her. "And I saw them in the spring when the MacDonald's took theirs to market." His tone was belligerent, daring Rose to disagree with him.

She didn't. Rose had learned a long while ago, at her mother's knee, to avoid locking horns with him over the MacDonalds. He loathed them and blamed Duncan MacDonald for every ill that befell him.

Instead, she handed out the bowls of pottage before taking a stool beside the fire. Then, with a sigh, she took a spoonful of supper. Swallowing, she tried not to wince. God's teeth, it was bland. Like Clyde, she wasn't fond of this meal either.

Her menfolk all started on their meals too, eating in silence. However, they were halfway through when her father snarled, "Satan's cods ... I'm sick of living like this."

Crouched over his bowl, using his left hand to spoon pottage into his mouth, for his right had been struck off months earlier, Graham wore a deep scowl.

"I'm sorry, Da," Rose murmured, her stomach tightening. "The pottage isn't my finest. I—"

"It's not yer fault, lass," he cut her off roughly. "It's *this* life." He waved the stump where his right hand had once been around. "This family was once prosperous ... but now look what we've been reduced to."

"Aye, Da, thanks to the MacDonalds," Clyde muttered. "If only a plague would carry the lot of them off."

Graham's face twisted, a pulse throbbing in his temple. "Duncan MacDonald and his lads are burs up our arses ... if we could rid ourselves of them, our lives would be much easier."

Inwardly, Rose groaned. Lord, they weren't back to complaining about the MacDonalds again, were they? She understood her father's frustration, yet her patience was stretched thin these days.

She hated how bitter he'd become, how petty.

When Graham MacAlister had moved into this cottage and taken over tending his own father's lands, life had been good. He'd been happily wed with three strong, healthy bairns. But slowly, with the years, her father's life had taken another path. He had a weakness for drink, and whereas *his* father had rubbed along with the MacDonalds, Graham couldn't bring himself to do the same.

He now resented the Mackays too, especially since their laird had struck off his hand for cattle thieving. Nonetheless, he had the wits to keep his resentment to himself. This cottage and the land they farmed belonged to Iver Mackay—and if he so wished, he could turf them out.

Rose watched her father's weathered face, noting the broken veins in his cheeks, which hadn't been there months earlier. Even in his anger, he looked defeated, for he sat, slumped in the sheepskins, his broad shoulders rounded. Something deep inside her chest twisted. He was a broken man, beaten down by life.

Her jaw tightened as anger rose to replace her sadness. It didn't help that he got the blame for every crime committed in the local area. There had been a period when the Dun Ugadale Guard made daily visits to their cottage to ensure Graham was behaving himself.

Kerr Mackay had it in for her father—he had for a while now.

Rose's pulse started to thud in her ears.

Curse him, the Captain of the Guard didn't consider everything that had befallen her father of late.

A succession of poor crops. Ewes that had died during lambing. The death of his beloved wife.

Rose dropped her gaze to her half-eaten bowl of pottage. It didn't help either that his offspring were a burden to him. Knox and Clyde were both idlers, and Rose hadn't found herself a man yet. Aye, she'd had offers, but none of them were from men she liked well enough to marry.

Captain Mackay was the only one to show interest in her of late—and she'd sooner marry a stinking billy goat.

Forcing down the last of her pottage, for she didn't waste a mouthful of food, Rose took the empty bowls from her father and brothers. They were still muttering about Duncan MacDonald and his four strapping sons, yet she barely heard them now.

Knox had recently had a run-in with one of them, and his broken nose had just healed. All the same, he'd have a bump on the bridge of it for the rest of his days, a reminder of Keith MacDonald's meaty fists.

Rose didn't pay much attention to their swearing and growled threats as she picked up the lantern with one hand and carried the bowls and spoons with the other. It was always the same. Anger, followed by vows of vengeance. It never came to anything though, thank the Lord.

Leaving them to it, she went outside to wash the supper dishes.

Graham waited until his daughter was out of earshot before leaning forward, his gaze sweeping over his sons' faces.

"Those were pretty cattle we spied today, weren't they, lads?"

Clyde grinned. "Aye, Da."

Knox nodded, his green eyes glinting in the firelight. "Duncan MacDonald's doing well for himself."

"He is, indeed," Graham growled. "Thank ye for rubbing that in my face, halfwit!"

Knox's gaze guttered, yet Graham barely noticed. As always, it felt as if a hot ember pulsed in his gut whenever he dwelled on how prosperous his nemesis was these days. Duncan's wife was fat and apple-cheeked, and two of his sons had just set up on their own. The bastard's influence was growing locally, while Graham's was waning.

He knew the truth of it. He was a drunk and a cripple—and nearly destitute. Rents were due again, yet he hadn't been able to pay the bailiff on his last visit. Luckily, Kyle MacAlister had given him extra time to find the coin. However, the bailiff would be passing by again soon, and they still didn't have the money.

Graham screwed up his mouth. He didn't like receiving charity and resented Kyle for his compassion. It was humiliating. However, it was just as well the new bailiff was a MacAlister. When Lennox Mackay had been bailiff, it had been harder to persuade him to be a little lenient.

The ember burned hotter still in his gut, and Graham reached down, rubbing his paunch. He'd been suffering from stomach pains for a few months now, although they were always worse when he was vexed.

Pushing aside worries about how he was going to pay his rent, Graham studied his sons' faces.

They were both a disappointment to him.

Duncan MacDonald's lads were independent and industrious, whereas Knox and Clyde lacked drive or ambition. If they were canny, they'd have gone after the daughters of prosperous farmers as Duncan MacDonald's brood had. But, instead, they depended on him for their futures.

If only they'd been born grafters like their younger sister. Rose worked harder than any of them, but unfortunately, she was a daughter, not a son.

The weight of responsibility was a heavy one. It meant that Graham found himself constantly scheming and planning.

And luckily for his useless sons, he had a plan.

"I've heard word that the MacDonalds intend to sell those cattle at Carradale market in February," Graham announced, lowering his voice as if he were afraid the walls might overhear him. "I think we need to take advantage of that, lads."

Both Knox and Clyde leaned closer, their expressions keen. Like hounds on the scent, they knew their father was plotting something.

Someone had to.

This plan didn't solve their immediate problems. They still had to survive the long and bitter winter ahead. But at least, come spring, they'd have coin.

"On the same week, there's another cattle market … at Clachan," he continued. "What say ye to stealing MacDonald's cattle while they're traveling to Carradale? We'll then herd the beasts across to the west of the peninsula, where we'll sell them off without anyone being the wiser?"

As far as plans went, it was a clever one. They couldn't arrive at Carradale with a head of stolen cattle—but if they made haste to Clachan and moved the livestock on quickly, they'd walk away with purses full of silver pennies.

Clyde was nodding vigorously, although Knox's expression shuttered, worry clouding his eyes. "We've never done anything this big before, Da," he pointed out.

"Why don't we just hide them in the Lost Valley and be done with it? No one will ever find them there."

Graham snorted. "No, but no one will ever pay us for the beasts either, idiot."

Knox flushed. "Maybe not … but it's less risky."

"No risk, no gain," Graham replied with a sneer.

"Aye," Clyde added, smirking. "What's wrong, Knox … have yer bollocks shriveled?"

Knox cast his brother an irritated look before meeting his father's eye once more. "If ye are set on this, Da … we'll need help."

"Aye, and lucky for us, I still have friends who'd be happy to be involved … for a cut of the profits."

Knox gave a slow nod, although he still didn't look as excited as his younger brother. "They'll hang us all if we're caught," he reminded them.

Clyde's grin slipped, as if he hadn't yet considered the possibility, while Graham swore under his breath. The devil's turds, he'd met sheep brighter than these two.

Leaning forward, he pinned them both with a steely gaze before a harsh smile tugged at his lips. Excitement quickened his blood then, as it always did when he came up with an idea that would kick his enemy in the cods. "And that's why our plan shall be watertight."

Kerr climbed the steps to the wall, pulling his cloak close as he went. It was a raw night, so cold that it hurt to breathe. Nonetheless, he wouldn't leave his men on the night watch on their own while he slept in a warm bed.

A few times a week, he made sure he showed his face for a while upon the wall. He'd recently recruited more warriors—all young men from nearby villages, the sons of cottars or fishermen mostly—and wanted to set a good example to them.

The political situation beyond this quiet corner of Scotland was worsening, and the king had continued his campaign against the Douglases. He'd already pulled some of the Highland clans into the conflict, and Kerr wondered how long it would be before he called upon the Mackays as well.

They had to be ready.

The cold dug through his layers of clothing. The glow of braziers on the ramparts lit up the night. It had been foggy earlier, yet the mist had lifted as dusk settled, the sky clearing. A hazy half-moon shone down, illuminating the world below in a silvery veil.

Kerr's breath steamed in front of him as he walked the wall, greeting each man-at-arms by name.

"All quiet, Ronan?" he asked one of the lads, an Irishman who'd recently moved across the water to Scotland.

"Aye, Captain," the young warrior replied, his breath clouding in front of him. "It's a still night … ye could hear an owl fart."

Kerr's mouth lifted at the corners. Nodding, he moved on, moving farther up the ramparts to where his brother stood.

"I can take ye off the night watch, if ye want?" he murmured to Lennox as he stopped, shoulder-to-shoulder with him.

Lennox raised an eyebrow. "And have the other lads accuse ye of favoring kin?"

"I imagine Davina would thank me though."

"Aye … although we'll be in our new home before long. I'll get someone else to watch my walls at night then."

Indeed, Lennox and his wife would soon be moving to their broch, which was currently being built on the western shore of Lussa Loch, inland from Dun Ugadale. Iver had gifted him a parcel of land that ran alongside the loch. His home would be ready mid-spring, but in the meantime, Lennox still worked in The Guard.

"Ye will make a good laird, I think," Kerr replied, adding. "Ye'll certainly enjoy ordering everyone around."

Lennox snorted before giving him a playful shove in the ribs with his elbow. "Leading is in *all* our blood, brother." He paused then, eyeing Kerr. "I saw Brodie ride out earlier for Ceann Locha. Why didn't ye join him?"

Kerr shrugged. "Didn't feel like it." In the past, he'd often accompanied Brodie for an evening drinking and dicing at taverns. The brothers watched each other's backs too. But these days, Kerr couldn't face it. "After Father Ross's passing, everything feels a bit" —he paused there, struggling to find the right word— "flat."

Silence fell between the brothers before Lennox spoke up. "Aye, it's been a sad time ... Davina is still inconsolable."

A week had passed since Father Ross's burial, yet the folk of Dun Ugadale still grieved. Kerr knew his sister-by-marriage was close to the priest. Father Ross had been one of the first to welcome her to the village, and she'd visited him regularly with flowers for the altar.

"Ross will be hard to replace," Kerr replied, even as guilt speared him. Aye, he had been out of sorts ever since Father Ross's death, but that wasn't the only thing bothering him.

His desire for Rose MacAlister had turned into a pining that twisted his guts and robbed him of joy. He had to master it, yet he didn't know how.

As if sensing something was amiss, Lennox turned to him fully. His brother's brow then furrowed. "Even since before we lost the priest, ye haven't been yerself, Kerr," he noted. "Ye've always been more serious than the rest of us ... but of late, I think yer face would crack if ye smiled."

Kerr snorted, even as his pulse quickened. Lennox was so taken up with Davina that he sometimes thought his brother noticed little else—but he had.

Kerr had always been known as the 'dependable' brother. Iver was charming, Lennox hot-headed, and Brodie brooding—whereas Kerr was the steady one. They'd all ribbed him mercilessly about it growing up, something he hadn't enjoyed.

Irritation speared his guts now at the teasing glint in Lennox's eyes.

This was why he kept his secrets close to his chest. His brothers didn't mean him ill, yet he tired of their mockery. Aye, he was dependable. Someone had to be.

"It's just the endless cold and grey of winter was getting to me," he lied with a shrug. "That and the prospect of seeing Graham MacAlister tomorrow."

"Why is that then?"

"Kyle's collecting overdue rent from a few farmers this week … and I'm accompanying him in case things turn nasty." He paused then. "I don't want Rose to lose her home."

Lennox nodded, even as his dark-blue eyes narrowed. "Yer compassion is commendable, brother," he replied, his voice lowering. "Although I don't understand it. Every time I've seen ye together, the lass looks like she wants to shove a pike up yer arse."

Kerr grimaced. He might have admitted how he felt about Rose then, and even weathered Lennox's teasing, if the thud of hoofbeats hadn't intruded.

The brothers turned their attention to the causeway leading up the hill from the village. A lone rider, hunched low over the saddle, was approaching the broch.

"A bit late for visitors, isn't it?" Lennox murmured.

Kerr frowned. "Aye," he replied, heading toward the guard tower that spanned the gate. "Let's see who it is."

4: ONLY A FOOL

"WHO GOES THERE?" The guard called down.

"The name's Bain MacEacharn," came the rough, answering croak. "I'm a merchant bound for Ceann Locha." The newcomer halted there as if having difficulty speaking. "I was attacked on the road south this afternoon."

"Raise the portcullis," Kerr ordered the guard before scaling the narrow steps leading down from the watchtower.

In the barmkin below, he helped Lennox unbar the heavy oaken gate, while the portcullis slowly rumbled up. Meanwhile, Kerr motioned to the other guards who'd descended the wall to form a semi-circle a few yards back from the gates.

With the civil unrest these days, one couldn't be too careful. This 'merchant' could be an outlaw—for there were plenty of them running from the crown at present—and he might have friends waiting in the darkness.

Kerr then took a flickering torch from where it hung on a chain by the gate and moved forward to get a look at the man.

As soon as the light found him, Kerr knew he was in a bad way.

The man's face was ashen, and he crouched over his horse's withers, one hand clutched at his belly.

Lennox stepped up and took the reins, leading the stocky horse into the barmkin, the interior courtyard that ran around the base of the broch.

"Who did this?" Kerr asked, even as he glanced over his shoulder at the open gateway. There didn't appear to be anyone else lurking outside, yet he motioned to his guards to lower the portcullis once more.

"They didn't introduce themselves," MacEacharn wheezed, attempting a rueful smile and failing. "But when I stopped at Claonaig yesterday, there was talk of a group of Douglases who've turned feral following a skirmish with the king's men." His face twisted then, his eyes glittering. "I'm sure it was them. They killed my brother and stole our cart of goods."

Lennox muttered a curse at this announcement, while Kerr's stomach hardened. Murder was a serious business.

"I'm sorry about yer brother," he said finally as he and Lennox helped the man down from his horse.

MacEacharn nodded, his throat bobbing.

"What were ye carrying?" Lennox asked then.

"Wine and ale," the merchant grunted. "They took what coin we had too. My brother and I tried to fight them, but they cut his throat ... and managed to stab me in the guts before I fled."

"Were they on horseback?" Kerr asked. His mind was immediately fixed on the details. He needed to know everything about these criminals, for they'd soon be out hunting them.

The merchant shook his head.

Kerr's mouth pursed. Somewhere in the darkness, there would be a merry band of thugs, drinking to their victory. It had been a vicious attack, and they would be punished for it.

But first, they had to help this wounded man.

"Come, Bain." Kerr pushed his shoulder under the merchant's armpit. "Let's get ye indoors and take a look at that wound."

"I fear it's too late," MacEacharn replied, his voice weak now. "I'm done for."

"Not yet, ye aren't," Lennox told him firmly.

The brother's gazes met then, and Kerr nodded to the broch. "Fetch Iver … he needs to hear about this."

Kerr's belly tightened as Graham MacAlister's cottage hove into sight. He never looked forward to these visits. In the past, being able to see Rose had made it bearable. But not these days.

Not when she couldn't stand the sight of him.

It didn't help that he was exhausted this morning, after having not slept the night before.

Bain MacEacharn had known he was doomed. The merchant had died just before dawn, after hours of agony. As soon as they got him indoors and examined the wound to his stomach, the gravity of it became clear. All they could do was make him as comfortable as possible. Both Bonnie and Davina had attended him, for there wasn't any time to fetch a healer from Ceann Locha.

But in his last hours, MacEacharn had managed to tell Iver all he could about those who'd attacked him. The assault had taken place in a wooded area. There had been six of them. The outlaws had all been armed with dirks and carried bows and arrows. Some of them bore bandaged limbs and scratches to the face as if they'd recently been in a skirmish.

And if they were indeed Douglases, they likely had.

Lennox had gone out that morning, with a band of men, traveling north to hunt them. Meanwhile, Kerr kept his word to the bailiff. It was now the beginning of December. Yule was closing in on them, and the king demanded his clan-chiefs deliver their taxes by then. Unfortunately, Dun Ugadale had a few farmers who hadn't yet paid their rent to the Mackays.

Graham MacAlister was one of them.

Kerr cast a sidelong glance at the man riding next to him. Kyle MacAlister's bearded face was unusually grim this morning, his gaze trained on their destination. No, neither of them was anticipating a pleasant meeting.

Shifting his attention back to the cottage, Kerr studied it. Located at the bottom of a shallow vale, a short ride from Dun Ugadale village, the dwelling appeared a bit ramshackle these days. Beyond the cottage, a row of narrow rectangular fields—*run rigs*—stretched down the glen. This time of year, there wasn't much growing. Although, unlike many of the fields they'd passed on the way here, these were either overgrown, fallow, or in need of mulching.

This glen formed part of a sizable *baile* that stretched around Dun Ugadale to the west, north, and south—where local families, the Mackay chieftain's tenants, farmed the land.

Drawing closer, Kerr spied dark smoke drifting from the chimney. And then his gaze alighted upon the comely figure drawing water from a well. Rose's chestnut-brown hair glinted, even on this dull day, tumbling down her back in heavy curls.

Kerr's gut twisted hard then as both dread and longing hit him.

"Good," the bailiff grunted. "At least someone is home."

"It's Graham we need to see," Kerr reminded Kyle. "He's the one owing the rent, not Rose."

"Aye ... but she's the best of the lot to deal with."

At the sound of their approaching hoofbeats, Rose glanced up. Her gaze swept over them, her face freezing when she saw Kerr.

He stared back at her, refusing to let her dislike penetrate his shield. He was doing his job; she'd just have to put up with it.

"Good afternoon, Rose," Kyle greeted her pleasantly. "Is yer father about?"

"He's inside," she replied cautiously.

"Can ye fetch him for me?"

She nodded slowly. "Is this about the rent we owe?"

"Aye, lass."

Lips compressing, Rose turned and retreated into the cottage, lugging the heavy pail of water with her.

"They work her too hard," Kerr murmured, watching her go.

"Aye," Kyle replied. "As they did her mother. Why do ye think she died so young? The men in this family expect to be waited on like princes." The bailiff paused then, casting Kerr a lopsided smile. "I tried wooing Rose, ye know ... last summer."

Kerr tensed, an unexpected shaft of jealousy lancing through his chest. "Ye did?" he said lightly. "What happened?"

"She made it clear my attentions weren't welcome."

"And now?"

Kyle inclined his head. "Now what?"

"Are ye still hopeful?"

The bailiff snorted. "Of course not. Only a fool pines after a woman who has spurned him."

Kerr stiffened.

Aye ... only a fool. If only he had Kyle's pragmatic approach to women. As a widower, left to bring up three daughters on his own, Kyle didn't have time for lasses who didn't want him.

Kerr should have taken his lead.

Even so, he didn't want to discuss Rose with the bailiff. Fortunately, their conversation ended then—for a big man with greying brown hair and a scowling face ducked out of the cottage.

Graham squinted at his visitors. His hair was tussled, and his clothing rumpled, indicating that they'd likely woken him up. Rose followed at her father's heels. Unlike Graham, she didn't look vexed, just worried.

Kerr didn't blame her for being concerned.

"What is it?" Graham barked.

"Ye know why I'm here, Graham," Kyle greeted him. His voice was pleasant, yet there was steel just beneath. His manner impressed Kerr. Lennox had said his friend would make a fine bailiff, and he did. He had the right balance of temperance and strength. "The final installment of yer rent is past due, while ye still haven't paid the last one."

The farmer screwed up his face, as if this was the first he'd heard of it. However, Kyle let the silence stretch out between them. Graham then glanced over at where Kerr sat, unspeaking, upon his courser. His grizzled eyebrows crashed together. "Why have ye brought *him*?"

"I decided it was a fine afternoon for a ride," Kerr replied before Kyle could answer, his tone dry.

In response, Graham spat on the ground. He then untied the leather purse at his waist. "Here ... ye might as well take the last coin I own." He threw it at Kyle.

The bailiff caught it easily before tipping the pennies out onto his palm. After counting them, he glanced up, meeting the farmer's belligerent gaze. "I'm sorry, Graham, but this is less than half of what ye owe. Ye know that."

Graham growled a curse. "I have nothing else. What do ye want me to do ... whore my daughter so I can pay Mackay's rents?"

Rose's hissed breath followed this comment, while Kerr's grip on the reins tightened into a fist. Of course, Graham wasn't speaking in earnest, yet it was a coarse thing to say all the same.

"When yer kin took over these run rigs, ye agreed to pay the laird of Dun Ugadale rents," Kyle answered calmly, deliberately ignoring the comment. "If ye can't pay, then Iver Mackay will have to take this land off ye and give it to someone else."

Graham's face turned the color of liver. "Over my dead body," he snarled.

"We have two pigs ... both sows," Rose blurted out, stepping up next to her father. "They are both due to farrow in the spring. If ye take them both, will that be enough?"

Kyle considered her offer, while the veins on Graham's forehead started to pulse. He'd focused his glower upon his daughter now and looked as if he wished to throttle her.

Kerr's breathing turned shallow. If he touched a hair on her head, he'd pummel him into the ground.

"Aye, lass," the bailiff said after a short pause. "That will make up the shortfall."

The relief on Rose's face was palpable. However, her father looked as if he were going to explode, like a pot of boiling water with the lid clamped on tight.

"Thank ye, Rose," Kerr said. "I will send some men tomorrow morning to pick up the sows."

She gave a stiff nod, although her gaze remained upon Kyle, as if he, not Kerr, had spoken.

The bailiff pocketed the coins Graham had given him, his brow furrowing as he watched the silently fuming farmer. "Is this agreeable to *ye*, Graham?"

"Aye," he croaked, choking out the word as if it cost him.

"Good." The bailiff nodded to Graham and his daughter and gathered the reins. "We'll be off then."

With that, Kyle and Kerr turned their horses around and set off back down the muddy road that led out of the valley.

Kerr had only ridden a few yards when he glanced over his shoulder to find Graham glaring after him. Rose watched him depart too, her lovely face pinched with worry.

Drawing up his gelding, Kerr twisted in the saddle to survey them. Truth was, he didn't like leaving Rose alone with her father, especially with the man nearly apoplectic with rage.

Seeing his hesitation, Graham's lip curled. "Want something, Mackay?"

Kerr held the farmer's eye. "Don't ye go blaming yer daughter for this," he called out. "Instead, ye should be thanking her for saving yer hide. It's lucky indeed that she has more wits than the rest of ye combined."

And with that, Kerr reined his courser around and urged it into a canter, following the bailiff down the path.

Rose stared after Kerr Mackay's retreating figure.

She hadn't expected him to defend her like that, hadn't wanted it—even though it wasn't the first time he'd spoken up for her—yet there was a part of her that appreciated his words.

Since her mother's passing, no one ever took her side. She had gotten used to fighting her own battles, alone.

Her father's muttered oath made her jerk her gaze from the Captain of the Guard.

Graham glared at her, his pine-green eyes glittering with anger.

Rose's pulse quickened as the reality of matters hit her. Mackay hadn't helped her at all—he'd just smacked the hornet's nest hard with a stick.

"What's this?" he growled. "Have ye been humping that whoreson?"

Heat flushed through Rose. "Of course not!" she gasped. God's bones. How could her father say such a thing?

"Then why would he defend ye?"

Humiliation prickled across Rose's skin as she remembered Mackay's interest in her at Samhuinn. She'd thought her reaction would have doused his attraction to her, yet perhaps it hadn't. "I have no idea," she replied. "But I'd thank ye not to accuse me of such things, Da."

Her father's face screwed up, although the heat in his eyes dimmed slightly. Rose didn't like the cunning look that replaced his anger. "However, if ye *were* to start humping him, Mackay might leave us alone in the future."

"Da!" Fire pulsed in Rose's stomach now. "How dare ye?"

Her father's jaw jutted belligerently. "I'm just looking out for our family," he growled. "Someone has to ... especially since ye have given away the last of our livestock. Those sows bring us in much-needed coin every spring."

Indeed, they did. He'd put them by a neighbor's boar just a fortnight earlier, and both sows were proven to give birth to large litters. Every spring, they sold the piglets at market.

But this year, they wouldn't.

"It was either that or lose this cottage," Rose pointed out between clenched teeth. She then swept a hand around, indicating to the land surrounding them. "And the run rigs." It embarrassed her to see the fields so overgrown. Before losing his hand, her father had spent most days laboring there—his sons, and Rose, at his side. Yet now, he seemed to have forgotten he was a farmer. Instead, he jealously guarded the small flock of black-faced sheep he owned and was forever trying to increase their number.

Knox and Clyde certainly preferred sheep farming to toiling in the fields, although Rose suspected that they often went off to Ceann Locha instead of watching the flock.

Her father glowered back, a muscle bunching in his jaw. His large hand clenched at his side.

Rose tensed. He hadn't lifted a hand to her since she'd been a bairn. However, he looked vexed enough to do so now. She didn't mean to humiliate him in front of the bailiff and the captain, but in her desperation to save their home, she'd done so.

"It's bad enough that those Mackays took my hand," he wheezed, eyes glittering, "yet ye'd let them rob me of my honor as well."

"I didn't, Da," Rose whispered, even as her belly twisted. Her father was already in the grip of melancholia. She didn't want to worsen things for him. "I was only—"

"Enough," he barked. "Ye've always had far too much to say for yerself. A good woman keeps her mouth shut and lets her menfolk deal with important matters. No wonder ye can't find yerself a man."

Rose's own hands clenched at her sides, even as his insult cut deep. Anger tightened her throat.

It took every bit of self-control not to let it all out, yet she managed to prevent herself. For all his bluster, her father was fragile. Life had hollowed him out. He was now like a brittle reed. Sometimes she worried that one particularly harsh gust of wind might snap him in half.

And so, she bit down on her tongue and let her father have the last word.

With one last baleful look at his daughter, Graham turned on his heel and stomped back inside the cottage.

5: THE NEW PRIEST

Three months later ...

ROSE HURRIED UP the path toward the kirk. The new priest had finally arrived, and she, like everyone else, was eager to meet him.

Father Ross's death had left a great hole in their community. There hadn't been any Sunday services ever since his passing either, a weekly event that the folk of Dun Ugadale had always looked forward to.

Reaching the end of the queue of excited villages filing into the kirk, Rose stood up on tiptoe to catch a glimpse of Father Gregor.

The priest waited before the steps of the kirk, welcoming his flock one-by-one, as they entered.

He was younger than Rose had expected, with short black hair shaved into a tonsure at its crown. Lean, with peat-brown eyes, he was handsome—something Rose wasn't the only one to note. At the head of the queue, Maisie MacDonald fawned over the priest, twittering like a young lass when he took her hand in his. Although the woman had grieved loudly and publicly over Father Ross's death, she appeared to have recovered now.

However, Maisie moved indoors, and soon it was Rose's turn to enter the kirk.

"Good morning, Father," she greeted him with a bright smile. "Welcome to Dun Ugadale."

The priest cast an eye over her, his dark gaze sharp as his mouth lifted at the corners. "What's yer name?"

The intensity of his stare made the fine hair on the back of Rose's neck stand up, and her smile faltered. "Rose," she murmured. "MacAlister."

"Rose," he spoke her name slowly, carefully, as if committing it to memory. "Ye appear to be on yer own ... where is yer kin?"

Rose's pulse quickened. "My father is poorly," she lied. "And my brothers are busy in the fields." Another lie. She had no idea where Knox and Clyde were. She'd asked all three of them to accompany her to the kirk this morning. It was an important day, and they should all meet the new priest.

But they'd refused to join her.

"Make sure ye remind them to join us next Sunday," Father Gregor said with another faint smile, his gaze still pinning her to the spot. "God's word must reach us all."

Rose swallowed. "Aye, Father."

She didn't like the way he looked at her; it was almost carnal. It certainly wasn't priestly—and when his gaze lowered to the swell of her breasts, she fought the urge to pull her woolen shawl across her front.

Nodding to him, Rose hurriedly climbed the steps and rushed forward into the kirk, allowing the couple behind her to greet the new priest.

Flustered, she hurried down the aisle between the pews. She usually was one of the first to arrive for the Sunday service, but she'd been delayed this morning after her brothers had left her to bring in the bricks of peat that had been drying in a lean-to behind the cottage. That was usually Knox or Clyde's chore, but they and their father had left the cottage before dawn. They'd gone out early on a few occasions of late, although, as usual, they refused to tell Rose what their business was.

It had gotten to the point where she'd stopped asking.

There were few spaces left in the kirk now, and Rose squeezed into the end of the first pew she encountered where there was room.

Right next to Kerr Mackay.

Rose's heart lurched into her throat. God's blood, she should have looked first. Sweating now, she glanced around, frantic to find somewhere else to sit, but since this was Father Gregor's first sermon, the kirk was much busier than usual.

"Morning, Rose," Kerr greeted her, his voice low and polite.

She gave a stiff nod in response before casting him a sideways glance. Clad in leather, a fur mantle about his broad shoulders, the captain was a striking sight—as always. His shaggy white-blond hair curled around his face, and his blue eyes were guarded as his gaze met hers.

He looked as surprised as she was, to find her standing next to him.

They hadn't spoken to each other since the day of his and the bailiff's visit to the farm three moons earlier. She'd caught glimpses of Captain Mackay from afar though, usually as he rode out on patrol with his men. Like the other locals, she'd heard about the outlaws who were terrorizing travelers on the Kintyre Peninsula. Unfortunately though, the Dun Ugadale Guard hadn't yet caught them.

There wasn't much space in the pew, and she and Mackay were standing so close their arms brushed. Without realizing what she was doing, Rose inhaled his scent: a blend of leather, spice, and pine.

Heat flushed over her as she resisted the urge to lean closer and breathe him in once more. She couldn't stand the man, yet her body and senses reacted to his closeness. Curse her, she liked how he smelled.

"How are ye faring?" he asked then, his voice almost drowned out by the excited chatter around them.

"Well enough," she replied coldly, shifting her attention forward.

"I know ye haven't had an easy winter."

Her cheeks started to burn. Of course, everyone in Dun Ugadale knew that Graham MacAlister had fallen on hard times indeed. If it hadn't been for the charity of others, they'd have starved during the harshest days of winter. "No, but it's nearly over," she replied, her tone clipped. "Now it's February, Da will soon be able to sell some of the sheep at market. There's a market coming up in a few days at Carradale. It's—"

Rose abruptly cut herself off. What the devil was she doing? Her exchange with the priest had clearly scattered her wits if she was babbling about her family's business to Captain Mackay.

She kept her attention facing forward, yet even so, she could feel Kerr's gaze still on her. Couldn't he look elsewhere?

"Ye can always come to me, Rose," he said after a pause, his voice roughening. "I'll help ye, if ye are ever in need. I promise."

She jolted as if someone had just stuck her with a pin, her gaze cutting to him once more. "Why?" she asked.

Lord, it felt strange indeed to be conversing with this man.

Their gazes fused, and the air rushed from Rose's lungs. She wished he wouldn't look at her like that. It wasn't like the priest's stare—which had made her uncomfortable—but a gaze that made her feel as if the ground were giving way under her.

Kerr's lips parted as he readied himself to reply, yet he was cut off by Father Gregor calling to them. "Silence in the house of God."

In an instant, the hum of excited voices cut off. All gazes swiveled to where the priest had positioned himself at the pulpit. Father Gregor's handsome face was creased into a stern expression. "When ye enter this kirk, ye shall do so in reverence and *silence*," he informed them, his tone sharpening. "This is a place of worship, not an alehouse."

Embarrassed coughs followed. Rose peered toward the front of the congregation, where the laird and his wife stood. She wondered at Iver Mackay's reaction to the priest's rebuke, although it was impossible to tell as the laird had his back to her.

Satisfied that his flock had settled, Father Gregor cleared his throat. "Since this is my first sermon, I wish to begin with a topic fundamental to us all: the avoidance of sin." He paused then, his gaze sweeping over the congregation. "These are evils that come from within a person and defile them ... sexual immorality, theft, murder, adultery, greed, malice, deceit, lewdness, envy, slander, arrogance, and folly ... ye must ward yerself against these evils ... for they will corrupt yer soul."

Rose tensed as the priest continued in this vein, giving detailed examples of all the sins. This service was nothing like the ones she was used to. Father Ross had been gentle-natured with a dry sense of humor, but Father Gregor's delivery was wooden, and it sounded as if he was reading a list.

Maybe he was nervous. He was much younger than his predecessor, after all.

The urge to glance Kerr's way, to see what his reaction to their new priest was, tugged at her. Rose quashed it. What did she care what he thought?

Eventually, the priest broke off his sermon, and they sang a couple of hymns. However, once the singing had ended, he drew himself up, his gaze sweeping the congregation solemnly. "It is an unfortunate fact that evil lives amongst us," he announced. "We must be on guard against it. This is an isolated corner of Scotland ... and ye may not have heard what goes on elsewhere, but I must be the sorry bearer of ill-tidings." Father Gregor halted then, his gaze flicking to the laird. There was a breathless silence before he continued, "In England and France, priests have unmasked many women as ... *witches*."

This comment brought a gasp to many in the congregation.

Rose's skin prickled. *Witches?*

"Aye, ye have heard me right," the priest said, shaking his head. "Ye must watch out for signs that the devil's handmaids live amongst us."

"What signs, Father?" A man called out.

The priest's youthful face tightened. "If yer crops spoil, if a draught strikes, or yer bairns turn wild ... these are all warnings ye should heed."

At the front, Maisie's hand shot up. "But how will we know *who* is causing these things, Father?" she asked breathlessly.

"A worthy question," he replied with a nod. "Be on the lookout for 'unnatural' women. Those who shun male company or do not wish to wed."

The urge to laugh bubbled up inside Rose. Her gaze traveled forward to where Eara's white-blonde hair gleamed in the light of the banks of candles lining the kirk. She wondered what her friend made of the new priest. Like Rose, Eara wasn't in any hurry to shackle herself to a man. Did that make them both *unnatural*?

"Such women will often keep an animal—a cat, rodent, or bird—as a consort," the priest continued gravely. "She will have strange ways and a sharp tongue. She will also think herself cleverer than her menfolk." He paused, surveying the rows of men, women, and bairns that filled the kirk. "And if her hair is red or her eyes green, be wary indeed."

Rose swallowed a snort. Surely, he was making a jape? Half the people in this village had red hair or green eyes. Everyone in her family was green-eyed, and her hair, although more brown than red, had streaks of russet through it.

However, the priest looked to be painfully earnest.

Rose's mouth pursed. The man was a fool. The laird's wife, who was standing but three yards from the pulpit, had flame-red hair. Was he implying that *she* was a witch? As Rose looked on, Iver Mackay ducked his head and whispered something to Bonnie.

Muttering started then, rippling through the kirk.

Rose couldn't help it; she even glanced over at Kerr. He was frowning, his gaze fixed upon the priest. "God's bones," he growled under his breath. "If only Father Ross were still with us."

Although it galled her to admit it, for she didn't want to side with Kerr Mackay on anything, Rose wholeheartedly agreed with him.

6: MARK MY WORDS

"WHY DID THEY have to send us Father Gregor?"

"No, idea ... I suppose he offered himself for the position. He's young and eager to make his mark."

Rose snorted and cast Eara Mackay a sidelong glance. "Aye, as well as pompous."

Her friend laughed. "All the same, he's attractive ... for a man of the cloth."

"I suppose so." Rose screwed up her face then. "Although ye should have seen the way he kept staring at my paps when I met him on the way into the kirk ... it was unpriestly."

Eara's grey eyes snapped wide. "Ye caught him ogling yer paps?"

"I didn't have to catch him at it, Eara. He was blatant."

"Ye should have scolded him!"

Rose sighed. "Aye ... I'm sure *ye* would have."

Eara's forthright manner was one of the many things she liked about her. Widowed nearly three years now, Eara's slender figure, flyaway tawny hair, and pretty face had fooled a few suitors into thinking she'd be easy to dominate. But she wasn't.

"Men don't ogle *my* chest," Eara muttered, glancing down at her breasts. "Unlike ye, I wasn't blessed in that area."

"I'm not sure it's a blessing," Rose replied. "It just gets me the wrong sort of attention."

In response, Eara pulled a face. Rose then stuck out her tongue, and the pair of them started laughing. The merry sound echoed across the road.

The two friends walked the way that led along the coast from Ceann Locha to Dun Ugadale. They were returning from visiting the morning market. Together, they pulled a handcart laden with sacks of barley for the ale that the alewife brewed.

Usually, Rose only assisted Eara in the mornings, but she needed help to tow the heavy cart today. It was mid-afternoon, and their destination was near. To the north, they now spied the craggy outline of the Dun Ugadale broch against a windswept sky.

"Did ye see the way Maisie was flirting with the priest?" Eara asked, breaking the companionable silence.

"I'd have to be blind not to. Everyone saw."

"Do ye think she hopes to warm his bed?"

"Eara!" Rose gasped. "She's old enough to be his mother."

Her friend giggled, waggling her eyebrows. "That's never stopped folk before."

A loud graunching sound intruded then, and the handcart they were pulling shuddered. Glancing over her shoulder, Rose saw that the wooden wagon had listed sideways.

"God's teeth," Eara muttered, her light-hearted mood dissolving. She stalked around to the side to see what the problem was. "The cursed wheel has come off its axle."

Rose breathed an oath of her own and drew near to inspect the damage. "How did that happen?"

"James built this cart years ago," Eara replied. As always, when she mentioned her dead husband's name, her voice flattened. "But I don't think he ever serviced it ... how am I going to get those sacks of barley home now?"

Rose didn't reply immediately, for she didn't have a solution either. The sacks were too heavy for either of them to carry. "We can't leave them out here, or someone will help themselves," she pointed out finally. "I shall go to the village and find someone to help."

Eara nodded. "Aye, ye could try—"

The thunder of hoofbeats interrupted Eara, and both women shifted their gazes right to where two men on horseback approached at a swift canter from the south.

Rose's stomach clenched when she caught a flash of white-blond hair.

Kerr Mackay.

The captain drew his courser up next to the bailiff. Both men's gazes swept over the listing handcart before the bailiff cocked an eyebrow. "Having some trouble, lasses?"

Eara placed her hands on her hips and eyed him. "Evidently."

Kyle MacAlister smiled, his teeth flashing white against his short beard. "It's always a pleasure to cross paths with ye, Eara."

The widow's pretty mouth pursed, making it clear she wasn't charmed by his easy manner. "Aye, well, I wish I could say the same. However, the only time ye knock on my door is to demand coin."

Kyle's smile slid into a grin. "That can be remedied," he replied. "I'm happy to pass by and try some of that fine ale ye brew."

"Aye, do that ... although it'll cost ye."

"Good afternoon, Rose."

Rose glanced away from watching her friend and the bailiff banter, to find Kerr watching her. His expression was serious, although his gaze was intense. It reminded her of the way he'd looked at her in the kirk a couple of days earlier.

Rose frowned. Perhaps he thought their brief exchange meant she was warming to him. She wasn't— and she'd make it clear.

"It *was*." Folding her arms across her chest, she held his eye. "Busy afternoon is it, Captain? Wringing more coin out of those who don't have any to give?"

Kerr's brow furrowed. "It's not a pleasant task, lass," he replied, "But rents have to be paid, all the same."

"Aye," she growled. "Of course, they do."

She wished the men would ride on. The sight of them was a jab in the eye.

But, of course, they were never going to do that, and both the bailiff and the captain swung down from their horses to come to their aid.

Kyle hunkered down, inspecting the wheel, before picking up something out of the dirt. "Looks like the pin came loose," he said, winking at Eara. He then nodded to his companion. "Lift the cart up, Kerr, and let's see if I can slide the wheel back on and secure it."

Kerr nodded and moved to the back of the handcart, readying himself to heft it up.

"Mind yer back," Eara warned him. "It's heavy."

To Rose's surprise, Kerr's mouth curved into a rare and unexpected smile. The expression lit up his face. The smile wasn't for her, although to her chagrin, the sight of it made Rose's heart thump against her ribs. "Luckily, I had my porridge this morning, lass," he replied. "Fear not, I can manage it."

And he did. Jaw clenched, Kerr hauled the cart upright, holding it while Kyle slid the wheel back into place and replaced the pin.

"Looks as if the axle's got some rust," the bailiff said to Eara, straightening up and brushing off his hands. "I'd get that looked at if I were ye."

"I will," she assured him, her mouth lifting at the edges as she met the bailiff's eye. "Thank ye."

He gave a bow before flashing another of his easy smiles. "My pleasure."

Eara shifted her attention to Kerr. "My thanks to ye too, Captain."

Kerr nodded, even as a groove appeared between his brows. "Just a warning," he replied quietly. "The outlaws are still at large ... and they grow increasingly bold." His gaze flicked to Rose. "I'd be wary of straying too far from the village these days."

Rose didn't answer, and an awkward pause drew out before Eara cleared her throat. "Very well, we appreciate ye telling us, Captain."

Remembering her manners, Rose forced herself to add, "Aye … thank ye."

Inclining his head, Kerr moved back to his horse and mounted. Kyle followed suit.

"Perhaps I *will* pass by and purchase some ale one day, Eara," the bailiff said then with another warm smile. "I hear ye brew it better than yer late husband."

Eara nodded, although her expression was veiled now. "I do."

The bailiff and the captain urged their horses forward then, departing with a nod to the women. Moments later, the horses quickened their pace to a canter, leaving them behind.

Watching them go, Rose unclenched her hands at her sides.

Next to her, Eara heaved a sigh of relief. "Well, that was fortunate."

"Aye," Rose replied weakly. "I suppose so."

Eara glanced her way. "They were helpful, were they not?"

Rose sighed. She then nodded to the sacks of barley. "Come, let's get going." The afternoon was waning; she needed to get back to the farm before her father and brothers did and put supper on.

Moving forward, both women grabbed hold of the rope and resumed towing the handcart along the rutted road.

As they walked, Rose cut Eara a veiled look. "The bailiff seems to have taken a shine to ye now," she observed.

Eara's mouth curved in response. "When Kyle MacAlister isn't collecting rent, he manages to be quite charming." She paused then, fixing Rose with a penetrating look. "Enough about the bailiff though … what was that between ye and Captain Mackay?"

Rose stiffened. "Nothing."

"Ye still hate him then?" Eara's voice took on a wry edge. She was the only person Rose had confided in about what had happened at Samhuinn.

"Aye."

"It's a pity. He's one of the few local men I'd consider a tumble with." Rose made a choking noise at this, yet Eara blithely continued. "Although I wouldn't have a chance. It's ye he wants. The man gazes at ye as if ye are the Virgin Mary herself."

Rose growled a curse and dug her elbow into her friend's side. "Wash yer mouth out with soap, Eara Mackay. He does not!"

Eara yelped. "Hades, yer elbow's sharp. I'll have a bruise on my ribs tomorrow."

"Aye, well … it'll teach ye not to talk rot."

Rose shot her friend a glare to see Eara was grinning, a devilish gleam in her eyes. "Deny it all ye like, but mark my words. That man's not done pining for ye."

7: WE RIDE AT DAWN

"YE SHOULD HAVE joined me yestereve," Brodie said, helping himself to a bannock. "The *Ardshiel* was packed to the rafters … and a group of traveling minstrels from Edinburgh played the harp for us while we diced."

Kerr swallowed his mouthful of porridge before shrugging. "Sounds entertaining, yet I couldn't get away."

Brodie met his eye across the table. They sat in the hall, consuming their morning meal just after dawn. The two brothers were alone at the chieftain's table, upon the dais, while men-at-arms, retainers, and their families lined the trestle tables below. As usual, the laird and his wife were breaking their fast upstairs with Lennox and Davina in the solar.

His brother shrugged. "Aye, The Black Wolves continue to elude ye," he replied. "But ye can't work all the hours the Lord sends. The occasional trip to Ceann Locha would do ye good."

Kerr's mouth pursed, as it often did when anyone mentioned The Black Wolves—as locals were now calling the outlaws. He didn't need reminding of his failure.

"Maybe," he said tersely, "but I won't rest until those whoresons have been brought to justice."

Brodie raised a dark eyebrow before dropping his attention to the bannock. Splitting it open, he spread butter and honey on thickly before taking a bite. "Anne asked after ye last night," he said when he'd swallowed his mouthful. "Wanted to know why ye no longer accompany me into town."

Kerr's hold on his wooden spoon tightened. He caught the teasing edge to his brother's voice but wasn't in the mood to entertain it. "And what did ye tell her?" he asked lightly.

Anne was a serving lass at the *Ardshiel Tavern*. Tall with a thick mane of chestnut hair and moss-green eyes, Kerr had once been struck by how much she looked like Rose MacAlister. One eve, after he'd downed too much ale, he'd tumbled her upstairs, in her attic chamber.

Anne was sunny-natured, passionate, and easy company—but she wasn't Rose. She didn't wish to be either, for the lass asked for coin from those patrons she let swive her. They'd lain together a couple of times before Kerr stopped accompanying Brodie into town.

"Nothing much," Brodie drawled, reaching for his cup of watered-down ale. "Only that ye have become a wet blanket of late."

Kerr snorted at the mild insult. "I'm sure she wasn't heartbroken."

"No." Brodie flashed him a wicked smile then, one that let Kerr know how his brother had spent the rest of his night once the dicing and music had ended.

Kerr wasn't jealous. There was nothing between him and Anne. Indeed, this conversation reminded him why he let his brother go off carousing on his own. Kerr no longer had the stomach for it.

These days, he was poor company anyway—easily irritated and impatient—even his men had earned the sharp edge of his tongue.

But the truth of it was, of course, that the elusive outlaws weren't the only reason for his moodiness. His longing for Rose MacAlister was starting to wear him down. He was sick of wanting someone who could barely look his way without curling her lip.

He thought about Rose often and worried what the future held for her—but when he and Kyle had come to her and Eara's aid the day before, Rose had made her disdain for him clear.

"Captain." Kerr glanced up to find one of the guards, Ronan, approaching the dais. "The horses are ready."

"Good." Kerr pushed aside the remains of his bowl of porridge. "Let's go."

"Off on another patrol?" Brodie asked.

Kerr nodded, rising to his feet. "Aye ... we're heading west this time to see if we can flush The Black Wolves out of the hills. A shepherd swears he spotted them yesterday, near the Drum Crags."

Drawing up his courser, Kerr swung down from the saddle. Prionnsa—Prince—tossed his head and sidestepped. Like Kerr, the gelding had been on edge all morning. Murmuring to Prionnsa, Kerr left his side, moving forward to inspect the prints in the mud. "They were here," he muttered. "Yet the curs still elude us."

Behind him, Ronan muttered a curse. It was in the tongue of Éire, his homeland, yet Kerr caught the meaning clear enough. "What are they ... wraiths?"

"The Wolves must have moved on, Captain," another of his men, Fingal, pointed out. "There's nowhere to hide out here."

"Aye, but where?" Kerr answered, straightening up.

"Maybe they've headed north again," Ronan said.

Kerr nodded. They could have, yet his gut told him that they hadn't. His gaze swept the bare glen they stood in. A burn meandered its way through the center of the wide valley, and after the recent rains, the path that led along its eastern bank was muddy. Beyond them, to the west, the Drum Crags rose against the sky. Black and rocky, the hills lived up to their name.

His belly tightened then. The attacks on travelers hadn't ceased. There had been another one, just a fortnight earlier—a couple traveling to visit relatives in Ceann Locha. The wife had been raped and her husband badly beaten. They'd stolen their ponies and all their coin.

Kerr and his men had set out in pursuit straight after the attack, but the outlaws had simply vanished.

"They can't run, or hide, forever," Kerr said finally, returning to Prionnsa and mounting. "Sooner or later, we'll flush them out."

Hazel hopped forward, picking up the small wooden spoon with her beak and tossing it off the window ledge.

Laughing, Rose crossed from where she was frying an oaten bannock upon a griddle to the window. She then stooped and retrieved the spoon before placing it back on the ledge. "Here ye are, lass," she said, stroking the owl's head affectionately. "However, I must warn ye ... I can't keep picking that up all night."

"Why is that owl still here?"

Rose glanced over her shoulder to see that her father was frowning, his gaze fixed upon the large eagle owl perched on the window ledge. Later, Rose would open the shutters to the tiny window so Hazel could fly outside and begin her nightly hunt.

Ignoring his grumpiness, Rose smiled. "Hazel likes living with us, Da," she replied.

"Aye, but its wing healed a while ago."

"It did ... but she and I have formed a bond."

Graham snorted.

"Careful, Rose," Knox said, from where he sat whittling a piece of rosewood near the fire. "Ye don't want to end up strange ... like Auntie Kenna."

At the mention of his sister, whom he never visited these days, Graham muttered something under his breath. Meanwhile, Rose shook her head. "There's nothing wrong with Kenna."

Guilt stabbed her in the ribs then. It had been a while since she had paid her aunt a visit. Kenna lived with her friend Ailis west of Dun Ugadale. Rose made a mental note to pass by in the next few days.

Knox merely cocked an eyebrow in reply, while next to him, Clyde smirked. However, the expression pained him, and the smirk turned into a grimace. Her youngest brother had a crusted, swollen lip this eve—after tangling with two of Duncan MacDonald's lads earlier in the day.

Her brothers often sported black eyes or split lips, for all it took was a half-penny in Knox or Clyde's hand and they headed off to the nearest tavern. And there, they found trouble.

Flipping the bannock onto a wooden plate, Rose inhaled the nutty aroma. Her belly rumbled in response. Their evening pottage would have a wedge each of bannock with it—a treat indeed, after her father's cousin had gifted them a small sack of oats.

"So ... ye are off to Carradale market tomorrow then?" she asked as she cut the bannock up into wedges. It was best to change the subject. Her father's mood always grew dark when anyone brought up his sister in conversation. They'd been estranged for a while now.

"Aye, lass," her father rumbled. Seeing that supper was nearly ready, he sat up properly on his nest of furs to receive it. He then cast a sharp look at his sons. "Although we might end up staying away for a night or two."

"Aye?" Rose ladled out bowls of pottage, placing a wedge of bannock in each, before handing them to her father and brothers. "Why is that?"

"I want to use the coin we get for the sheep wisely," he replied. "Perhaps I'll get us a milk cow, in addition to some sows."

Rose nodded, pleased by this news. It had been a while since her father had taken such a practical approach. A cow would allow her to make cheese, and she could even sell any surplus at market, which would mean extra income for them.

"We should be paid well for our sheep," Clyde added, winking at his brother. "They're the best on the peninsula."

"Aye, well, just look after the coin ye get for them," Rose replied, her gaze narrowing as she continued to regard Clyde. "And do us all a favor—stay away from the alehouses in Carradale."

After a long day in the saddle, Kerr was exhausted. He'd just finished his dish of blood sausage and bread and was washing the delicious supper down with a tankard of ale, when a tall, rangy man with short brown hair and keen grey eyes loped into the hall of Dun Ugadale broch.

Duncan MacDonald halted a few feet from the door, his gaze sweeping the interior. He was looking for someone.

An instant later, the man's attention settled upon Captain Mackay.

Kerr stifled a sigh. He hoped MacDonald hadn't come here to complain about the MacAlisters again. After a long, fruitless day of searching for the outlaws, he wasn't in the mood to hear it. The constant bickering between the MacAlisters and the MacDonalds was wearing indeed, and with those Douglas criminals still at large, he had bigger problems to deal with at present.

"What's this?" Lennox said from next to him. He sat with an arm loosely slung across his wife's shoulders. "We rarely get a visit from MacDonald at this hour."

Farther down the table, the laird had noticed their visitor. Usually, the guards would keep newcomers at the gate and announce their arrival first to Iver, but not with the likes of MacDonald. The farmer was well-liked and respected locally.

He approached the laird's table now, his long legs crossing the rush-covered floor quickly. "Good eve, all," he greeted them before favoring Iver with a respectful nod. "And apologies if I've interrupted yer supper."

"We've just finished," Iver replied. Bonnie sat on his lap, her arms wrapped around her husband's neck. "Take a seat, Dunc, and pour yerself an ale."

The farmer's weathered face creased into a smile. "Thank ye, Mackay, but I cannot stay. We're off to market tomorrow, and I must ensure all our livestock is ready to move at dawn." His gaze flicked back to Kerr then. "I came to ask a favor of The Guard, Kerr."

"Aye?" Kerr put down his tankard, meeting his eye.

"The February market at Carradale is the biggest of the year," Duncan said, his features tightening. "I'm going to be selling off some of my best cattle." He paused then, his brow furrowing. "My sons will be accompanying me, as always, but I must admit I'm nervous this time."

"The cattle rustling has been dealt with," Kerr reminded him. Indeed, the culprit—the man who'd rallied his friends to steal from the MacDonalds—Graham MacAlister, had lost a hand last summer. "MacAlister won't cause ye any more trouble."

"Maybe not." Duncan's expression soured at the mention of his nemesis. "But with all the civil strife of late, the roads aren't as safe as they once were." He paused then, his brow furrowing. "It's been a hard winter ... empty bellies make men desperate."

Kerr sighed. MacDonald had a point. There was a reason why the farmer was one of the most prosperous in the area. He was clever and cautious.

"I'm happy for ye to provide an escort, Kerr," Iver said as he gently stroked his wife's back. "None of us want anything to befall Duncan's cattle on the way to market tomorrow." The laird paused then, his brow furrowing as he regarded MacDonald. "And we don't want ye to encounter those outlaws still roaming the hills either."

Kerr tensed. Of course, his brother was right. It was wise to keep men like Duncan MacDonald happy. He was a good tenant, always paid his rent on time, and kept his rowdy sons in check—most of the time, anyway. Kerr hadn't missed the note of chagrin in his elder brother's voice either. Iver was disappointed the Dun Ugadale Guard hadn't yet dealt with the brigands.

"Very well, Dunc," Kerr said with a nod. "I'll have a company of men ready at dawn. We'll meet ye at yer farm."

A relieved smile spread across the farmer's face. "Thank ye, Captain. I shall see ye at first light then." His gaze swept over the table, where the rest of the laird's kin sat, before he nodded to Iver. "Good eve, Mackay."

Kerr watched the farmer stride from the hall, greeting some of the men he passed as he went. He then turned back to his ale.

"Do ye want any company?" Lennox asked.

Kerr nodded. "We'll be making an early start though."

This comment brought a snort from Brodie, across the table. "Aye, yer wife will have to kick ye out of bed, Len."

"Fear not, I'll make sure he doesn't oversleep," Davina quipped.

Lennox winked at her, grinning. "Who says we'll be sleeping at that hour, lass?"

Davina laughed, even as her cheeks turned pink.

Watching them, Kerr felt a familiar tug of envy under his ribcage. He didn't resent Lennox or Iver. Instead, it warmed him to see them so happy. Iver had suffered years of ill luck with women before meeting Bonnie, while Lennox had once been too selfish to give his heart to anyone. Bonnie and Davina had softened his brothers, had changed their lives for the better.

Only a hard-hearted bastard could resent them that. Nonetheless, their contentment sometimes made Kerr feel as if he was on the outside looking in.

Taking a large gulp of ale, he shifted his attention to tomorrow's task. He then scowled.

Across the table, Brodie met his eye. "Something worrying ye, brother? Ye have the look of a man who's just sat his arse down on a thorn."

Kerr snorted. "Aye, well, I'm sore that the outlaws still elude us … they're bold enough these days to try and steal MacDonald's cattle."

"They can try," Lennox replied. He then lifted his tankard, a grim smile tugging at his mouth. "But let's see them succeed."

8: LOST WITHOUT YE

"OUT YE GO, lass ... happy hunting." Rose opened the shutter, wincing as a blast of freezing air entered. Hazel didn't appear to notice though, for, with a soft coo of thanks, the owl hopped forward before taking flight into the night.

Rose watched Hazel go. It was part of her daily routine she always looked forward to. The owl flew silent and swift into the star-sprinkled sky, and she found herself envying Hazel her freedom.

Unlike the eagle owl, Rose was very much tethered to the earth.

She lingered at the window for a short while longer, gazing up at the waxing crescent moon that had risen high. It was a clear night, promising a hard frost the following morning.

Yawning, Rose relatched the shutters and turned around. It was getting late. Her brothers had both fallen asleep in front of the hearth, wrapped in sheepskins. However, her father was still awake, his left hand curled around a cup of broth. His gaze was on the fire, his expression pensive.

The cottage was cramped, although Rose was used to living in such close quarters with her kin. She had a wee alcove in one corner, and a sheepskin hanging on the opposite side of the space shielded what had once been her parents' sleeping area. These days, her father retired there alone.

"I'm off to bed, Da," she announced. "Is there anything I can get ye first?"

Graham blinked, coming out of his reverie before he glanced her way. "No, lass."

"Very well ... I'll see ye in the morning then."

He shook his head. "We'll be getting up early and will try to be quiet. Don't fash yerself ... stay under the blankets."

Surprised, for he usually liked her to add fuel to the fire and prepare him and the lads something to eat in the mornings, Rose nodded. "I shall see ye when ye get back then."

"Aye."

Rose's brow furrowed. Her father was in an odd mood tonight. It was as if he wasn't quite there.

Deciding to let him be, she moved toward her corner. She'd almost reached it when he spoke once more. "I'm sorry, Rose."

Halting, she glanced over her shoulder, meeting his gaze. "What about, Da?"

He huffed a weary sigh. "Everything, lass. I've been a poor father ... but I want ye to know that I appreciate all that ye do for us." He paused then, his green eyes darkening. "We'd be lost without ye."

Rose's throat thickened. It was unlike her father to be so sentimental, and she found it both worrying and touching. Moving across to him, she leaned down and placed a kiss on his whiskery cheek. "I love ye, Da."

"Are the lads ready?"

"Aye." Knox's breath steamed in the frigid air as he answered. "We've loosened the last of the rocks. Once the MacDonalds reach this end of the gorge, the lads are going to allow the cattle to pass first before they let the rocks fall."

"They need to time it right," Graham replied, his gaze surveying the shadowed, deep-sided valley before them. The sun was about to crest the edge of the hill to the east. He'd chosen this spot carefully. It was an hour's ride from Dun Ugadale, and the narrow gorge would force the MacDonalds to spread out along the rocky road, to send their cattle ahead of them. "The men need to be trapped *behind* the rockfall, not in front of it."

"They will be," Clyde assured him.

The bluff confidence in his youngest son's voice made Graham scowl. Not for the first time, he wished Rose had been born a lad. Kerr Mackay was a meddling whoreson, yet he was right about one thing: Rose was worth more than any of them.

Guilt tightened his gut then. His daughter deserved better than the life he'd given her.

Once ye sell these cattle at Clachan market, ye'll be able to make things easier for her, he assured himself. This is a solid plan.

It was also a clever one. Rushing down the gorge, dirks drawn, and fighting the MacDonalds man-to-man wouldn't be wise. Duncan and his sons were strong fighters, but the greater risk was that if Graham, and those who joined him, revealed their identities, there would be a price on all their heads. A rockfall would make it look like an accident. There would be dust and debris, and some of the MacDonalds would be crushed under rocks. And while they were dealing with the commotion, Graham and his lads would herd the frightened cattle out of the gorge and push them west, away from Carradale.

And no one would even know it had been them.

A whistle sounded then, twittering like a lark's call.

It echoed down the cold, still gorge, shattering the dawn silence. Anticipation twisted in Graham's gut. Finally. After years of struggle, of watching others prosper while his life fell to pieces, he had a chance to even the scales. Not only that, but he would strike a blow against his archenemy.

Duncan MacDonald would taste defeat for once.

Turning to his sons, and marking the same excitement in their eyes, Graham flashed them a grin. "It's time."

"This is kind of ye to take so much trouble, Lady Bonnie … thank ye."

Rose took the basket the laird's wife passed her, even as humiliation twisted like a blade to the chest. As kind as the gesture was, she'd grown tired of seeing the pity in the eyes of those who brought her food.

Bonnie and Davina were doing their best to hide it, yet she saw their concern.

The three women stood outside the door to the cottage. A frost sparkled around them. Rose had just drawn water from the well in the garden and was carrying it back inside, when she'd spied the two women riding garrons approach.

Irritation had bubbled up within Rose at the sight. She'd slept in later than intended and was now running late. Eara would have already lit the large cauldron in her bothy. Right now, she'd likely be readying the trays of malted barley for the next stage in the ale-making process, and Rose was eager to join her. She enjoyed working at her friend's side. Brewing ale gave her a sense of purpose. It was *hers*. At home, she felt like a servant, but with Eara, she was an apprentice alewife.

But now, she'd be very late, and Eara would wonder where she was.

"It's no trouble at all," Bonnie replied, her blue eyes studying Rose intently. "We have more than enough food to share. We don't want ye fading away."

Rose gave a soft snort. Fortunately, she was of tough farming stock—she was a hardy, sturdily-built lass. Aye, she'd gotten thinner over the past months, but now Rose had survived the winter, she'd fatten up over the warmer months; she always did.

"Aye, well, food has to be shared between the four of ye," Davina added with an arch look. "And we all know what hearty appetites men have."

Rose stiffened. Was that a veiled criticism aimed at her menfolk? Did they think her father and brothers scoffed all the food and left nothing for her? Her father and brothers could be selfish—and there had been times over the years when she'd wished she'd been born into a different family—but she was as protective of them as a she-wolf over her cubs.

"I get my share," she finally replied, shattering the uncomfortable silence.

The aroma of sweet buns tickled Rose's nose then, rising up from the cloth-covered basket. And an instant later, to her embarrassment, her belly gave a loud growl.

Davina gave a soft laugh. "I'd say it's time ye broke yer fast."

"Aye." Cheeks warming, Rose tightened her grip on the basket. "Ye have both been kind to my family," she said awkwardly. *Kinder than yer menfolk have been.* "I know Da and the lads are never here to thank ye, but they do appreciate yer generosity."

Bonnie smiled. "It's the least we can do, Rose," she replied, a note of chagrin in her voice now. "Ye live on Mackay lands ... and whether or not ye realize it, that makes ye family."

"Can ye believe Lady Bonnie said we were *family*?" Rose glanced up from where she was using a heavy wooden rolling pin to crush malted and kilned barley into 'grist' and met Eara's eye. "Is that what we are?"

Not waiting for her friend's answer, she clenched her jaw and resumed rolling the barley in long sweeping motions. It was hard labor, although Rose welcomed it today—for irritation pulsed through her. Kneeling on the floor of the alewife's bothy, Rose crushed the grain upon a large flat stone.

Meanwhile, the alewife's black cat, Ember, watched Rose with narrowed amber eyes. The over-fed feline hadn't taken kindly to her daily presence in the bothy and, even months on, treated the alewife's assistant like an interloper.

A few feet away, Eara sighed and pushed a lock of flaxen hair out of her eyes. The alewife's cheeks were flushed, as she too had been working vigorously, smashing grist and water into a paste using a large pestle and mortar. "I'm sure Lady Bonnie meant well."

Shoving herself upright, so that she sat on her heels, Rose scowled. "Really? Family cut off the hand of their own flesh and blood, do they?"

The raw resentment in her voice—as well as the chagrin in Eara's eyes—jolted her out of her ill-temper.

Don't be such an ungrateful chit, she berated herself. *Bonnie and Davina are lovely women who genuinely care about folk.*

Indeed, her family's ruin wasn't their fault. It wasn't fair to take her frustration out on them.

"God's blood, just listen to me," she muttered. "If I'm not careful, I'll end up like my Da."

"Or like auld Margie Mackay," Eara added, her tone wry now. "Although Lord knows, the woman has plenty of reasons to be angry ... what with her feckless husband and a brood of ungrateful sons."

Rose scrubbed a hand down her face. "Aye, but she never misses an opportunity to complain about her lot to anyone who'll listen." She pulled a face. "I don't want to turn into someone like that."

Silence followed her statement, and Eara's expression turned pensive. "Aye, we *all* have to ward ourselves against bitterness." After a pause, she then favored Rose with a whimsical half-smile. "Few folk go through life without disappointments, Rose ... the trick is not to dwell on them."

Later, as Rose walked up the path to her family's cottage, she reflected on her friend's words. Sometimes, she envied Eara her sanguine attitude. They were both strong-willed and practical women, traits that had drawn them together in friendship—yet Rose had inherited her father's dogmatism.

If she was to follow his lead, she'd end up raging against the world.

Eara was right. She couldn't let life's setbacks sour her character.

Entering the cottage, Rose set down the large bag full of skins of ale on the worktable. Her father and brothers would have plenty of cool ale to quench their thirsts when they returned from the Carradale market. She glanced over at where Hazel was roosting on the window ledge. The eagle owl was fast asleep, and she wouldn't disturb her.

Rose's gaze alighted on the basket of sweet buns she'd left on the table earlier.

With a sigh, she helped herself to one and took a bite. She'd already had a bun and should really leave the rest for her menfolk. Nonetheless, her belly was still growling. Sweetened with honey and dried plums, it was delicious.

Rose took the bun outside and lowered herself onto a stool on the edge of her rambling cottage garden. She'd planted the first of the spring greens the day before, yet there was still much work to be done. She ate the bun slowly before standing up and brushing the crumbs off her skirts.

There was no hurry to put the noon meal on today, as her father and brothers weren't likely to be back until the following morning at the earliest. Nonetheless, she couldn't sit idle—there were always chores to be done and a garden to be tamed. She'd also collected reeds from a nearby burn the day before and planned to weave some baskets, which she could then sell at the village market.

Her father and brothers were doing their best to get a good price for their sheep, and she'd do her bit too. She appreciated the ale she received from Eara, but she needed coin as well.

Rose was about to turn and go inside when the ground started to vibrate.

Glancing up, she spied a lone rider approaching down the glen, fast.

It was still a bright, cold day, and the sunlight had a silvery quality. As such, Rose squinted as she tried to make out the identity of the rider.

As they drew closer, she saw it was a man, clad in dark leather, shaggy white-blond hair streaming behind him.

Rose's breathing stilled, and she tightened her grip on her trowel.

"The devil's turds," she growled. "What's *he* doing here?"

She'd seen far too much of Kerr Mackay of late. Everywhere she turned, there he was. As he approached, she was tempted to go indoors and bolt the door, yet she resisted the urge. Instead, she held her ground, watching as he drew his courser up a few yards away and swung down from the saddle.

She noticed then that his horse was lathered and breathing hard, as was he. Mackay's leathers were coated in dust, and streaks of grime marked his face. His handsome face was set in harsh lines.

Rose folded her arms across her chest and lifted her chin as he approached. "What do ye want?" Her tone was rude, yet she didn't care. He wasn't welcome here.

Kerr stopped before her, his chest rising and falling sharply. His sea-blue eyes were darker than usual. His gaze burned into her.

She spied a cut above his right eye then, and foreboding prickled across her skin like an army of marching ants. It looked like he'd been in a fight—but with whom?

They stared at each other for a few moments before Rose eventually muttered, "Well ... are ye going to speak?"

Kerr's throat bobbed. "I'm sorry, Rose."

Her breathing caught, nausea sweeping over her. The roughness in his voice warned her she wouldn't welcome the news he was about to deliver.

"Is it my father?" she whispered.

He nodded.

"Tell me."

"He, yer brothers, and five others tried to steal the MacDonald's cattle on the way to Carradale."

Rose's heart kicked against her ribs. "What? That can't be right. Da and the lads are taking *our* sheep to market this morning."

He shook his head. "They caused a rockfall in a gorge north of here ... it killed a few men, but most of us got through." He broke off then, his gaze guttering. "There was a fight afterward ... yer father and brothers were killed."

Rose took a step back, staggering slightly. "No," she whispered.

Sadness flickered across Kerr's face. "I wish it weren't so, lass," he said softly, "but it is."

Her legs gave way under her then. She'd have collapsed if Kerr hadn't leaped forward and caught her under the arms.

"Why?" she croaked, hanging in his grip as shock rolled through her. "*Why?*"

He didn't answer. Moments passed, and then a terrible suspicion dawned. Heat swept across Rose, and she struggled out of his grip. She then pushed herself away from him. "Did *ye* kill them?"

"No," he said roughly, alarm sparking in his eyes.

"Liar! Ye have always hated my family ... this was the chance ye were waiting for, wasn't it?"

"No, Rose," he rasped. "Do ye really think me such a beast?"

Rose swallowed down bile. Aye, she did.

"When the fight turned against him, yer father skewered himself on Duncan MacDonald's dirk." A nerve flickered in Kerr's cheek as he spoke. "Yer brothers died by the hands of two of my guards."

"No!" Rose's wail echoed across the garden, splintering the bright, still day.

Grief barreled into her, like a mailed fist to the stomach. She doubled over, unable to withstand the pain. All three of them gone—just like that. She hadn't been able to take it in initially, yet now the truth flattened her.

"Dear Lord, no!"

A red haze blinded her then, fury erupting. She flew at Kerr, fists clenched. She caught him by surprise, and one fist slammed into his stomach, while the other smacked him in the jaw. He grunted, reeling back under the force of her rage.

She swung at him again, but this time, he was ready. He caught her wrists, pinning them against his chest as she writhed against him. Her knee came up sharply, aiming for his cods, yet he shifted, and her kneecap dug into the hard muscle of his thigh instead.

Her cry, rage blending with grief, ripped through the air, and she struggled against him.

Damn him for being so strong. She was no weakling, yet it was impossible to wrest herself from his iron grip. But still, she fought him, snarling curses.

Kerr didn't budge, even if his face had gone taut with strain.

Finally, exhaustion dragged at her, and she went limp against him—and as soon as she did, the sorrow that her anger had momentarily eclipsed slammed into her.

A painful sob rose up, ripping from Rose's throat. And once the dam broke, there was no keeping the tears back.

Suddenly, Kerr disappeared, as did the rest of the world.

All that existed was pain.

9: SOMEONE TO WATCH OVER HER

KERR CAUGHT ROSE as her legs gave way under her
once more.

Picking the woman up, he carried her toward the
cottage. She didn't fight him now; she no longer saw him
at all.

Shouldering the door open, he took her inside.

A lump of peat smoldered in the hearth, casting its
golden glow over the dark space. The single small
window was open, allowing a stream of pale sunlight to
filter in also. The interior of the cottage was cluttered,
the walls lined with shelves. A sheepskin hanging,
presumably leading through to the sleeping area, broke
up the space, yet Kerr didn't take Rose through.

Instead, he lowered her down on the pile of
sheepskins in front of the glowing fire.

Ignoring him, she curled up in a ball, sobs tearing
from her. Kerr knelt before her and placed a reassuring
hand on her shoulder. However, it was pointless, Rose
was lost in grief; he couldn't reach her.

Maybe its for the best, since she thinks I'm Satan.

Aye, he knew she hated him, yet he remained there
for a while, watching over her while she wept. The winter
had taken its toll on Rose, he noted. She'd lost flesh. Her
cheekbones were sharper than in the summer, and the
kirtle was loose on her. She looked achingly vulnerable

curled up there, her face in her hands, her shoulders shaking.

She'd had an awful shock. There was no good way to deliver news like that. He'd steeled himself to do it the entire journey to the MacAlister farm—but when he'd finally stood before her, words had deserted him.

He hadn't been surprised when she'd accused him of killing her father, although it had still stung all the same. Kerr's jaw clenched then as he let himself think about what had happened in that gorge.

They'd been three-quarters of the way through it—riding in twos along the narrow road, driving the cattle before them—when a deep rumble shattered the peace of the morning.

He'd glanced up to see dust rising from the rocky hillside above.

An instant later, the first of the boulders hurtled toward them.

He hadn't told Rose, but those heavy rocks had caused carnage, killing three MacDonalds and their horses.

Kerr and his men, who'd been in the lead, just escaped being flattened, as did Duncan MacDonald and his sons. If MacAlister had been planning on killing his nemesis, he failed.

The skirmish that had followed was quick yet bloody.

Kerr would never tell Rose how desperate her father was, as he slashed clumsily, his dirk clenched in his left hand. Roaring curses, Graham had run at them—and when he realized the fight was lost, he'd thrown himself on Duncan's blade.

In the end, all eight would-be cattle thieves lay dead at the bottom of the gorge, their blood soaking into the dirt. Meanwhile, the bellows of frightened cattle, and Duncan MacDonald's enraged cursing, echoed around them.

A scraping sound drew Kerr's attention then, and he looked away from Rose to see movement on the ledge next to the window.

A large eagle owl perched there. The bird was beautiful, with speckled brown feathers and faintly comical ear tufts. It blinked drowsily, moving forward, its claws scraping across stone. The bird had clearly been sleeping when they entered, yet Rose's weeping had awoken it. The owl then cocked its head, its dark-golden eyes fixing upon him. Kerr could almost imagine it was concerned about Rose.

"She'll be fine ... in a while," he murmured. "Although she needs someone to watch over her."

The bird continued to stare at him, unblinking.

Sighing, Kerr rose to his feet, his gaze returning to Rose. He didn't want to leave her like this, yet he was expected back at Dun Ugadale. The MacDonalds were in an uproar right now.

He needed to find someone to stay with Rose, to help while her grief ran its course. To his knowledge, the only kin she had remaining was a reclusive aunt. If he remembered correctly, the woman lived west of the broch, deep within the Red Deer Hills.

He'd fetch her.

Kerr glanced over at the owl once more to find it still watching him with disconcerting focus. "Look after her," he said softly. "I'll be back with help soon."

"Sit up lass, I've got some hot broth for ye."

Kenna's soft voice roused Rose from her misery. Opening her eyes, she pushed herself up into a sitting position. Her stiff limbs protested, and her head throbbed. Lord, she felt terrible. How long had she been curled up on these sheepskins, weeping?

It felt like forever.

She vaguely remembered Kerr Mackay bringing her in here and laying her down. She also recalled the rumble of his voice, although she couldn't remember what he'd said. She supposed she should be embarrassed about losing control like that around him, yet she was too drained now to care. Mackay had left eventually, and the silence had pressed in, making her sorrow even keener. But then, a while after he departed—she wasn't sure how long—her aunt arrived.

Kenna held her close and stroked her hair, and eventually, the storm had passed.

In the aftermath, Rose felt weak, as if she'd just emerged from a fever.

Sitting in silence, she watched her aunt ladle out a cup of broth from the pot steaming over the fire. Her belly growled then. "How long has it been?" she asked. The question came out in a croak, and Kenna's heart-shaped face creased into a gentle smile as she handed over the cup.

"Just a day. Here ... ye'll feel better after ye've had this."

Wrapping her hands around the wooden cup, Rose took a sip of the hot broth. It was delicious, for her aunt had made it with pork bones. A rare treat these days.

"Thank ye," she murmured. "It's kind of ye to come to me so quickly."

"I wouldn't have known what had happened if Captain Mackay hadn't ridden to fetch me," her aunt replied with a rueful shake of her head. "He was worried about ye."

Heat flushed over Rose, and she dropped her gaze to her cup of broth. Of course, her aunt didn't know that she couldn't stand the man.

God's bones, he was like a bad penny, always turning up when things went ill. Was it any surprise he'd been the one to tell her of her father and brothers' fate?

Moments slid by, and when Rose glanced up, Kenna was settling herself onto a stool near the fire. Her green eyes, so like her brother's, guttered. "I'm sorry, Rose ... it's a terrible thing."

"Aye," Rose whispered, her chest constricting. Part of her couldn't believe her father and brothers were dead. She half-expected them to throw open the door to the cottage and walk in, their rough voices shattering the peace.

But they wouldn't. Never again.

Swallowing more broth, she steeled herself to ask the question she dreaded. "Where are they?"

Kenna's face tightened, and she brushed a lock of red-brown hair streaked with grey off her forehead. "At Dun Ugadale broch. The laird has agreed to keep them there for the moment ... until the burial."

Rose approached the kirk. A crisp wind tugged at her skirts and the woolen shawl she'd wrapped around her shoulders. She did her best to ignore the cold, her gaze remaining fixed upon the steepled roof of the stone kirk piercing the sky.

Her body ached from grief, and her throat and eyes were raw from weeping—but she had a burial to organize.

Rose found Father Gregor indoors. He was praying before the altar, head bowed. Inhaling the musky scent of incense, she halted behind him. If he'd heard her approach and the whisper of the door closing, he gave no sign.

Rose waited for a short while before clearing her throat. "Father Gregor."

The priest straightened up, his gaze flicking her way. "Rose MacAlister," he murmured. "I was wondering when ye would pay me a visit."

Rose wilted a little under the intensity of those peat-brown eyes. "Ye will have heard what happened?" she asked huskily.

He nodded, his gaze narrowing.

"I wish to bury my father and brothers tomorrow."

Father Gregor rose smoothly to his feet and dusted off his robes. "Ye can bury them when ye wish," he said coolly. "Just not on holy ground."

Rose's heart jolted against her breastbone. "What?"

The priest's mouth pursed. "I will not allow criminals to be buried alongside Godfearing folk."

"My father and brothers were part of this congregation," she choked out as grief and anger battled for dominance. "Baptized like everyone else."

"Maybe … but they all strayed from the path."

Rose swallowed as bile stung the back of her throat. Her pulse pounded in her ears, and her legs trembled slightly. She couldn't believe the priest was denying her family this. When she finally spoke, her voice was hoarse, pleading. "Didn't Jesus himself preach compassion and forgiveness?"

"Aye."

"Well then, why won't ye show some to my family?"

His dark eyes hardened. "Do ye defend their behavior, Rose?"

She shook her head. Of course, she didn't. When Kerr told her what they'd done, she'd been horrified. She'd later learned that three MacDonalds had died in the rockfall. She was deeply ashamed of her father's act. "Never," she gasped. "But to refuse them a Christian burial is cruel indeed."

Father Gregor approached her then, his robes whispering as he moved. He stopped when they were just a couple of feet apart. His closeness was unnerving and deliberately intimidating. However, they were of a similar height, so she didn't need to raise her chin to hold his gaze.

"An eye for an eye, Rose," he murmured, his mouth lifting into a humorless smile. "And yet … I *could* be swayed to change my mind."

She tensed, fighting the urge to step back and widen the gap between them. "Ye could?"

"Aye, lass." He reached out, stroking her hair. He entwined a lock between his long fingers, tugging gently.

His gaze softened then, his lips parting. "Although my generosity will come at a price."

Rose froze. She knew without asking exactly what he wanted.

Trembling now, she stepped back so he was forced to let go of her hair. "Something tells me yer price will be too high, *Father*," she replied, not hiding the anger and disgust in her voice.

In an instant, the softness in his eyes vanished. "Then there will be no Christian burial," he ground out. "Yer father and brothers will burn in hell."

In the end, she buried her father, Knox, and Clyde on the eastern side of the glen, where they'd lived and farmed all their lives.

Ailis and Eara joined Kenna and Rose, and together, the women dug three graves. They then wrapped the men in sheepskins and lay them inside, covering them with soil and piles of stones, creating three small cairns on the hillside.

It was hard work, yet the morning was cold and damp, which helped cool the sweat on their brows. And when they were done, Ailis whispered a prayer for the dead.

Head bent, Rose was surprised to find she was dry-eyed.

She'd wept a loch of tears over the last two days and digging the graves had helped get rid of the rage and grief that still boiled inside her.

When she'd told Kenna and Ailis that Father Gregor had denied her menfolk a proper burial before trying to blackmail her into lying with him, they'd both been furious.

"A wolf in sheep's clothing indeed," Kenna growled. "How dare he?"

"Oh, he dared," Rose had replied.

"Be careful with the priest in the future," Ailis had warned, worry shadowing her hazel eyes. Small with curly dark hair and an impish face, Ailis had been uncharacteristically grim as she met Rose's gaze. "He'll have an ax to grind against ye now."

Rose had nodded. It was best she stop attending the Sunday mass for a while.

The women fell silent as they remained before the cairns, listening to the cry of kites wheeling above and the whine of the wind. Then Rose stepped forward and placed a hand on the stones of her father's cairn. "At least he'll be at peace now," she murmured.

"At last," Eara said, sadness tinging her voice. "Yer Da was a tormented man."

"Aye," her aunt murmured. "Especially toward the end." She paused then. "He was happy once though ... when he first wed yer mother, Graham was always smiling."

Rose glanced Kenna's way to see the grief etched upon her aunt's proud face. The siblings might have been estranged, yet Kenna had loved her brother, all the same. And now she'd never have the chance to mend things with him—just as Rose hadn't been able to say goodbye to her father and brothers. Knox and Clyde were wastrels, yet their lives had been cut tragically short. It was such a waste.

"What will ye do now?" Ailis asked then.

"Sell Da's sheep," Rose announced firmly. Sorrow had consumed her over the past days, yet she had to be practical. "That should give me enough to live on for a while. I will also start weaving more baskets to sell at the village market."

"Ye can always come and live with us." Kenna offered gently. "We'd welcome yer company."

Rose's chest started to ache. Kenna and Ailis's cottage was a tiny one, yet they wouldn't hesitate to share it with her. However, just like Eara, Rose was proud and independent. "I appreciate yer kind offer, auntie," she replied huskily. "But I will find a way through this."

10: PRIDE

STANDING IN THE hall of Dun Ugadale, before the dais where the laird sat, Rose blinked.

Surely, she'd misheard Iver Mackay?

She hadn't wanted to attend the chieftain's weekly audience. After all the trouble between her family and the Mackays, she tried to avoid their broch whenever possible. However, when she'd gone out to retrieve her family's flock of black-faced sheep that morning and found them missing, she'd been forced to walk to the broch in the rain.

And when it was Rose's turn to speak before the laird, he'd informed her that the sheep now belonged to Duncan MacDonald.

"What?" she croaked.

Iver Mackay loosed a heavy sigh. Seated upon a carven chair—a fur mantle wrapped around his broad shoulders, his white-blond hair pulled back from his face—he was an intimidating sight. And just as threatening was the tall, leather-clad figure standing to his right: his brother Kerr.

"He shouldn't have taken them without informing ye first," the chieftain continued. "And I shall have a word in his ear about that ... but it is MacDonald's right, Rose." Mackay paused then. "After what yer father did."

Rose's pulse started to hammer in her ears. "But those sheep were all I had left," she whispered.

"I'm sorry, lass," the laird replied, his features tensing. "But I have other ill-tidings." He paused then, glancing at Kerr. The two brothers shared a long look before Mackay focused on Rose once more. "I was going to send Kerr out to give ye the news … but yer appearance now saves him a trip. MacDonald will also be taking possession of yer cottage and lands."

Rose's gasp echoed through the hall. Around her, she could feel the stares of the laird's retainers and the other folk waiting for an audience with the laird. She hated being the center of attention, for many of the gazes upon her weren't friendly, as if she had been part of her father's plot.

"But *why*?" she finally managed.

Mackay held her eye. "Yer father's attack robbed Duncan of much. A flock of sheep and some land is little in recompense … but it is his due nonetheless."

Rose started to shake. She wanted to scream at him, yet she choked the words back.

She wouldn't heap more humiliation upon herself. Her pride was the only thing she had left.

"Ye have an aunt, do ye not?" the chieftain asked, his brow furrowing.

Rose managed a jerky nod. She couldn't speak. Her tongue felt cloven to the roof of her mouth.

His expression softened. "Well, I'm sure she will take ye in."

Rose already knew she would, yet that wasn't the point. The Mackays were ripping away the only home she'd ever known and giving it to the MacDonalds.

Something twisted deep in her chest. Lord, she couldn't believe she was about to lose her cottage and garden.

"I can send men to help ye clear things out?" Mackay said after an awkward pause.

Another wave of heat rolled over Rose. Hades, that was the last thing she needed.

"No," she gasped out the word. "I need no assistance."

And with that, choking back rage and grief, she swiveled on her heel and stormed from the broch.

On the way, she passed Maisie MacDonald.

Maisie glared at her as she walked by. "Someone's got to pay for what yer Da did," she growled. "And someone *will*."

Rose's breathing quickened. Eara had told her that one of the three MacDonalds who'd died in that gorge was Maisie's younger brother. The woman had never liked her before, yet now there was hate in her eyes.

Dread fluttered up then, causing her belly to clench. How many other villagers would turn on her?

Hurrying on, Rose left the broch and made her way down the slippery steps into the barmkin. Hot tears stung her eyelids, yet she blinked them back. She wouldn't weep—not until she was outside the broch.

Sheets of rain swept over Dun Ugadale now, and the clouds pressed close. It would be a wet walk home, yet Rose was too upset to care. Let the heavens open. Let lightning strike from the sky and smite her dead. What did it matter anyway?

"Rose!"

A man's voice hailed her as she crossed the barmkin, head bowed against the rain. However, she walked on. It was only when a hand caught her by the arm that she was forced to stop.

Whipping around, she came face to face with Kerr Mackay.

"Satan's cods," she choked out. "Not *ye* again."

"Please, Rose," he gasped, out of breath from sprinting after her. "I have to talk to ye."

"No." She tried to twist out of his grip, but he held her firm. His hold was surprisingly gentle, although his fingers had locked around her arm, and she couldn't budge them. "Let me go *now*, whoreson!"

Her grief and anger spilled over then. Blinded by tears, she shoved hard at his chest.

The bastard didn't budge.

Jaw bunching, Kerr towed her out of the rain, and into a narrow passage between the granary and the stables. The roof overhung here, protecting them from the weather. An instant later, Rose found her back pressed up against damp stone, Kerr looming over her.

Her throat was aching cruelly now, and she swallowed a sob.

Was there no end to her humiliation? The Mackays had ruined her life—and now one of the men responsible was watching tears stream down her face.

Still holding onto her arm, for he knew that she'd bolt if he didn't, the captain stared down at her. The rain had wet his face and slicked his hair back. "Ye aren't alone, Rose," he said softly. "There's no need for ye to go to yer aunt's, if ye don't wish to. I've just spoken to Iver … and he'll give ye a position here, in the broch."

Rose jolted. "What?" That must have been a quick exchange, for she had just left the hall.

He swallowed. "Aye, lass. Bonnie requires another chambermaid. The job is yers … if ye want it."

"Well, I don't," she rasped, scrubbing at her tears with her free hand.

A nerve flickered in his cheek. "Why not?"

"I don't want any charity from ye!"

"Don't let pride ruin ye, Rose. This is yer chance to start again. Don't throw it away."

"Ye need to stop interfering in my life," she cried, fury pulsing like a living thing in her breast, eclipsing her grief. "Haven't ye realized that ye are the last person in heaven and earth I wish to receive help from?"

His blue eyes guttered. "Is this what ye want then?" he asked hoarsely, leaning in and placing his free hand on the stone wall, next to her head. It was a dominant move and one that made her breathing hitch. Even now, his closeness affected her, as it had that day in the kirk. And as they stared at each other, a mask slid over Kerr's features, his own anger rising now. "For the whole world to turn its back on ye?"

"No," she replied, her voice barely above a whisper. "Just *ye*."

His blue eyes darkened. "I'm not responsible for yer father and brothers' deaths, or for the choices they made in life. Open yer eyes, Rose. None of them were saints.

They died as they lived ... trying to take from others instead of earning an honest living."

His words sliced into her like boning knives, and Rose cringed back against the wall. "Release me," she gasped. "Or I shall start screaming like a banshee."

A strong emotion, one she couldn't quite place, rippled over his handsome features, and the anger in his eyes banked. "I'd never hurt ye, Rose," he rasped, letting go of her arm as if scalded. "And ye know it."

Curse him, she did. But that didn't mean she'd admit it. All she wanted now was to run from this place.

Seizing her chance, she rushed back out into the rain and sprinted toward the gate leading from the broch, passing under the metal teeth of the raised portcullis without looking back.

Breathing hard, Kerr watched her go.

God's blood, it seemed that with every encounter he had with Rose, she hated him more. He was only trying to help, but each time he opened his mouth, he offended her.

Ye are the last person in heaven and earth I wish to receive help from.

Even in her grief, the lass didn't bandy her words. She really did loathe him, and no matter how he tried to mend their relationship, he just made things worse. And to nail the coffin shut, he'd just gone and insulted her family. Everything he'd said was the truth, but such was Rose's devotion to her father and brothers, she wouldn't hear a word against them.

Of course, sorrow still had her in its grip—and it had blinkered her.

Her loyalty was something he'd always admired. When Rose MacAlister loved, it was for life. But the other side of the coin was that she hated for life too. There was no changing her mind about him.

Kerr's gut twisted then, nausea rolling over him, and he leaned against the wall, waiting for it to pass.

"Enough," he muttered. "Ye have to let her be now."

Rose hated him. It was pointless to try and help her.

Exhaustion pressed down on him then, and he pushed himself off the wall and walked back into the rain, crossing the barmkin, climbing the steps, and entering the broch once more.

His brother was finishing up inside, talking to Maisie MacDonald. Whatever answer he'd given the woman had disgruntled her, for she stalked away muttering to herself.

Wiping rain off his face, Kerr approached the dais. "Another unhappy conclusion?"

Iver grunted before nodding. "She's vexed that her cousin Duncan has been given all Graham MacAlisters run rigs. She wants half of them."

"And ye denied her?"

"Aye ... I promised the land to Duncan, and I'll not go back on my word." Iver eyed him then, taking in his soaked clothing and wet hair. "Did ye catch up with Rose?"

"Aye."

"And?"

"She'd rather kiss a leper than accept any help from the likes of me."

Iver's dark-blue eyes widened. "She said that?"

"No ... worse."

His brother shrugged. "At least ye tried."

Kerr didn't answer, and Iver's expression changed, his gaze glinting. "Ye are soft on her, aren't ye?"

Heat washed over Kerr. God's teeth, if Iver had noticed he was pining for Rose, who else had?

"Don't look so pained about it," Iver said, reading his face. "Rose is a comely lass, and ye are of the age to find yerself a wife. It's only natural ye'd be interested."

"I'm wasting my time," Kerr said roughly. "Rose believes I hounded her father ... and made things worse for him."

Iver's gaze narrowed. "Ye didn't, did ye?"

"Of course not. Graham MacAlister set fire to his own life, as ye well know."

"Well, just explain it to her."

Kerr snorted. "I did ... and now she despises me."

11: DEFENDING THE INDEFENSIBLE

ON HER LAST morning in the cottage, Rose awoke early and started clearing up. Eara arrived to help her, and together the two friends worked in brittle silence. There was little either of them could say that would bring solace to this day.

The night before, Rose had packed everything of sentimental value and a few essential items—for she was wary of cluttering up Kenna's cottage with her belongings. With the dawn, she and the alewife carried anything remaining outside, built a pyre, and set fire to it.

Tears filled Rose's eyes as she watched the pyre burn, while Eara put a comforting arm around her shoulders. There wasn't much, as they'd been forced to sell many of their belongings to pay for food over the winter.

Among the items she'd kept was a small wooden horse Knox had whittled out of rosewood for her years earlier. There were also half-finished items he'd been still working on, as well as her mother's amber brooch— an item she'd had to hide from her father, to stop him selling that too.

Dark smoke drifted into the pale dawn sky. The rain had spent itself overnight. "It looks as if our journey to Kenna's cottage will be a dry one," Rose murmured. "Thank ye, Eara ... for suggesting we use yer handcart. I don't have many things to bring to my aunt's, but it will be easier with the cart."

"It was the least I could do for a good friend," Eara replied, squeezing her shoulders gently.

Rose cast Eara a sidelong glance then. "I feel guilty about ye missing this morning's market." Indeed, the alewife always sold ale at the twice-weekly market in the village square—it was where she earned most of her coin.

"Don't worry about that," Eara replied firmly. "It's not the end of the world if I miss it once."

As the fire burned down to embers, they went back inside to collect the last of Rose's things.

Hazel watched them curiously as they worked, from her perch by the window, and eventually Rose approached her. Reaching out, she stroked the owl's soft feathers. "Do ye wish to come with me, lass?"

The owl shuffled forward and gave a soft hoot as if answering 'aye'.

Rose tried to rouse a smile, for she appreciated Hazel's company, especially now—but failed. She didn't have much to smile about these days.

While Eara carried a few packs and bags outside, Rose wrapped her father's sealskin cloak, one he'd used for rainy weather, around her shoulders. Putting on a heavy leather glove, she moved to the window and lowered her wrist to the ledge so that Hazel could climb on it.

The eagle owl was smaller than some, yet the bird was still weighty. Rose wouldn't be able to carry her for long on her wrist, so she lifted the owl up, allowing it to step onto her shoulder.

Hazel's claws dug in, yet the thick sealskin protected Rose from any damage. The bird's soft feathers tickled her cheek as she made her way toward the door. The cottage's interior was stark without the familiar objects surrounding her. Now that she'd cleared everything out, she just wanted to be gone.

Strangely, it no longer felt like her home—and later in the day, the MacDonalds would reside within it.

Stepping outdoors, she found Eara waiting for her, handcart at the ready. Immediately, her friend's gaze went to Hazel. "Well, look at that," Eara murmured, her mouth quirking. "She's so tame."

"Hazel doesn't want to be left behind," Rose replied. "But hopefully Kenna and Ailis won't mind her moving in with me."

Eara's gaze met Rose's. "Ye can live with me, ye know ... my bothy is a bit cramped, but I'd make space for ye."

Warmth suffused Rose's chest at her friend's offer. However, she was aware how unpopular she was in the village at present. Just the day before, a group of young lads, all MacDonalds, had heckled her as she walked up the street to Eara's.

No, it was best for all if she went to her aunt's—even if that meant she had a lengthy walk into the village. She'd still make the trip to Eara's a few times a week. Some things could continue as they had.

"I don't think Ember would appreciate Hazel," she said deliberately making an excuse that wouldn't set her friend to worrying. Indeed, the alewife's well-fed black mouser stalked around Eara's bothy like a queen.

Eara snorted. "She'd just have to get used to it."

"All the same, Kenna might take offense if I didn't stay with her."

That wasn't true—her aunt wouldn't mind either way—and Eara's gaze narrowed a fraction as if she'd seen right through Rose's excuses. Yet she didn't press the matter.

"Well then," she said, picking up the rope to tow her handcart. "We'd better get moving."

They walked down the path, through the rambling garden Rose had done her best to keep productive since her mother's death. They then took the rutted road back toward Dun Ugadale.

The two women traveled in silence for a spell, and soon enough, the outline of the broch shadowed the sky. Smoke rose from the roofs of the bothies below.

However, when Rose saw a group of women standing together by the roadside, she cursed under her breath.

"That's Maisie MacDonald and her friends," Eara murmured. "What do they want?"

Rose's pulse quickened. "Reckoning."

"There she is," Maisie called out, her voice carrying across the road. "The *criminal's* daughter!"

"Aye, turfed out of her home," another MacDonald woman added smugly.

"And rightly so," Maisie replied. "After what her kin did, she should be run off these lands."

Heat washed over Rose, a mix of humiliation and anger, yet she managed to bite her tongue. She didn't want an argument with these women—not this of all mornings.

Self-righteous muttering followed these words as Rose and Eara drew close, the handcart rattling behind them.

"Enough of this heckling," Eara greeted them with a scowl. "Why don't ye get yerselves off to market like most folk and leave Rose be?"

Maisie's round face tightened. "Ye'd be wise to distance yerself from this one, Eara Mackay," she replied, placing her hands on her hips. Eara snorted, yet Maisie plowed on. "Look at her, carrying an owl about with her. I'd say she's going a bit strange in the head."

Rose's heart started thumping against her ribs. "No, I'm not," she growled. "This is Hazel ... I healed her of a broken wing."

"Really?" one of Maisie's friends chortled. "What is it, Rose ... yer *consort*?"

"Aye, we should tell Father Gregor about ye," Maisie added. "He told us to be on the lookout for *unnatural* women."

"Why don't ye mind yer own business?" Eara snapped. "I'm sure the priest has better things to do than listen to a gaggle of witless geese."

Rose's jaw clenched. She appreciated Eara defending her, yet her friend was just riling Maisie up. She seemed to have forgotten too that Father Gregor was likely looking for a reason to cause problems for Rose.

"And *ye* mind yer tongue, alewife," Maisie snarled, her cheeks flushing red. "Or I'll see to it that no MacDonald buys from ye at market in the future."

"Do yer worst," Eara shot back. "And save yer threats for those weak-minded enough to heed them."

Rose and Eara walked on, although when they were out of earshot of the MacDonald women, Eara muttered a salty curse.

"Aye," Rose muttered. "I did warn ye."

"How dare they gather at the roadside to insult ye?"

"Ye know how it is between the MacDonalds and the MacAlisters. And after what my father and brothers did, some of them want blood."

"Well, they can look elsewhere for it."

Silence fell between them then, broken by the rattle of the cart and the thud of their booted feet on the dirt road.

"I don't want them to turn on ye, Eara," Rose said finally. "Maybe I *should* distance myself from ye for a while." Her stomach twisted as she said these words, for she loved helping Eara brew ale and didn't want to give it up. "Just until the dust settles."

Eara shook her head, her slender jaw tightening. "Absolutely not. We're not going to let the bullies win."

Sitting in front of the hearth, a bowl of pottage balanced on her knee, Rose ate hungrily. Her aunt was a good cook; she could even make pottage tasty.

Eara perched on a stool next to her, dipping pieces of bannock into her stew.

The women had arrived close to supper time, so Kenna had insisted that the alewife stay the night. With the outlaws still terrorizing travelers, it wasn't safe to travel alone after dark.

As she ate, Rose's gaze slid around the interior of the cottage. Guilt constricted her chest. The space was half the size of the one she'd left behind. It was already cramped with Kenna and Ailis living here, but with Rose and the few things she'd brought with her, it felt overflowing. Hazel now perched on the ledge before the tiny single window and was dozing.

Despite that the cottage was small, the two women had made it homely. Fresh rushes covered the earthen floor, and bunches of dried herbs and flowers hung from the smoke-blackened rafters. The scents of sage, lavender, and thyme mingled with the more pungent smell of peat-smoke.

A hanging, made from a patchwork of fabrics, divided the living space from the sleeping area.

Rose's attention shifted then to Kenna and Ailis. They sat opposite her and Eara, with their shoulders touching, in a wordless gesture of intimacy.

"I'm so sorry to impose on ye both like this," Rose said awkwardly.

Ailis waved her away. "Och, lass ... ye can stay here as long as ye wish."

"But—"

"No argument, Rose," Kenna said firmly. "Ye don't need to worry about the future, at present. Ye need time to heal yer grief. Ye have lost much of late."

A lump formed in Rose's throat. "The Mackays offered me a position in their broch," she admitted huskily, "but I refused it."

"What?" Eara gasped, turning to her. "Ye didn't tell me that?"

"It slipped my mind earlier," Rose replied weakly. In truth, she'd done her best to forget her encounter with Kerr Mackay in the barmkin and the argument that had followed.

"When did ye receive this offer?" Kenna asked, her green eyes wide.

"Captain Mackay followed me out of the hall after my audience with the laird ... there's a position as chambermaid available."

All three women stared back at her, their expressions bemused. "Why didn't ye take it?" Ailis asked gently.

"This isn't because of yer resentment toward Kerr Mackay, is it?" Eara's brow furrowed then. "Surely, ye wouldn't cut off yer nose to spite yer face?"

"I'm not, Eara," Rose replied, her fingers clenching around her spoon. "But the Mackays broke my Da. The past two years, Captain Mackay and his men did nothing but hound him ... and then the laird struck off his hand."

A brittle silence followed these words. Eara shifted uncomfortably on her stool, while Kenna and Ailis exchanged glances.

However, when Kenna's gaze met Rose's once more, her expression was grave. "The Mackays would have left Graham alone had he worked his land and lived honestly," she pointed out gently. "I know ye loved him, lass ... as did I ... but he wasn't without his faults."

Heat ignited under Rose's ribcage. She couldn't believe her aunt would dare take the Mackays' side on this. They were kin, and family had to stick together. "Ye sound like Kerr Mackay," she said bitterly. "He tried to tell me Da wasn't worth protecting."

"I'm not saying that," Kenna replied, her gaze shadowing. "However, the captain was only trying to help ye, lass. He's always struck me as an honorable man."

The heat under Rose's ribcage intensified. "Honorable?" she gasped. "His men slew my brothers ... *yer* nephews."

"Aye, after *my* brother and nephews launched a rockfall that killed three men," Kenna countered, her voice sharpening as her own anger quickened. "Blood *is* thicker than water, Rose, but that doesn't mean we should defend the indefensible."

12: CARE FOR SOME EGGS?

"WHAT A SLOW morning," Kenna muttered. "It looks as if no one needs eggs today."

Standing next to her aunt, Rose stiffened. Of course, the locals needed eggs. However, they didn't want to buy them from *her*.

It was a breezy spring morning. Clouds scudded across a robin's egg-blue sky, and the smell of blossom sweetened the air. Two months of cold weather had crawled by since Rose had gone to live with her aunt. The chill had dragged on for so long, they'd begun to believe spring would never come. But then it had, in an explosion of color. Kenna's fowls had been laying well over the past weeks, and they had plenty of eggs to sell.

Kenna and Ailis often came into Dun Ugadale for the Saturday market, where they sold eggs and, occasionally, furs from the stoats that Ailis trapped. Kenna had admitted to Rose that they sometimes struggled to sell their wares here, for locals whispered about the two strange women who lived together out in The Red Deer Hills.

However, *Rose's* presence at Kenna's side this morning was the kiss of death.

Rose's belly tightened. Usually, she let her aunt and Ailis sell the eggs on their own at market, but since Ailis wasn't feeling well this morning, Rose had accompanied her aunt instead.

That was a mistake. Her presence was chasing folk away.

On the opposite side of the village square, Rose spied a small woman with white-blonde hair wearing a tall cloth hat—Eara had a stall at the market on this fine spring day. Marking the solemn expression on the alewife's face, Rose frowned. Usually, there would be a queue of locals to buy her fine ale. But not so this morning. Her friend stood alone.

Rose's jaw tightened. Despite that she now lived a good walk from the village, she still went in four mornings a week to help Eara.

But they would have been blind not to notice the changing mood in the village toward them both. No one greeted Rose as she walked the tangle of streets to the alewife's bothy, and those who did notice her scowled.

Just a few days earlier, someone had thrown a dead rat over the fence into Eara's garden. Eara's cat, Ember, hadn't been impressed, although the alewife had shrugged the incident off. However, it bothered Rose.

"Eara's not selling anything either," she murmured to her aunt. "She's paying the price for her friendship with me."

Kenna sighed. "Folk can be as fickle as sheep, lass. Pay them no mind."

"I don't ... but if they ruin Eara's livelihood, I shall feel responsible." She paused, motioning to the surrounding crowd. "Ye know how much influence the MacDonalds have here. And now it seems they've scared off the Mackays as well."

It was true. Apart from two nervous MacAlister women and Eara, they'd had hardly any buyers for their eggs.

Kenna snorted. "Worried they'll make themselves unpopular too, are they?"

"Aye." Rose heaved a sigh. "I will speak to Eara later ... and tell her I won't be helping her for a while." Her aunt frowned, but Rose added. "It's not forever ... just until things settle."

"Careful, Rose," Kenna replied softly. "If ye let her, Maisie MacDonald will turn ye into an outcast."

Considering her aunt's words, and wondering at Kenna's treatment at the hands of these people over the years, Rose's gaze traveled across the crowd to where the woman herself was in a huddle with a group of friends. Maisie had clearly been hard at work, and Rose wondered if she'd spoken to Father Gregor about her as she'd threatened.

A sickly sensation washed over Rose then. Of course, Maisie had.

As if summoned, a slender, black-robed figure appeared in the crowd, moving briskly through the press of shoppers just a few yards away. Father Gregor greeted the locals with nods before stopping to chat to the MacDonald women for a few moments.

Maisie leaned close, her gaze bright, speaking quickly to him.

A moment later, Father Gregor turned, his dark gaze spearing Rose's.

Her pulse quickened before she chastised herself. *Goose ... he doesn't have any power over ye.*

However, her heart started to race when the priest murmured something to Maisie and stepped away. He then cut his way through the milling crowd, skirting around where a man was selling a gaggle of honking geese, toward Rose and Kenna.

"What's this?" Kenna murmured, seeing him approach. "Does the priest want some eggs?"

"I think not, auntie," Rose replied, schooling her features into a veiled expression.

An instant later, Father Gregor halted before their stall. His dispassionate gaze surveyed the baskets of eggs sitting on the small trestle table.

"Good morn, Father," Kenna greeted him brightly. "Care for some eggs?"

He shook his head dismissively, his gaze coming to rest upon Kenna's companion. "Ye no longer attend the Sunday services, Rose?"

Holding his gaze, she lifted her chin a fraction. "I live quite a distance from the village these days, Father."

"But that doesn't stop ye from coming here on other days," he replied, his tone sharpening. "To work with the *alewife*." His mouth puckered then as if he'd just tasted something sour.

Rose stilled. It discomforted her to know that he'd been paying attention to her routine.

"I am merely helping a friend in need, Father," she said, her own voice cooling, "and learning a valuable skill too."

His dark brows knitted together. "A *good* woman finds herself a husband and lets him provide."

"Sometimes that isn't possible," Rose replied. "And sometimes women enjoy having something of their own."

His jaw tightened. "Ye have been drawing attention to yerself of late ... if ye are not careful, ye will gain yerself a reputation."

"There's nothing wrong with my niece, Father," Kenna interjected crisply. "She's a good-hearted, hardworking lass who has never done anyone wrong."

Father Gregor favored Kenna with a look of cold disdain before he focused on Rose once more. "Locals have brought to my attention that ye have taken an eagle owl into yer care."

Rose frowned. "Aye."

He shook his head gravely, clearly pained to hear her admit this. "Then I counsel ye to set the bird free," he replied. "Eagle owls are demonic ... they are the devil's helpers. It is unwise to have such a creature under yer roof."

Rose huffed a sigh, her irritation rising now. Aye, some folk might believe the bird's large eyes and tufts of feathers that looked like horns made it look demonic, but she wasn't so foolish. She was about to point out to the priest that she didn't believe such superstition when

Father Gregor continued, "I would resume yer visits to the kirk, Rose, if I were ye." His eyes glinted. "Call on me whenever ye wish ... I will help ye purify yer soul."

Rose ground her teeth. Aye, she was sure he would.

The priest stepped forward, although the table between him and Rose prevented him from crowding her. A hungry look flickered across his face then. He seemed to forget that he and Rose weren't alone, that Kenna was watching. "Ye have strayed from the path, lass ... but I will put it right. A woman like ye should—"

"Good morning, Father." A male voice, low and powerful, interrupted the priest mid-sentence.

Their gazes snapped to where a tall, broad-shouldered man with white-blond hair strode toward them. It was a warm morning, and Kerr Mackay wore a leather vest and braies. Leather bracers covered his wrists, while sweat gleamed on his bare, muscular upper arms. He looked as if he'd just come from training.

Rose's heart kicked against her ribs.

They hadn't set eyes on each other in the two moons since the Mackays had taken her family's cottage and lands from her and given them to the MacDonalds. Since that fateful day in the barmkin of Dun Ugadale.

In truth, she'd started to regret how harshly she responded to him. Maybe he'd only been trying to help, after all.

"Captain Mackay," Father Gregor greeted him stiffly.

"Buying some eggs are ye?" Kerr asked, drawing up next to the priest.

Two high spots of color appeared on Father Gregor's cheeks. "No, I was merely exchanging pleasantries with these women."

Kenna's soft snort followed, and the priest's blush deepened.

"Well, ye should try Kenna's eggs," Kerr replied, his expression inscrutable. "Ye won't find any better elsewhere."

Father Gregor gave a quick, jerky nod. "Perhaps another time." He then ducked his head and moved backward. "Captain."

Then, without sparing Rose or her aunt another glance, the priest walked off.

Kerr watched him go before his gaze shifted to Kenna, who pulled a face. The captain's brow furrowed. "Was he bothering ye?"

Kenna huffed a sigh. "Not me especially. Father Gregor doesn't approve of Rose working with the alewife ... or her independent ways."

Rose cut her aunt a quelling look. God's blood, did Kenna have to be so open? "It's nothing," she said quickly. "He's just been listening to petty gossip ... that's all."

Kerr's attention shifted to Rose, and his brow furrowed. "Have the MacDonalds been heckling ye?"

"Not really," she lied, wishing he'd drop the subject. They were attracting a few stares now—something she didn't need.

"Relations between the MacAlisters and the MacDonalds have never been so strained," he replied, his frown deepening. "The lads and I had to break up a brawl in the fields yesterday."

Rose swallowed. Her father and brothers had caused this. Unfortunately, folk had long memories—it would be a while before she was accepted here again.

"Just bang their heads together, Captain," Kenna muttered. "Maybe that'll knock some good sense into their thought cages."

Kerr snorted, his brow smoothing. "I've tried, Kenna ... unfortunately, they've all got thick skulls." He paused then, focusing on Rose once more. "But if the priest or any of the villagers give ye any bother, ye are to tell me ... things can sometimes get out of hand."

Rose nodded stiffly, guilt tugging at her. She wished he wasn't always so *noble*—he sometimes made it hard for her to hate him.

"We will," Kenna assured him. "Thank ye, Captain."

Kerr's mouth lifted, just a fraction, at the corners, in the barest hint of a smile. "I'll take two dozen of yer eggs then," he said, reaching for the purse at his belt. "Our kitchen always needs them."

13: HUNTING WOLVES

KERR WAS SHOEING his horse when the lad ran into the barmkin.

"Captain!"

Glancing up from where he'd just hammered in the last nail on the gelding's rear hind hoof, Kerr's gaze alighted upon a youth's red face. He was breathing hard, his face slick with sweat. "What is it?"

"The Black Wolves ... me and my Da spotted them."

Kerr's pulse quickened as he lowered the horse's leg and stepped away from the beast, straightening up. "Where?"

"West of the village ... at the edge of the Red Deer Hills."

"That close?"

"Aye, Captain. We saw them ... a group of six, all on horseback."

Kerr scowled. Of course, they were on horseback. Months earlier, the outlaws had been forced to flee on foot. However, over the winter, they'd stolen horses from those they attacked. It had made them harder to chase, although easier to track.

"Which way were they riding?"

"West ... straight into the hills."

Kerr's stomach clenched, and he swallowed a curse. That would take them right by Kenna MacAlister's cottage, for it lay amongst the green folds of the Red Deer Hills.

"This is our chance, Captain." Ronan stepped up next to Kerr, his face taut. "We need to catch the bastards up ... before they go into hiding again."

Kerr nodded, swiveling, before he shouted up to the walls. "Evan, Athol, Rae, Lorcan ... get down here." He glanced over at Ronan still waiting beside him. "Fetch Tavish, Murtagh, and Coby. We ride out now."

A short while later, the party of nine warriors clattered out of Dun Ugadale.

Kerr led them down the causeway before turning his gelding west. They rode briskly through the village and then pushed their horses into a gallop up the hillside, spitting up turf behind them.

Crouched forward over his horse's withers, Kerr wished Lennox was with them this afternoon. Like him, his brother had become increasingly frustrated by their inability to catch The Black Wolves.

However, Lennox was currently overseeing the final work on his broch at Loch Lussa. He and Davina would be away for another fortnight, at least.

They'd face The Wolves today though—Kerr knew it in his bones.

Worry gnawed at him, all the same. Rose, Kenna, and Ailis lived in a remote area, something that made them vulnerable to brigands. The outlaws had already raped travelers, and Kerr's blood ran cold at the thought of what they might do if they discovered Kenna's cottage.

Rose.

Seeing her days earlier at the market had been a kick to the gut, yet he'd done his best to mask his visceral reaction to her. He'd spent the past months telling himself that he had to let his infatuation for Rose MacAlister go.

But the moment he'd spied her standing next to Kenna in the village square, the same want had twisted within him.

No, he hadn't cured himself of this affliction.

Lord, Rose had been a feast for the eyes too. She'd clearly eaten better over the past weeks and had regained her curves. She also had a bloom to her cheeks and a sparkle in her eyes that had been absent of late; life with her aunt appeared to suit her.

The warm afternoon air feathered Kerr's face as he rode, his gaze scanning the gently unfolding landscape around them for any sign of the outlaws. Nothing.

They entered the Red Deer Hills, the first of which were strewn with tussock and ferns, their horses leaping over a meandering burn at the bottom. However, there still wasn't any sign of The Black Wolves yet.

Fear now cramped Kerr's guts. If the outlaws continued directly west, they'd find Kenna's cottage. He let the courser have its head as it crested the top of the next hill. "Come on," he shouted to his men.

The cottage lay ahead at the bottom of a valley, surrounded by a well-tended garden and a livestock enclosure. Smoke drifted lazily from the sod roof.

Kerr's heart was in his throat as he closed the distance. But when he saw a woman standing in front of the cottage, scattering grain for fowl, his breathing caught, relief washing over him.

Rose was safe and well.

Seeing Kerr and his men approach, she halted her task, her body tensing.

Of course, they rode fast. She would be alarmed.

Drawing up Prionnsa, Kerr dispensed with greetings and got straight to the point. "Outlaws are said to have passed this way," he announced. "Have ye seen them?"

Rose swallowed, her eyes snapping wide. She then shook her head.

"What is it, Captain?" Kenna emerged from the cottage, wiping her hands on her apron, Ailis following close behind.

"It's not safe in these hills at present," Kerr replied, his voice roughening. "The Black Wolves are here."

All three of the women drew together at this news. Aye, despite their sheltered existence, they'd all heard of the bloodthirsty outlaws.

"There's been no sign of them," Kenna assured him.

Kerr nodded. "Go indoors and bolt the door," he instructed. "Don't open it until we come back and tell ye it's safe."

"Aye, Captain," Kenna answered, gesturing to Rose and Ailis to follow her indoors.

However, as Rose turned to go, she glanced over her shoulder, her gaze meeting his. The moment froze, and just for an instant, Kerr could have imagined he saw a flash of concern there. But then she turned away, and he blinked.

No, his mind was playing tricks on him.

"It's been a long while ... they should have returned by now."

Across the fire, Kenna nodded. She sat huddled together with Ailis. Both women's expressions were pinched. And like Rose, they kept glancing at the bolted door as the hours wore on.

Where are they?

Of course, even locked inside the cottage, the three women were vulnerable. If the outlaws found them here, they could set fire to the dwelling to force them out or burn them alive. Rose didn't feel safe here, although her thoughts kept shifting away from her own situation to the fate of Kerr Mackay and his men.

Something has happened to them.

The conviction had taken root in her mind, and as the afternoon crawled into evening, and evening into night, she became increasingly certain the Dun Ugadale Guard had fallen foul of The Black Wolves.

When she'd gone into Ceann Locha a week earlier, to pick up supplies, she'd heard fishwives gossiping on the dock about the brigands. Douglases run off their lands by the king and filled with bitterness and rage, they were dangerous men.

Once night had fallen, Rose opened the window and let Hazel out. She'd then bolted the shutters tight and returned to the fireside to wait.

But no one came.

Eventually, Kenna and Ailis went to bed, retreating behind the hanging to the pile of sheepskins they shared. Rose stayed by the hearth as she always did, wrapping herself in blankets.

But she couldn't sleep.

The sense of 'wrongness' within her merely increased as the night wore on.

Whatever she might think of him, she knew Captain Mackay was a man of his word. If he said he'd be back, he would. The fact that he hadn't returned made her breathing grow shallow, foreboding prickling her skin.

Not long before dawn, a scratching noise outside the window roused Rose from where she'd just drifted off into a fitful doze. Rising from the ground, she padded over to the window and unlatched it, letting Hazel in.

"Did ye see anything out there?" she asked the owl. She knew it was foolish to talk to Hazel as if she were a person. Nonetheless, there were times when she felt that the owl could understand her.

Hazel's dark-gold gaze met hers. The owl then inclined its head and let out a sharp whistle. It was different from the soft coos and hoots she usually made indoors.

The sound was a warning.

Rose's pulse started to race.

Glancing around the shadowed interior of the cottage, lit by the dying embers of the fire, she made a decision.

If the others awoke, they'd never let her go outside. But instinct drove her now.

She *had* to go. She had to find The Guard.

"Lead me to them," she whispered to Hazel.

The eagle owl gave a soft coo.

She let Hazel fly out the window before closing the shutters again. She then helped herself to the sharpest of Ailis's boning knives. It wasn't much of a weapon, but she'd feel better carrying it. Her father had shown her many a time how to defend herself using a knife if necessary. She then grabbed her woolen shawl, wrapping it around her shoulders, pulled on her worn leather boots, and crept to the door.

Sliding the wooden bar free without making a noise was a difficult task indeed. Sweat beaded on her skin, and Rose kept stealing nervous glances over her shoulder as she inched it free.

No one appeared to be stirring behind the hanging.

After a short while, she managed to open the door wide enough to squeeze out. Walking out into the early morning dew, Rose hesitated. She'd have preferred to lock the door behind her, yet there was no way to do so, and she really had to go.

Stopping a moment to put on her boots, she drew in a few steadying breaths of the crisp early dawn air. The sun was on the verge of peeking above the hills to the east. The valley lay in shadow, although the sky was beginning to lighten.

She looked around before spying Hazel perched upon a stunted apple tree behind the cottage, as if waiting for her.

Rose hurried toward the tree, and Hazel took off, flying up and over the hill, heading northwest.

Breaking into a jog, Rose followed.

The valley after theirs was wilder and narrower, covered in a carpet of soft green ferns, clumps of brambles, and a scattering of pines.

Hazel disappeared then, yet Rose kept walking. She blindly stumbled on through the press of trees. She guessed she was traveling north now, following the valley as it narrowed, and the press of pines grew thicker. Ahead, bracken crackled underfoot, causing Rose to skid to a halt. Heart pounding, she reached for her boning knife.

However, an instant later, two red deer burst into view. The deer, young hinds, watched her with wide eyes before bounding away into the trees.

Rose watched them go, heart thumping.

Goose, she chided herself. *Stop jumping at shadows.*

"Hazel!" she called out then, hoping to hear the owl's hoots echoing through the pines, guiding her in the right direction. However, no such call was forthcoming; it appeared Hazel had deserted her.

Sighing, Rose walked on. She was starting to feel a bit foolish, expecting the owl to lead her. Nonetheless, she'd come this far—she couldn't turn back now.

She'd gone another dozen furlongs when the trees drew back, and the valley opened out into another carpet of bright green ferns.

Rose stopped abruptly. Yet this time, it wasn't deer that startled her—but the sight of bloodied, leather-clad bodies strewn across the valley floor.

14: AMONGST THE FERNS

MOMENTS PASSED, AND then Rose breathed a curse. Several arrows protruded from the prone bodies, and the iron tang of blood tainted the morning air.

From this distance, it was impossible to tell who the men were. They could have been The Black Wolves—or the Dun Ugadale Guard.

However, as she stood there, a chill feathered down Rose's neck. She started to tremble.

If they were the bodies of the outlaws scattered here, Captain Mackay and his men would have already ridden back to Kenna's cottage to tell them what had happened. The Guard wouldn't have left the dead scattered about like this either. She glanced around, pulse hammering in her ears now.

Where were their horses?

And most importantly, where were the men who'd done this?

Cold sweat slicked Rose's skin, and she glanced about nervously.

The last thing she wanted was for the outlaws to find her. The knife she carried would do her no good against men capable of such violence.

Steeling herself, Rose crept forward over soft ferns, to where the first of the fallen men lay sprawled on his back.

He was young, with long black hair. His blue eyes stared sightlessly up at the lightening sky, his face locked in a grimace of agony. An arrow jutted from his left thigh while blood covered his chest and belly, from two terrible wounds.

Bile stung the back of Rose's throat.

She recognized him. He was one of Kerr's men—the warrior who hailed from Éire.

Aye, these were the men of the Dun Ugadale Guard.

Rose started to sweat, nausea rolling through her as she moved on, going from man to man.

The third one she checked, a big warrior with wild brown hair, was still breathing, barely, although the gaping wound to his abdomen warned he wouldn't be for much longer. His face was chalk-white, and he was insensible.

Rose removed her hand from his cold brow. Death was only a whisper away. She could do nothing for him.

Straightening up, she counted the bodies strewn around her.

Nine.

How many of The Guard had ridden west? Were they all accounted for? Their horses had all disappeared, no doubt taken by The Wolves, and they'd been stripped of weapons.

Rose sucked in a deep breath and moved on to inspect the last of the fallen. She caught a flash of pale hair, and her breathing hitched. Only two men at Dun Ugadale had hair that color. One of them was the laird. The other was Kerr Mackay.

Of course, she'd known it would be him. She'd dreaded this moment.

Rose clenched her jaw. She didn't want to draw closer, to see the agony frozen on his face. When she did reach him, the captain's expression was hidden from her. He lay face-down upon the ferns, spreadeagled. Two arrows pierced his left shoulder, one just below the other.

Rose's brow furrowed. Moving close, she took hold of his uninjured shoulder and gently rolled him onto his side, bracing herself for the worst.

To her shock, he was breathing. A large purple lump had come up on his forehead, and when she examined the ground, she saw he'd hit his head upon a large stone as he fell.

It had knocked him senseless.

Unlike the warrior lying just a few yards away, Kerr wasn't doomed—not yet anyway.

Breathing an oath, as a strange weakness flooded her body, Rose reached forward and placed a hand on his brow. It was warm, yet clammy, and his breathing was shallow. Fear clenched her belly.

He might not be close to death, yet Kerr was in dire need of a healer.

"Thank ye for acting so quickly, Rose." Iver Mackay's voice rumbled through the cottage. The laird of Dun Ugadale crouched at his brother's side, his dark-blue gaze haunted as he watched him sleep. "Ye took a great risk venturing out into that valley alone."

"When they didn't return, I knew something was wrong," she admitted softly.

Rose didn't admit, however, that instinct had driven her from the cottage and into the dawn. She'd known, even hours earlier, that something was wrong. It had gnawed at her, urging her to search for The Guard.

"We've sent for the healer at Ceann Locha." Brodie, Kerr's younger brother, spoke up then. He stood behind the laird, his face creased with worry. "He shouldn't be too far away."

Rose nodded, relieved. Kenna's healing skills were good enough, and Rose had assisted her, yet they lacked the herbs needed to make sure the wounds didn't fester.

After discovering Captain Mackay was still alive, she sprinted back to the cottage, where Kenna and Ailis were already awake and panicking about what had happened to her. She'd stilled their questions with a rushed explanation. Ailis had then run off, heading toward Dun Ugadale, while Rose and Kenna cautiously returned to the clearing.

They didn't expect the outlaws to return—but they were careful to move as quietly through the pines as possible.

As Rose had predicted, the badly wounded warrior had died in the meantime.

Kerr still breathed, although a sheen of sweat had covered his skin while she'd been away.

Trying to be as gentle as possible, the women had pulled him up, placing their shoulders under his armpits, and dragged him back to the cottage. It had been a slow and laborious journey. All the while, Kerr remained unconscious, his head lolling against his chest.

And no sooner had they gotten him inside the cottage, when the thunder of hooves outdoors warned them that the laird had arrived.

Iver and Brodie helped Rose and her aunt snip off the ends of the arrows and remove them. Kenna had poured vinegar into the wounds, yet they were deep and would need tending or they'd surely fester. They'd then laid Kerr back on the sheepskins in the corner where Kenna and Ailis usually slept.

He still hadn't awoken, which was worrying.

"The blow to his head was a hard one," Brodie muttered, dragging a hand down his face. "It's a miracle it didn't split his skull open."

"The rock he hit was rounded rather than sharp," Rose replied softly. "Otherwise, it would have."

Brodie's hazel gaze met hers, and she witnessed the pain, the worry, there. The folk of Dun Ugadale all knew the history of the broch's blacksmith. He was half-brother to Iver, Lennox, and Kerr—the result of the former laird's dalliance with a cook. Brodie Mackay was somewhat of an enigma to most folk. He kept to himself usually, worked hard, and was known to be dour and easily irritated.

Rose had to admit the man was quite intimidating. The blacksmith's broad shoulders and brawny body barely seemed to fit in the cramped confines of the cottage. He loomed over the three women standing with him.

"Butchers," Iver growled, straightening up. The laird's face was tight, fury burning in his eyes. His gaze then speared the blacksmith's. "Ride back to Dun Ugadale and gather what's left of The Guard, Brodie. We're going after The Wolves." His attention shifted to Rose then. "Can I leave Kerr in yer care?"

Silence filled the cottage, broken only by the crackling of the hearth.

"Here, lass, grind this up for me." The healer passed Rose a pestle and mortar. "The woundwort needs to be mashed into a paste."

Nodding, Rose did as bid, stealing glances at where Malcolm was cleansing the two arrow wounds once more with vinegar. Kerr lay on his side on the sheepskin-covered bed, still insensible.

Malcolm, the healer, was a serious man of middling age, who'd arrived with a basket of tinctures, herbs, and bandages strapped to his garron's back. His long-fingered hands worked deftly as he examined the wounds.

"Here," Rose murmured, passing him the bowl of mashed woundwort. "Is this what ye wanted?"

"Aye, thanks." Malcolm took the mortar from her and shifted closer to his patient. He then stuffed the herb pulp into the arrow wounds, packing them tight.

Straightening up, the healer reached for a damp cloth and wiped his hands clean. "I'm going to need yer help once more, Rose," he announced. "To put on the bandage."

"Aye ... what do ye want me to do?"

"We need to pull him upright ... so he's sitting."

Together, the pair of them managed to get Kerr sitting up. However, he slumped against the healer's shoulder, his head lolling. Then, under Malcolm's instruction, Rose bound a bandage around Kerr's injured shoulder.

Once that was done, they laid him back against a nest of pillows.

Gazing upon Kerr's pale face and the swollen purple lump on his forehead, Rose frowned. "What about his head?" she asked, shifting her attention to the healer.

Malcolm huffed a sigh. "There's little we can do about that." He started digging through his basket and produced a small clay container. "This is a salve of chamomile and goatweed. It will help with the bruising and the pain." Rising to his feet, the healer then ran a critical eye over the captain. "He should wake up soon."

"And if he does not?"

Malcolm glanced her way, his brow furrowing. "Well ... then we shall have cause to worry."

Rose swallowed, her gaze flicking to where a light sheen of sweat still covered Kerr's naked chest. "Does he have a fever?"

"Aye ... a slight one, although it will likely worsen as his body seeks to heal itself." Malcolm pushed himself to his feet, grimacing as his stiff joints pained him. "Ye tended him well before I arrived ... and so I shall leave him in yer care now." The healer motioned to his basket. "I will leave ye more woundwort, salve, and bandages."

Rose nodded, even as her pulse quickened.

Noting her nervousness, Malcolm's brow smoothed, and his mouth curved into a kindly smile. "Just wash the wounds with vinegar every morning and then apply fresh woundwort and bandages ... the rest is up to him."

"Can he go home?"

"Not yet ... I wouldn't move him until he is awake and strong enough."

Rose watched as the healer packed up, leaving the items he'd promised behind. She followed him outside to where his fat garron waited.

Kenna glanced up. She was weeding around patches of onion and garlic, in an attempt to keep busy and not fuss, while the healer tended Kerr. Meanwhile, at the other end of the garden, Ailis was scattering grain for their fowl. "How fares the captain then?" Kenna asked, concern shadowing her green eyes.

"Well enough, for the moment," Malcolm replied, strapping his basket onto his mount's back. "But only time will tell."

15: HEALER'S ORDERS

KERR AWOKE TO a blinding headache.

Rising from the darkness with a groan, his eyes flickered open. Firelight burned his pupils, and he winced.

The pain pulsed in time with his heartbeat.

Wherever he was, it wasn't brightly lit. Nonetheless, his eyes watered, and the thumping in his head intensified. Unbidden, another groan tore from his throat.

"Good. Ye are awake," a woman's soft voice greeted him. "Are ye thirsty?"

"Aye," he croaked.

"Here ... lift yer head a little."

Kerr did as bid, even though the movement made his pounding forehead hurt even worse. An instant later, the rim of a wooden cup nudged against his lips. He took a few grateful sips of what tasted like stale boiled water before sinking back down against the pillows.

His left shoulder twinged painfully then, and he muttered a curse. "What happened to me?"

"Don't ye remember?"

The woman's voice intruded, and Kerr stilled.

Rose MacAlister sat at his bedside, her proud face bathed in firelight. She was watching him closely, a groove furrowed between her brows.

Kerr stared back at her, his mind scrabbling through the pain to claw back his memories.

A heartbeat later, it hit him with the force of a charging bull.

Cursing, he closed his eyes once more.

Riding through the valley, weaving in and out of pines, following the trail The Wolves had left north. They'd all been wary, the entire company had fallen silent as they traveled. But the attack had come as a surprise, nonetheless.

Arrows had flown in all directions, peppering the company, and knocking two of Kerr's men from their horses. The rest of them had swung down to the ground, drawing their weapons as they went.

But The Wolves were clever, they continued to fire arrows from the shadows, and when they'd taken down another three of The Guard, they burst out of the undergrowth and ran at Kerr and his men, howling like banshees.

The fight had been violent and swift.

Kerr had managed to bring one of them down—a big bastard with a pike—but then something punched his shoulder, throwing him forward. A second blow knocked him off his feet, and he remembered no more.

"The others?" he eventually croaked.

"I'm sorry, Kerr," Rose whispered. "Ye are the only survivor. They took yer horses, stripped ye all of weapons, and left ye to bleed out in that clearing."

Pain lanced across his chest, and he squeezed his eyes shut, fighting against grief so powerful it threatened to claw him apart.

He'd grown up with many of those men, and three of them—Ronan, Tavish, and Coby—were recent recruits.

They'd all trusted him with their lives, and he'd led them to death. What a cruel twist of fate that they'd all die while he lived. The sorrow was almost too much to bear—and yet underneath it, rage flickered to life.

It had been a trap. They'd lured Kerr and his warriors into that clearing, had lain in wait for them. The Wolves wanted to assert their dominance over this corner of the peninsula.

"Whoresons," he growled as rage pulsed through him like the pain in his head. It was a salve, galvanizing him. "I won't rest until I impale each of their heads on pikes."

It was a bloodthirsty thing to say, yet he didn't care.

Jaw clenched, Kerr finally opened his eyes again, to find Rose watching him, her gaze shadowed. "Yer brothers and the rest of The Guard are hunting the outlaws," she assured him.

"I should join them," he ground out.

She pulled a face. "Ye are in no condition to go anywhere. The arrow wounds in yer shoulder risk souring, ye have a fever ... and ye have just awoken from a massive knock to the skull." She paused there, her cheeks flushing, as if embarrassed by her response. "The *healer* wants ye to stay here for the meantime."

Kerr frowned—a mistake, for the expression made the throbbing in his forehead grow worse still. Swallowing a moan, he tried to breathe through the pain. "I can't stay here," he muttered.

"Those are Malcolm's orders, Kerr," Rose replied with a sigh, rising to her feet. "I have broth simmering over the fire. Would ye like some?"

"Aye," he grunted. In truth, he wasn't hungry. All he wanted was to get up and go in search of The Wolves. But his body felt frustratingly weak, and it did seem overly warm inside this cottage.

Nevertheless, it wasn't lost on him that he was imposing on a woman who couldn't stand him. Another bitter irony.

He watched Rose ladle broth into a large wooden cup. She then carried it over to him, setting the cup down on a ledge by the bed. "We'd better ensure ye're sitting up for this," she said briskly, avoiding his eye as she reached for the pillows. "Come on."

Kerr did his best to aid her, although the act of pushing himself up a little made him break out in a sweat. He sank back against the wall, heart pounding, his shoulder throbbing. Dizziness swept over him, a high-pitched whine starting in his ears.

"Kerr." Rose's voice sounded as if it were coming from down a long tunnel. "Are ye well enough to take some broth?"

He opened his eyes to see she was watching him now, her face taut, her lovely pine-green eyes shadowed. He could have almost believed she was worried about him—if he didn't already know the truth of things.

Grateful the dizziness was passing, he eventually forced a nod.

Wordlessly, Rose picked up the cup and perched next to him on the bed. She then raised the cup to his lips and lifted it so he could sip.

He choked it down. The broth was tasty enough, yet he had no stomach for it. However, if he wanted to regain his strength and get out of this bed, so he could go after those who'd killed his men, he needed to drink every drop.

Kerr was in a bad way. He was doing his best to hide it, yet the pallor on his cheeks and the pain in his eyes told the truth. He'd reacted as Rose had expected to the news that the rest of his company was dead. Badly.

The raw grief that had rippled across his face moved her—although his rage was worrying.

He shouldn't blame himself for what happened, yet it was clear he did.

Those men were his responsibility, and Captain Mackay was a man who took his duties seriously. She wasn't sure what to say to him. There was nothing she could say that would put things right.

"Did Iver find me?" he asked eventually, sinking back onto his pillows. He'd drunk the broth she'd given him, although his eyes now had a haunted cast to them.

"No," she murmured. "I did."

Kerr glanced her way, his features tightening. "Didn't I tell ye to keep indoors?"

Rose held his eye. "Aye, but when have I *ever* heeded ye?"

He snorted and then winced.

"When ye didn't return as ye'd promised, I knew something was wrong," she continued. "So, I sneaked out just before dawn and went looking for ye all."

Kerr nodded, swallowing. He was likely imagining the scene she'd found upon that carpet of ferns. Nonetheless, she wasn't going to describe it to him. She wanted to forget the grisly sight, not relive it.

"Ye were fortunate they left ye for dead," she said after an awkward pause.

A muscle feathered in his jaw. "Aye," he growled. "Although I'll make The Black Wolves regret it soon enough."

"How is he faring?" Ailis whispered, casting a glance over at where the hanging had been drawn across the corner.

Rose grimaced before taking the bowl of stew Kenna passed her. "His fever worsens," she murmured, trying to ignore the knot of worry that had lodged under her ribcage. "He's sleeping now."

"A fever is not uncommon after such an injury," her aunt said, careful to keep her voice low. "He's had a shock ... and those arrow wounds need to settle."

Kenna's tone was reassuring, yet it didn't ease Rose's tension.

She'd once sworn to hate Kerr forever, and yet here she was, concerned about his welfare. However, her perspective had altered of late. Things weren't quite as black and white as they had been. These days, she couldn't dredge up the venom she had in the past. Her aunt was right—Kerr Mackay wasn't the devil. And if she was honest, he'd done her a few kindnesses over the years.

She'd just been blind to them.

Rose took a mouthful of stew and forced it down. In truth, she wasn't hungry. The laird and his men hadn't yet returned from hunting the outlaws, and she feared they might meet the same end as Kerr's company had.

But her disquiet was deeper than that. Different.

Searching her thoughts, she realized that she felt guilty.

Her aunt's reprimand months earlier had stuck with her. And with the passing of the weeks, and the worst of her grief for the loss of her father and brothers blunted, she was able to see clearly again.

The truth was she'd been desperate for someone to blame for their deaths. But her menfolk had known what they were doing. They'd set out to kill MacDonalds so they could steal their cattle.

It was a reprehensible act, and the fault was theirs alone. Kerr wasn't responsible for it.

After supper, Rose took the dirty dishes out to the burn and washed them. It was a cool, foggy evening. Tendrils of milky mist crept down the bottom of the valley, swirling around her as she worked.

The days were longer now, although dusk was closing in.

There was still no sign of Iver Mackay and the warriors who'd followed him.

Rose's mouth thinned. She hoped grief and rage hadn't made the laird reckless.

Filling a clean bowl of water from the burn, Rose returned indoors. She found Ailis laying out a sheepskin near the fire. All three of them would sleep out here tonight, for they couldn't move Kerr from his current position.

Yawning, Rose put away the dishes on a shelf near the tiny window, where Hazel still roosted. She hadn't slept at all the night before, and exhaustion was finally catching up with her. However, she couldn't retire just yet.

Rose ducked around the hanging. In one hand, she carried the water and drying cloth, and in the other, a small lantern. Careful to be as quiet as possible, she hooked the lantern above Kerr's head before running a critical gaze over her patient.

He'd thrown off the sheet covering him. Naked to the waist, the skin of his torso and arms gleamed with sweat.

Rose's brow furrowed, worry fluttering up. Aye, a fever had him in its grip. But, the Lord willing, it would burn itself out overnight.

Seating herself on the edge of the bed, she wet the cloth in the cold water and squeezed it out. She then leaned forward and gently wiped the sweat from his brow. The purple lump there had gone down slightly. Nonetheless, she kept her touch as light as possible.

Kerr let out a soft moan and then murmured something in his sleep.

Rose halted her ministrations, observing his face. She'd never seen Kerr this vulnerable before. It brought up unsettling sensations within her.

Waiting until he settled once more, she wiped the sweat off his face and neck before rinsing out the cloth. Yet as she smoothed it over the heavily muscled expanse of his bare chest, careful to avoid the bandage that protected his shoulder, Rose's cheeks warmed.

There was an intimacy to this—one she'd taken on without question. Indeed, she hadn't given Kenna or Ailis the opportunity to look after Kerr. Why hadn't she?

Gritting her teeth, she struggled to regain her equilibrium as she dipped the cloth into the water once more. *Goose, get ahold of yerself.*

16: NOTHING TO FORGIVE

ROSE STAYED WITH Kerr all night, dozing on the edge of the nest of sheepskins where he lay. Her sleep was fitful though, and she found herself waking often to check on him.

As the first rays of morning light caressed the valley outside, Rose slipped out from behind the hanging and opened the shutters for Hazel. "Did ye have a good night's hunt?" Rose whispered to the owl, caressing its soft feathers with the back of her hand. In response, Hazel gave a soft hoot. She then hopped up onto the shelf Kenna had cleared for her roost and settled in.

Rose's mouth curved. Hazel had been a friend indeed over the past months. However, now that her grief had subsided, she felt a little less reliant on the owl. In addition, she was no longer put upon, as she had before—although there was a part of her that would have welcomed going back to the way things had been before, if it would bring her father and brothers back.

Slipping back behind the hanging, Rose perched next to Kerr and placed a hand upon his brow.

A sigh of relief then gusted from her. His fever had broken. In the middle of the night, he'd burned hot like an ember, but the fire raging in his veins eventually died.

Kerr's eyes flickered open then, and their gazes met.

It occurred to Rose that she was sitting very close to him, so close she could see that his eyelashes were blond with dark tips. Drawing back a little, she favored him with an embarrassed smile.

"Good morning."

"Morning," he rasped. "Why do I feel like a wrung dish rag?"

"Ye were burning up with fever for most of the night," she replied. "But fortunately, it has spent itself now."

Their gazes held, and his blue eyes darkened. "Have ye been looking after me?"

Rose cleared her throat, her embarrassment rising further. "Aye."

"Thank ye."

She swallowed, not sure how to respond. "Aye, well … it was the least I could do," she said softly, even as her pulse started to race. "After the way I've treated ye." His eyes widened at these words, yet Rose rushed on. Guilt had sat like a crow on her shoulder all night. She had to say this. "When ye offered me a position in yer brother's broch, I responded harshly." She broke off, swallowing as heat crept across her chest and up her neck. "And I have regretted the things I said, ever since."

Kerr didn't reply immediately. Instead, his gaze roamed over her face, as if he wasn't quite sure if Rose MacAlister sat before him and not a changeling.

"Rose," he said gently. "I—"

"Don't mistake me," she interjected, her pulse hammering now. Lord, this was awkward. "I still have no wish to work for yer family … but there was no need for me to throw the offer back in yer face the way I did."

Another silence swelled between them before Kerr eventually answered, "There's nothing to forgive, lass. Grief does strange things to us all."

Rose stared back at him. God's bones, why did he have to be so decent?

Of course, he *was* decent. He always had been.

If he'd hounded her father, it was because he'd been doing his job. Not out of spite or cruelty. Kerr Mackay could be obstinate and overly serious, but he was a good man. She admitted it now.

Straightening her shoulders, Rose attempted to school her features into an expression of composure. It was hard though, for his steady gaze now flustered her. "Aye, well, I just wanted to say 'I'm sorry'," she murmured, rising to her feet.

His mouth lifted at the corners—although his gaze remained solemn, shadowed—before he nodded.

"The Wolves have eluded us … again."

His brother's news, delivered roughly, made Kerr sit up in bed. His heart kicked against his breastbone, and heat rolled over him. "Let me get out of this bed, Iver," he snarled. "I'll hunt them down … and gut each shit-eating bastard."

Iver's gaze widened at this angry proclamation, while Brodie shifted awkwardly next to him.

"Fear not, we'll deal with those outlaws, Kerr," Brodie assured him firmly. "But ye aren't in a fit state to go after them."

"No, he isn't," Iver agreed, his gaze still on Kerr's face. "We followed them west for a spell … but then the ground grew rocky as we approached the Drum Crags, and we lost their tracks. They just disappeared." He paused then. "We need reinforcements … and since The Black Wolves are Douglases, I shall write to the king and ask him for assistance."

Kerr stiffened, logic fighting with instinct. He knew Iver's plan was a solid one. It made sense to ask King James for help, as the crown was currently locked in a struggle against the Douglases. Nonetheless, there was a part of him that wanted the reckoning to be his own, and his alone.

But of course, that would never be the case.

Murmuring another curse, he sank back against the pillows. His gaze then flicked to Rose. She stood back from his brothers, and the furrow to her brow warned him that his reaction had shocked her as much as it had Iver and Brodie.

In truth, Kerr didn't feel himself at all.

Two days had passed since he'd awoken, and he couldn't shake the anger, the guilt, that he'd survived when the rest of his band hadn't—and the raw humiliation of being bested by The Black Wolves.

"My men," he croaked then, his throat thickening. "Have they been buried yet?"

Iver shook his head. "Their burial is today, at noon." He paused then, his gaze roaming over Kerr. "Are ye strong enough to attend?"

"Aye," Kerr grunted. "Of course." Wild horses wouldn't keep him from paying his respects to those brave warriors.

"Kerr."

Rose's voice drew his attention as he prepared to let Brodie and Iver help him up into the saddle. It was humiliating to be assisted like he was an old man, yet his limbs were still shaky after the walk from the cottage to where the horses waited.

Kerr turned to see that Rose had followed them down the path.

"Aye," he replied tersely. He wished she'd go inside. He didn't like her seeing him in this state.

"I'd like to attend the burial too ... can I?"

There was a brittleness to her voice that made him still. It was as if she expected him to deny her.

He never would. Despite that she wasn't to be his, he'd never deny Rose anything.

"Aye," he murmured. "Ye don't need to ask permission for such a thing, Rose."

"Ye can ride with me, lass," Brodie offered then.

Wild, irritational jealousy spiked through Kerr at these words. His brother's face was earnest, and there was no lust in his eyes as he regarded Rose, but Kerr couldn't fight the response that boiled inside him.

He wanted to punch Brodie in the guts for making such an offer.

God's bones, what was wrong with him these days?

He felt as if he'd awoken a different man than he'd been before the attack. Right now, he wanted to rage against the world.

Kerr would have suggested she rode with *him*. However, she wouldn't have been comfortable with that, and it might knock his injured shoulder.

As such, he swallowed his foolish jealousy, while Rose nodded and flashed Brodie a grateful smile.

A cool, salt-laced breeze whipped in from the sea, ruffling the hair and clothing of the group of mourners gathered around eight mounds of fresh earth.

Rose stood near the back of the crowds, careful to wait behind a group of MacAlisters. When she'd ridden into the village, perched behind Brodie Mackay, she'd seen the curious stares of the locals and heard the whispers that had followed them. Dismounting from Brodie's horse, she'd distanced herself from the Mackays as quickly as she could. She didn't want to draw any more attention to herself than she already had.

Today was about mourning eight brave men, not about creating fodder for gossip.

Father Gregor stood at the center of the circle of graves, his black robes fluttering around him as he spoke the burial rites for each man. The sounds of sobbing accompanied his words.

One of the women, a lass called Esme, who'd been wed to Tavish MacAlister, knelt at the edge of her husband's grave. She covered her face with her hands, her shoulders trembling as grief consumed her. Meanwhile, the wife and bairns belonging to another guard, Athol Mackay, sobbed loudly at his graveside.

Rose's throat grew painfully tight.

It was awful to watch, and since she'd recently lost kin, she understood their sorrow. She knew how it pierced the heart like a blade, how it was impossible to believe the pain would ever subside.

Her vision blurred, and she swallowed hard, attempting to ease the lump in her throat. Like most of the locals, she knew these men. Indeed, she'd grown up with some of them.

Struggling not to break down, Rose sought something to cling to, and without meaning to, her gaze shifted to Kerr Mackay.

He stood next to the laird and lady of Dun Ugadale, his gaze unfocused as he listened to the priest's words.

Two days earlier, she'd witnessed his grief at the news that the rest of his band had died at the hands of the outlaws. But there was no outward sign of grief now. Only the way his throat worked and the tension in his jaw betrayed him. Kerr's expression was carved from stone. His eyes glittered, not from sorrow, but banked rage.

Rose's belly clenched. His anger made her worry about him. She knew first-hand what hate and bitterness did to folk. She'd seen it ruin her family, and it had threatened to destroy her too.

She wished, for his sake, that Kerr would let it go, but the man was stubborn.

He'd not rest until The Black Wolves were brought to justice.

The burial service ended, and, one by one, the mourners drifted away, leaving the kin of the dead alone to grieve in peace.

Rose waited for a little longer than she should have, for part of her had wanted to talk to Kerr, to remind him he wasn't to blame for his men's death. However, Father Gregor was now speaking to Iver Mackay, and she didn't want the priest to see her.

With a sigh, she decided it was time she began the walk home.

Kerr wouldn't be returning with her as he'd finish his healing inside the broch. She was relieved that he was no longer her responsibility, yet at the same time, a strange hollowness settled in her gut.

Irritated by her reaction, she set off down the path that would take her out of the kirkyard.

Unfortunately, it took her straight past Maisie MacDonald.

The woman had spied her amongst the crowd and had been waiting for her.

"Wicked lass," she hissed as Rose drew near.

Rose's step faltered, and her spine snapped straight. "Excuse me?"

Maisie's round face flushed. "Yer father was a bad seed, but ye are even worse. Ye are behind all of this, aren't ye?"

Rose scowled. "Behind what exactly?"

Maisie fisted her hands at her sides. "Ye lured Captain Mackay and his men into the hills and then set the outlaws upon them ... admit it!"

Rose stared at Maisie as if she'd slapped her. The accusation was as ridiculous as it was offensive.

17: THE KING'S MEN

THE KING'S MEN arrived on a bright spring morning, with the clatter of hooves and rattling of armor.

Kerr watched them approach from atop the guard tower with mixed feelings.

He was conflicted, for as much as he appreciated the king's swift response to Iver's request for assistance, there was a part of him that railed at needing it.

All the same, with eight of their men gone, it would take time to train new warriors. Time they didn't have.

Kerr's gaze narrowed as he surveyed the column of warriors. King James had been generous, for he'd sent twenty men. Kerr wasn't sure where they were going to house all of them though. He'd have to clear out the barracks. The members of The Guard would have to sleep on the floor in the hall for the time being.

Brow still furrowed, he turned and made his way down to the barmkin, to where Lennox had ordered a guard to raise the portcullis.

Kerr met his brother's eye, and they exchanged a grim smile. Of course, Lennox was of the same mind as him. They wanted to be the ones to bring The Black Wolves to justice.

"I appreciate ye coming home for a while, Len," Kerr said then, as they watched the soldiers reach the causeway below. "I know ye'd prefer to be looking after yer new broch."

Lennox snorted. "No, I'd rather be here for the moment," he replied. "I'll not sleep easy until we have the bastards."

Kerr nodded, noting the glint in his brother's eye. It was the same anger that he felt, although Kerr's rage burned deeper. It sat with him day and night. Every eve, he lay abed seething, tossing and turning until sleep eventually found him. And when he awoke at dawn, he had barely a moment of peace before rage surfaced once more.

He remembered Ronan's cheeky grin, and how Athol used to sing for them, his deep baritone drifting over the walls. While watching Evan and Tavish's widows weep at their dead husbands' gravesides had cut him deep.

His shoulder throbbed painfully through that lengthy burial service, yet it paled into insignificance compared to the ache in his chest.

Three weeks had passed since that day, and the shoulder was healing well, as was his head. The headaches that plagued him initially had faded. He'd been forced to rest a few days, yet as soon as he was able, he'd busied himself in recruiting new warriors and beginning their training. He'd also increased the patrols around the perimeters of the fort, including the Red Deer Hills—to keep Rose, Kenna, and Ailis safe.

The first of the king's men reached the top of the causeway and passed through the gate.

A big man clad in leather and mail, a forest-green cloak rippling from his broad shoulders, with a domed iron helmet jammed upon his head, grinned down at Kerr and Lennox.

"Which one of ye lads is Iver Mackay?"

"Neither of us," Kerr replied, stepping forward. "I'm Kerr Mackay, Captain of the Dun Ugadale Guard, and this is my brother Lennox."

The soldier's grin widened. "Good afternoon to ye, Captain Mackay ... Captain Fergus Stewart at yer service."

Kerr favored him with a nod, although he couldn't bring himself to answer the captain's cocky grin with one of his own. He wouldn't smile while the outlaws were still at large.

"Ready to go hunting for wolves, Captain?" Lennox asked, a challenge in his voice. Like Kerr, his brother didn't appreciate the intrusion.

Captain Stewart glanced his way, his dark gaze narrowing a fraction. "Aye … although since we've ridden a week to get here, we'd like to fill our bellies and slake our thirst first … if ye don't mind."

"Aye, and ye will." Irritation spiked through Kerr then. It was irrational, since none of them were ready to ride out today, but he resented these men making themselves comfortable here while the Wolves were still at large. If they had to be here, they could at least make themselves useful.

Swallowing his annoyance, he motioned to the stables behind him, where three lads were mucking out stalls. Somehow, they'd have to find the space to accommodate these new arrivals. "The lads will help ye see to yer mounts," he said curtly. He then nodded to the broch that loomed above them, its lichen-covered walls bright in the noon sun. "And I shall inform the laird of yer arrival."

It was loud inside the broch, much more so than usual.

The soldiers sent by the king were rowdy, and no sooner had they seated themselves at the long trestle tables than they were downing tankards of ale.

Fortunately, Fergus Stewart was more measured in his drinking.

The captain sat with Iver and his kin at the chieftain's table, listening intently while Kerr told him all they knew about the outlaws.

"Sounds like Lachlan Douglas and his brothers to me," Stewart said when Kerr had concluded. "They were troublemakers … even before their clan fell afoul of the king."

Kerr's mouth thinned. Of course, no one mentioned that 'falling afoul of the king' meant *disagreeing* with him. King James had stabbed the former earl of Douglas to death at Stirling Castle after the man had refused to break with two of his allies. The incident had left a stain on the young king's reputation, although the behavior of some of the Douglases since then did little to garner them sympathy. The summer before, Lennox's wife, Davina, had been robbed by one of them.

"So ... eight of them, ye say?" Stewart asked, rubbing his stubbled chin.

"As far as I could count on the day of the attack ... although I brought down one of them," Kerr replied. Restlessness churned through him. He didn't want to be sitting here discussing the outlaws; he wanted to be hunting them. "We thought there were six ... but it seems they have increased their number."

"And they were well armed?"

"Aye ... and they'll be even more so now, for they took all our weapons." The loss of Kerr's dirk and claidheamh-mòr, both gifts from his father upon his sixteenth birthday, had galled.

"And they now have fine horses too," Iver added.

Captain Stewart nodded, his expression turning thoughtful as he considered this. Kerr was relieved to see that, since his arrival, the man's arrogance had ebbed a little. Some of his men had started singing loudly now as they clamored for more ale, yet the man who led them was focused on the reason they were here.

"There has to be an explanation for how they can appear and disappear so easily," he murmured.

"Aye," Kerr muttered, his irritation rising once more. "They're like ghosts."

"And yet, ye all know these lands better than they do."

There was a slight chagrin to Stewart's voice, one that brought a frown to all the Mackay males sitting around him. Meanwhile, Bonnie and Davina, who'd listened silently to this discussion, exchanged looks. Brodie too was scowling. Of late, he'd put aside his work as blacksmith to help hunt The Wolves.

"Ye'll see for yerself, Stewart, that the valleys and mountains of this peninsula have plenty of places to hide," Brodie growled.

Fergus Stewart flashed another one of his arrogant smiles Brodie's way. "Then we shall just have to find a way to flush them out," he replied. "Like pheasants hiding in the bracken."

Picking up the dirk, Kerr held its thin blade up to the light, admiring its wicked sharpness. He then tested the claidheamh-mòr, feeling its balance and weight by holding it two-handed. Finally, he did a practice-strike and a feint. His left shoulder gave a warning twinge as he moved, yet he ignored it.

The long blade sliced through the air, and a harsh smile tugged at Kerr's lips.

"Ye have done well, Ian," he said finally, meeting the weaponsmith's eye. "This is some of yer finest work." It wasn't idle praise. No sword, even his old one, had ever felt so right in his hand.

It was the day following the arrival of the king's men. After breaking his fast, Kerr had ridden for Ceann Locha, to see if his new weapons were ready, and to his relief, they were. Ever since the attack, he'd made do with a dirk and a light sword from the armory, yet he wasn't comfortable wielding either.

He was impressed to see how fast the weaponsmith in Ceann Locha had worked, without any sacrifice to quality.

Ian accepted the praise with the nod of a man who knew his own worth, a smile tugging at the corners of his mouth. "Aye, well, I worked night and day to get them both right."

"Aye, and I appreciate yer dedication." Kerr sheathed the dirk at his hip before sliding the claidheamh-mòr into a scabbard on his back. He then untied a bag of coin from his belt and handed it to the weaponsmith. "Thank ye, Ian."

The weaponsmith's smile widened. "Can ye do me a favor, Captain?"

Kerr inclined his head. "Aye?"

"Name the claidheamh-mòr 'Wolf-slayer'."

Kerr stilled. Of course, Ian's younger brother, Rae, was one of the men who'd fallen on that fateful day. Guilt twisted hard in Kerr's gut then. No one had blamed him for the deaths of his men, yet he still secretly condemned himself. Moments passed before Kerr nodded. "I shall," he assured the weaponsmith gruffly. "And I will make sure it lives up to the name."

Making his way purposefully back to Ceann Locha's docks, where his horse was tied up, a short while later, Kerr burned with impatience. The following day couldn't come soon enough. His left shoulder was still stiff, the arrow wounds, although healing, sore when he exerted himself. Fortunately, he wielded his dirk with his right arm. If he had to draw his claidheamh-mòr, he might have problems, but he didn't care.

He'd rip open those old wounds, if necessary, to bring The Wolves down.

Head bowed, deep in thought, he quickened his step, moving out of the narrow space between two buildings—and barreled straight into someone.

"Oof!" The woman sprawled backward, her basket spilling its contents over the cobbles. She'd have hit the ground too, if Kerr hadn't leaped forward and caught her.

His gaze met a pair of startled pine-green eyes. "Rose," he grunted. "I'm sorry, lass. I wasn't watching where I was going."

"Clearly," she muttered, extricating herself from his grip and turning to retrieve the things she'd dropped. "Ye hit me like a battering ram."

"Here," he replied, stooping to pick up her basket. "I'll help ye."

"There's no need." Rose's cheeks were pink as she crouched and retrieved the cloth sacks of onions, carrots, and dried beans. The latter had scattered all over the cobbles.

"I think there is," he replied, cursing his lack of attention.

Together, they retrieved the items, although it took a while to pick up all the beans. In truth, Rose's nearness made it difficult to concentrate. For the first time since the attack, he forgot about The Black Wolves and his vow of reckoning.

All he could think about was how the sun caught the strands of red in her long brown hair, how pretty she was when she blushed, how bright her green eyes were, and how delicious she smelled, both fresh and sweet like the summer's dawn after the rain.

He hadn't forgotten her kindness either, the way she'd tended to him in her aunt's cottage. Or the apology she'd given him.

His breathing grew shallow. Satan's cods. He still wanted her as much as he ever had. Longing gnawed at him, and he wished he could pull Rose into his arms right now and kiss her senseless, uncaring of the locals passing by.

He ached to do so—but, of course, he didn't.

Instead, he rose to his feet, watching as she fussed over her basket, ensuring she had everything.

"Ye are a good distance from home," he said awkwardly, suddenly at a loss of what to say. Indeed, Kenna and Ailis's cottage was a lengthy walk from here.

"I walked here yesterday," she murmured, still avoiding his eye, "and stayed overnight. Folk in Ceann Locha are more kindly disposed toward me than at Dun Ugadale, so Ailis asked me to sell the furs she cured over the winter."

Kerr frowned. "Are the locals mistreating ye, Rose?"

Rose glanced up. "Not really ... well only Maisie MacDonald and her friends ... but they appear to wield quite an influence." The blush on her cheeks deepened as their gazes held, and Kerr wondered at her embarrassment. In the past, she didn't have a problem meeting his eye, even if it was usually in anger.

But Rose wasn't vexed this morning, even though he'd nearly knocked her over. Instead, she almost seemed timid around him.

Clearing her throat, she took a step back from him. "I'd better get going … like ye said, I've got a good distance to travel."

Rose went to move away, yet Kerr stepped toward her. "Wait, Rose. Ye really shouldn't be traveling on yer own … especially with outlaws still at large. Let me take ye home."

She shook her head. "I don't want ye to go out of yer way … and the road is well-traveled enough."

"Maybe … but the path through The Red Deer Hills isn't." He paused then, his gaze holding hers. "Yer aunt's cottage isn't far out of my way … and I've concluded my business in Ceann Locha."

Rose huffed a sigh, clearly wavering. "Only if it's not too much trouble," she murmured.

Kerr's mouth curved. "It isn't." He then motioned to the *Ardshiel Tavern* farther down the dock. "I was going to get myself something to eat before traveling … would ye care to join me?"

18: STOLEN MOMENTS

SETTLING INTO THE booth opposite Kerr, Rose
questioned the wisdom of accepting his offer.

Time was, she'd have told him to choke on his noon
meal, yet today she'd meekly accompanied him into the
Ardshiel. In truth, she was grateful for the offer. She'd
slept badly the night before. The inn she'd stayed in was
noisy and the bed lumpy, yet it was all she could afford.
After a busy morning haggling over the price of furs and
loading her basket with provisions, she didn't relish the
journey home. The basket was much heavier than on the
way here, and even strapped to her back would tire her.

"How is it ye are in town on yer own?" Kerr asked,
leaning back in his seat.

"Ailis offered to come with me," Rose admitted,
hoping her burning cheeks had cooled a little. She wasn't
usually prone to blushing and was unsure what had
come over her earlier. "But she and Kenna have done so
much for me of late, I wanted to make myself useful.
They're busy with the garden now, so I said I'd go." She
paused then before grimacing. "However, I
underestimated just how tiring the trip is on my own. I
could have done with Eara's handcart."

"I haven't seen ye with the alewife in a while," Kerr
observed. "Have ye stopped working with her?"

A hollow sensation settled in Rose's belly at this
question. She missed her friend. Eara hadn't been happy

about her decision, even when she'd explained her reasons for it.

"Aye," she murmured. "Eara's association with me was harming her business."

Kerr frowned. "So, ye are staying away from the village?"

Rose tensed, catching the edge to his voice. "I'm not letting them intimidate me," she replied crisply. "This isn't about *me* at all … but Eara."

Kerr nodded, although his brow remained furrowed.

A serving lass, comely with a thick mane of auburn hair and a twinkling moss-green gaze, bustled across to the booth then. "Well, if this isn't a bonnie surprise," she greeted Kerr with a grin. "It's been a while since ye graced the *Ardshiel* with yer presence, Kerr Mackay."

"Good day, Anne." Kerr smiled at the serving lass, although Rose marked the way he shifted awkwardly in his seat as he did so. "I didn't expect to see ye serving at this hour."

"Aye, well, Elspeth's got a bad head today, so here I am."

He nodded stiffly. "How are ye faring?"

"Well enough," she replied before favoring him with a saucy wink. "Although yer absence has been felt." She glanced over at Rose then, acknowledging her for the first time. "This lad doesn't say much … but he knows how to treat a woman, if ye know what I mean," she said, smirking now. "Ye're a lucky lass."

Heat rolled over Rose. Her lips parted as she stared back at Anne, at a loss for words. Clearly, the woman thought she and Kerr were together. An awkward silence drew out, while neither of them corrected her.

Meanwhile, faint spots of red appeared on Kerr's cheekbones, and he made a soft choking sound. "We'll have the braised mutton, oaten bread, and two tankards of ale, thanks, Anne."

The serving lass flashed him another grin, this one wicked. "Aye … right away."

Anne then sashayed off, hips swinging. After her departure, silence fell over the table.

Rose leaned back in her seat and observed the man opposite. "Ye two seemed ... familiar," she noted.

"Aye." His blush hadn't yet faded, and Rose found his embarrassment oddly endearing. "We were ... *familiar* once."

Rose continued to watch him. In the three weeks since the attack, she'd often wondered about Kerr and had even found herself worrying about his wounds. She'd been irritated with herself whenever she caught her thoughts straying in his direction, but they still did.

He looked well enough, if a little thinner in the face than the last time she'd seen him.

"Whatever there was between Anne and me... it ended a while ago," he added, his tone brusque now.

Rose shrugged, smiling. He didn't need to explain himself to her. "Ye are healed from those arrow wounds then?"

He nodded. "I never thanked ye properly for taking care of me so well."

"I'm sure ye did." Now it was her turn to be embarrassed.

His sea-blue gaze never wavered. "I didn't ... but I will now. Thank ye, Rose."

Another pause followed, and Rose looked away. "Ye are welcome," she murmured.

A heavy silence settled over the table, although Kerr made no attempt to break it. The serving lass was right about him. He was quiet, yet with an intensity that simmered just beneath the surface.

Eventually, Rose cleared her throat and forced herself to meet his eye once more. "So," she said, feigning a nonchalance she didn't feel. "Any progress with the outlaws?"

His gaze narrowed, and she immediately regretted bringing up the subject. Of course, speaking of The Black Wolves would remind him of that savage attack and the loss of his fellow warriors. "No," he replied, his jaw tightening. "Although, now that the king's men have arrived, that should hopefully change."

Her gaze widened. "The king's men?" Since Rose lived apart from everyone these days, she had little idea about the goings-on in Dun Ugadale.

"Aye, King James has loaned us twenty of his soldiers." His tone roughened then. "We're all riding out tomorrow ... heading toward the Drum Crags, where we always seem to lose them."

Rose stilled. His mention of those rocky hills northwest of her aunt's cottage made a memory tickle in the back of her mind. However, before she could retrieve it, Kerr spoke once more. "I've got a new dirk and claidheamh-mòr now." His gaze shifted to the sword he'd unstrapped from his back before sitting down, and propped up next to him. His handsome face hardened, violence sparking in his eyes. "I'm ready to face them."

Anne arrived then, bearing platters of food and drink.

Rose expected the serving lass to tease Kerr again. However, Anne cut him a quick look, marked his shift in mood—for the glower upon his face was intimidating—and departed without a word.

Glancing down at the large dish of braised mutton, accompanied by a generous wedge of oaten bread, Rose's mouth watered. Her belly was empty, for she'd eaten nothing more than a few bites of dry bread upon waking at dawn. The inn charged extra for fresh bannock with butter and honey, and she couldn't afford it.

Taking a bite of mutton, Rose suppressed a groan. It was delicious and tender. It had been a long while since she'd eaten a dish as good as this. Across the table, Kerr began his meal, and so Rose dug in too. Neither of them spoke as they ate. However, when Rose wiped up the dregs of gravy with her last piece of bread, she heaved a satisfied sigh. "That was a meal to remember."

"Aye," Kerr replied, lifting his tankard to his lips. "Ye always get hearty fare at the *Ardshiel*." His mood seemed to have righted itself again. The fire in his eyes had dimmed, and the groove between his eyebrows had smoothed.

"I can't remember the last time I ate roast mutton," she admitted.

His features tightened. "Ye have had a hard time of late, Rose."

She shrugged. "Some have had it harder." It was true. At least she hadn't been widowed and left with bairns, as Athol Mackay's wife had been. And she had a roof over her head, although she was imposing at her aunt's. Kenna and Ailis were both too kind to say so, yet they often tripped over her in that small cottage. She sometimes went outdoors to prepare food and eat, just to give them some time alone together.

As if reading her thoughts, his mouth quirked. "Things are a little cramped at yer aunt's?"

She sighed. "Aye … as soon as I'm able, I shall find my own lodgings."

"I'm sure Kenna doesn't mind."

Rose took a sip from her tankard. The ale was stronger than she was used to, yet delicious. It also relaxed her, easing the awkwardness between them.

"Ye shouldn't be made to feel like an outcast in yer own village," Kerr grumbled then, his brows drawing together. His gaze hardened, the anger that seemed close to the surface these days bubbling up once more. "Next time ye come in, I can accompany ye, if ye like? No one's going to insult ye with *me* as yer shadow."

Despite herself, Rose's mouth curved into a smile. "My own bodyguard?" she teased.

He nodded. "If that's what it takes, lass."

Their gazes held, the moment stretching out.

Warmth crept across Rose's chest. However, it wasn't embarrassment this time, but another sensation. He'd touched her. She wasn't used to being taken care of. Her father and brothers had treated her like their lackey most of the time. They'd never looked out for her. Their treatment had given her a tough hide, one few people ever manage to penetrate.

But at that moment, Kerr did. His words gave her a taste of what it would be like to be protected. Cared for.

"I've misjudged ye all these years," she said dropping her gaze to her tankard. "Haven't I?"

Silence followed her question, stretching out so long that Rose eventually glanced up to find Kerr watching her. His gaze was veiled. "Ye had yer reasons."

Rose swallowed. "I was awful to ye at Samhuinn ... when ye asked if ye could woo me." She inwardly cringed as she recalled how viciously she'd spurned him. "I'm ashamed of it."

His head inclined, a challenge sparking in his eyes. "So, ye no longer think I'm Lucifer?"

"No." She faltered then. "But I've never understood why ye were so taken with me."

He huffed a soft laugh. "There are plenty of reasons for me to like ye, lass." His eyes softened then as their gaze drew out. "Ye are strong, loyal, and courageous ... and lovely enough to make a man lose his wits."

Warmth crept up Rose's neck before she cleared her throat, embarrassed. "Ye exaggerate."

He held her eye. "No, I don't."

They lapsed into silence again. Moments passed, and Rose took another gulp of ale, noting that she was nearly finished. Her chest constricted then, not because she wanted another—although she wouldn't have said no—but because it signaled their time together was ending.

After the initial awkwardness, she'd enjoyed sharing a meal with Kerr. Strangely, his company relaxed her and loosened the tension in her shoulders. And his words just now had thawed something deep inside her.

But their meal was at an end.

Kerr drained the rest of his tankard and set it down on the table. It was a signal that he was ready to leave, and so Rose finished her ale.

They then rose from their booth, and Kerr picked up his sword and handed over a penny to Anne.

"Hopefully, ye'll pay us a visit one eve, Kerr," the serving lass said, flashing him a coy smile.

Kerr's gaze met hers before his mouth lifted at the corners. "I don't think that's likely," he replied gently. "All the best, Anne."

He turned then and walked outside. Rose nodded to Anne before following him.

The wind had gotten up while they were indoors, and the scream of gulls and the slap of water against the quayside greeted them. As usual, fishermen were hawking their wares from baskets along the quay that thrust out into the water, where fishing boats bobbed. Local women haggled with them for the best price, their voices mixing shrilly with the gulls.

Rose pushed her hair out of her eyes as she walked after Kerr to his horse, a magnificent bay stallion tied up a few yards distant. She recognized the beast—it was the laird's. Above, the sky had clouded over a little, and she wondered if rain was on its way.

Hefting her heavy basket against her hip, Rose waited while he unhitched the horse from the railing and tightened the saddle's girth.

"Are ye sure about this?" she asked, hesitant now. "My basket is a bit cumbersome."

Kerr glanced over his shoulder, his eyes crinkling at the corners as he favored her with a proper smile—his first in a long while.

Rose's breathing hitched. The Saints forgive her, that smile lit up the day like the sun, and the warmth in his eyes revealed that her company pleased him. She was relieved to see she'd chased away his anger for a short while at least.

"Aye," he assured her. "The horse won't mind the extra weight. I'll tie the basket to the back of the saddle ... while ye ride in front of me."

Rose nodded, even as her belly fluttered at the prospect of sitting so close to him. She'd never been in such proximity to Kerr before and wasn't sure if accepting his offer was such a wise idea now.

Kerr took the basket from her and used a length of cord hanging from the back of the saddle to tie it into place. He then vaulted lightly into the saddle before reaching down a hand, favoring Rose with another smile. "Yer turn, lass."

She reached up, her fingers wrapping around his. The contact made her breathing catch once more, yet she tried to ignore it. Instead, she gathered her skirts with her other hand, placed her foot on his boot, and let him pull her up in front of him.

The moment Rose settled into the saddle, adjusting her skirts so that they covered her legs, she was aware of just how close they were sitting. The curve of the saddle brought her bottom up against his groin, her legs pressing against his thighs, and the front of his body was flush with her back.

It was intimate, and yet at the same time comfortable. Strangely, it felt right to sit with him like this.

All the same, Rose's breathing grew shallow and fast, and an odd fluttering began in her lower belly. Lord, how was she supposed to sit like this with him all the way home?

Seemingly oblivious to her reaction, Kerr adjusted the reins so he held them one-handed, his free hand resting on his thigh. He then turned his mount right, and they headed off down the dock, weaving their way through the throng.

19: REFUGE FROM THE RAIN

OFFERING TO TAKE Rose home had seemed a gallant idea at the time.

However, as he urged Iver's stallion into a trot, Kerr began to doubt the wisdom of his chivalry. Indeed, the moment she'd settled onto the saddle in front of him, her plump, firm rear nestling against his groin, he'd made a silent prayer to the Virgin to keep his rod from stiffening.

Her body was warm and soft against his. That sweet yet fresh scent that was uniquely hers filled his nostrils now, and her soft hair tickled his nose.

It was torture sitting with her like this—yet one he welcomed.

Kerr inhaled deeply, trying to ignore the friction of Rose's backside against his groin as they settled into a trot and then a smoother canter.

He'd enjoyed Rose's company over the past couple of hours. It had been difficult to look away from her in the tavern. And for a short while, she'd distracted him from the thoughts of reckoning that plagued him day and night.

But even the warmth of her body pressed up against his couldn't dampen the rage completely.

It was still there, pulsing like a stoked ember.

There had been times over the past three weeks when he'd wanted to explode. He hated that he needed to recover from his wounds and that the king's men had been called upon to assist in hunting The Wolves.

With each passing day, tension coiled tighter in his gut.

Kerr's mouth thinned, heat igniting under his ribcage. Tomorrow couldn't come soon enough.

They cantered out of Ceann Locha, following the road north along the coast for a spell. Kerr then turned inland, taking the less traveled way that cut south of Dun Ugadale and would bring them to the Red Deer Hills.

Above, the sky clouded over, and spots of rain blew in with the wind. Rose kept glancing up as they traveled. It wouldn't be long before the heavens opened. Fortunately, they were riding through woodland now and could take shelter if necessary.

Kerr said little as they rode. For a while, Rose welcomed the silence. Eventually though, she murmured, "Ye have gone very quiet."

"Just thinking."

"Ye aren't brooding, are ye?"

Kerr snorted. "About what?"

"About The Black Wolves and how ye are going to make them pay."

"And I will." His voice took on a flinty edge.

"I know," she replied gently. "But be careful, Kerr."

"Don't worry, I can handle myself," he assured her.

Rose frowned. *Curse men and their bullishness.* Kerr had clearly forgotten how close he'd come to dying in that glade. "I wasn't talking about ye fighting the outlaws," she said crisply, "but about yer *anger*. I've seen what it does to people."

"I need this rage, Rose." Kerr's voice sharpened. "It's keeping me going."

"Aye ... that's what worries me."

A pause followed, and when Kerr answered, his tone had softened. "I didn't realize ye worried about me, lass."

Rose snorted, even as warmth flooded through her. "Don't go getting all conceited about it," she muttered.

"But ye *do* worry?"

"Only because I'd hate to see a good man destroy himself," she shot back.

Water splattered across her face then. The rain began gently, although within moments, it thundered down.

Kerr turned his horse off the road and under the shelter of an alder.

Relieved, both to get out of the rain and to end the frustrating exchange between them, Rose threw her leg over the pommel and jumped down from the saddle. Likewise, Kerr dismounted, and they huddled against the trunk of the tree as the rain pelted down around them.

Standing close to Kerr, Rose kept her gaze downcast. She felt embarrassed now, as if she'd said too much and risked being mocked for it.

However, Kerr didn't tease her.

Moments passed, and then he murmured. "Rose ... please look at me."

Swallowing, she lifted her chin, meeting his gaze. He was staring down at her, his blue eyes burning.

Rose's pulse started hammering in her ears. Mother Mary save her, she wished he wouldn't look at her like that. Her legs suddenly felt shaky and her skin feverish, as if she were ailing.

Kerr lifted a hand to touch her cheek. "Yer concerns are noted."

Rose swallowed. "Good," she said weakly. She wished her breathing wasn't so ragged, or that she wasn't so acutely aware of him. It felt as if she were melting on the inside.

And the feel of his fingertips lightly tracing her cheek didn't help. Not at all.

To her chagrin, she leaned into his touch, craving more.

He caressed her cheek and the line of her jaw before sliding to her neck, pushing the curtain of her hair aside so he could touch her there. "Ye have skin like milk," he whispered. "And as soft as a rose petal."

Rose made a choked noise in the back of her throat, her lips parting as hunger twisted within her belly. If he kept touching her like this, she'd dissolve into a puddle at his feet.

A heartbeat passed, and then another, before his fingers cupped the back of her neck, and he drew her closer. Kerr lowered his head then, his lips brushing across hers. It was tentative, a question. He wanted to know if she'd welcome his kiss.

A sigh escaped Rose as she raised her face to his. Aye, she did.

His mouth met hers again, firmer now, a sensual discovery. An instant later, his tongue flicked along her lower lip.

Rose gasped, her lips parting to admit him, and then suddenly she was in his arms, crushed hard against his chest, and he was kissing her fiercely.

She was drowning in the taste and feel of him, willingly, helplessly. Her hands went up, sliding around his neck as she gave herself to the embrace. Her tongue slid against his, shyly exploring his mouth.

Rose had never kissed anyone like this. Aye, she'd had a few fumbles with lads at fire festivals, yet she'd found most of them invasive and had been relieved when she'd been able to disentangle herself and make an excuse to go home.

But she didn't want *this* kiss to ever end.

The feel of his strong body pressed flush with hers, the iron bar of his desire against her belly, made lust pulse inside her. He'd set her on fire, and she wanted to burn.

However, as the kiss drew out, and his hands slid down from her shoulders, exploring the curve of her back before possessively cupping her buttocks, anxiety bubbled up, intruding on the haze of desire that had wrapped itself around her.

As delicious as this was, they were both on the brink of forgetting themselves.

Part of her—a reckless part she'd never known existed—wanted him to push her back against the tree trunk, lift her skirts, and take her there under the drumming rain. Aye, that wicked side to her craved it.

But things were moving too fast.

Today had healed the rift between them, yet she was afraid to go any further. Rose had never given herself to anyone. The unknown scared her. She unlocked her arms from around his neck and slid her hands down to his chest.

"I think we should stop now," she whispered against his mouth.

"Aye, lass," Kerr sighed. His hands lifted then, resting upon her shoulders as he slowly drew back. "Sorry, I got carried away."

Rose met his eye, her breath catching at the need that smoldered there. "We both did," she murmured.

He smiled then, and he lifted a hand, cupping her cheek gently. "I didn't frighten ye, did I?"

She bit down upon her lower lip, noting how his gaze dropped to her mouth, before shaking her head. "No ... I think I just scared myself."

His expression grew serious then. "We can go slowly, Rose. I'd never rush ye."

Pressure built in her chest at these words. Suddenly, she felt as if she could weep. His gentleness almost undid her.

"I know ye wouldn't," she whispered huskily.

His blue eyes gleamed as he gazed down at her. "So ... may I woo ye then?"

The vulnerability in his voice made her throat constrict, and her vision blurred as she nodded.

20: SOLVING THE RIDDLE

ONCE THE RAIN stopped, Kerr led Iver's stallion out onto the road and mounted. He then helped Rose up after him.

The feel of his arms around her was both comforting and unnerving. This man had set a fire ablaze inside her that wouldn't be easily cooled. She appreciated that he would let her dictate the pace between them, although that didn't ease her hunger for him.

Trying to ignore it, she focused instead on the way the sunlight sparkled off the droplets of water covering the surrounding vegetation.

"I love the air after rain," she admitted then. "It smells like a new beginning."

"It does," he rumbled in her ear. His free hand moved from his thigh then, sliding across to cup the gentle curve of her belly. The gesture was protective, rather than lustful, yet the feel of his warm palm against her stomach just made the restlessness in her womb coil tighter.

The clip-clop of their mount's hooves on the wet road echoed through the trees, as did birdsong.

Rose sighed, relaxing against him. They would reach her aunt's cottage soon. She wanted to make the most of the contact she had with Kerr while it lasted.

"This has been the most surprising day of my life," Kerr admitted then, a smile in his voice.

Rose's mouth curved. "And mine. I didn't imagine when ye barreled into me earlier that we'd end up kissing under a tree in the rain."

He gave a soft laugh, his breath feathering across her ear. "I'm just grateful ye didn't slap me for taking advantage."

"I wouldn't," she assured him, placing a hand over the one he'd rested on her stomach. "I welcomed it."

Silence swelled between them before he eventually broke it. "I've dwelt in darkness of late, Rose," he murmured. "But yer company today is like stepping out into the sunlight."

She squeezed his hand. "Ye *will* bring those outlaws to justice."

"Aye." He exhaled sharply then. "I'm just frustrated the bastards have eluded us so easily. I don't understand how. It's as if we chase them to a certain point and then they just ... disappear."

Rose considered his words, her brow furrowing. They'd spoken of this at the *Ardshiel*, and something had been niggling at her ever since. "Where did ye say ye always lose them?"

"Around the Drum Crags area."

Rose's pulse quickened. *The Drum Crags*. Aye, that was it—she remembered now. The simmering awareness between her and Kerr had addled her wits, yet suddenly, the memory she'd been searching for slid into place.

Over the years, she'd heard her father speak to her brothers about that place. It was never in her presence. He'd always thought she was asleep in her alcove, yet she overheard him.

"Have ye ever considered that they might be hiding in plain sight?" she asked after a pause.

Kerr snorted. "How's that possible?"

"My father knew of a place in the Drum Crags," she began, careful now. "Somewhere he called 'The Lost Valley'. My Grand Da had shown it to him, as *his* Da had done before him ... they hid livestock there."

Kerr tensed against her, and when he replied, his voice had tightened. "Go on."

"It's a narrow valley at the heart of The Crags," she replied, digging into her memories to help him. "I never saw it myself, but Da would brag that it was impossible to spot from a distance. Ye must ride into The Crags and make for the biggest of them ... and just when ye think ye must surely start climbing, the valley will open up before ye." She paused then. "My Great Grand Da found it many years ago, while he was out hunting ... and it's been a family secret ever since."

Kerr didn't answer, and Rose's heart started to race as she wondered if he was angry with her. "I know Da got up to a lot of mischief," she said hurriedly. "But I can assure ye, he had nothing to do with The Black Wolves."

Of course, she had no proof, as such, just a gut instinct. Her father had taken a dishonest path, yet even he had a line he wouldn't have crossed. He would never have stooped to killing merchants and raping their wives.

She'd stake her life on it.

"Don't fret, lass," Kerr replied. She could hear the raw excitement in his voice now. His hand on her stomach had clenched. "I don't blame him ... or ye. I just can't believe ye may have just solved the riddle that's had me chasing my tail for months."

More rain was threatening when Kerr drew up Iver's stallion in front of Kenna's cottage. Dismounting, he then helped Rose down, enjoying the feel of her soft curves sliding against him as he did so.

Her cheeks were flushed as she lifted her gaze to meet his, her full lips parting.

Hunger kicked Kerr in the guts, as it had earlier when they'd sheltered together under that alder. How he wanted to haul her into his arms again and kiss her until they were both gasping for breath.

However, he restrained himself.

Kenna or Ailis could appear at any moment, and he didn't want to embarrass Rose.

Instead, he untied her basket and handed it to her.

A different kind of excitement rose within Kerr then, one that hardened his stomach and sharpened his senses. Finally, he'd discovered where The Black Wolves were hiding. "Thank ye for helping me, lass," he said, grinning as he met Rose's eye. "It will make the outlaws much easier to hunt."

His pulse quickened to a march. He could kiss her again, just for telling him about the lost valley that lay amongst the Drum Crags. With Captain Stewart and his soldiers' assistance, they'd catch The Wolves this time.

"So, ye will go in search of them tomorrow?" she asked. Her pine-green eyes were shadowed. Aye, she *was* worried about him.

The realization made him feel like the luckiest man in Scotland.

Reaching up, he stroked Rose's cheek with his knuckles, his grin softening to a smile. "Aye."

"Ye'll mind that shoulder, won't ye? It's still mending."

"I will."

Rose might think he took a careless approach to his own safety—yet there was no way he was getting stuck by a dirk tomorrow. Not with this woman waiting for him.

The rain started to patter down then, a strong wind buffeting them. Leaning in, Kerr brushed his lips lightly over hers before stepping back. "Go on, Rose. Ye'll get drenched out here."

"Will ye let me know the outcome of tomorrow?" she asked, clutching her basket against her as she backed toward the rickety gate that would lead her up the garden path to the cottage. "I'll have no way of knowing how things have gone otherwise."

"I will," he promised. He then swung onto the stallion's back and angled it toward the road that would take him east back toward Dun Ugadale. "As soon as I have word, I shall bring it to ye."

Rose watched as the horse and rider disappeared over the hill—and only then did she turn and hurry inside.

The rain was hammering down now, and her clothing was soaked through.

Yet she'd been unable to stop herself from remaining there to see Kerr off.

Daft lass, she inwardly chided herself as she pushed open the wattle door and stepped into the warm, smoky interior of the cottage. *What's come over ye?*

She wasn't sure exactly, although she liked it.

That morning as she'd hawked Ailis's furs in Ceann Locha, she'd been a little melancholy. Her life in the village had been curtailed of late, and she felt an intruder in the life Kenna and Ailis had made together. But her unexpected meeting with Kerr had turned everything on its head.

It made her face what she'd been trying to deny for a while now—that instead of loathing the man, she'd formed a connection of sorts with him. If she'd been honest with herself in the past, she'd always found him attractive. Tall and strong, with that wavy ice-blond hair she'd run her fingers through as they'd kissed, he was just the sort to turn many a lass's head.

Anne, the serving lass, was clearly taken by him, and it surprised her that he wasn't yet wed.

It was lucky for her that he wasn't.

She didn't know what the future would bring, or if, indeed, their paths were meant to be entwined. All she knew was that today had felt right—and she couldn't wait to see him again.

"Ye are home early, lass," Kenna greeted her with a relieved smile. She sat near the fire, shelling peas for supper, while Ailis wound wool onto a spindle. "We didn't expect to see ye back for a while yet, especially with the rain."

"Kerr Mackay brought me," Rose replied, careful to keep her voice light as she placed the basket on the bench against one wall. "I got a good price for those furs, Ailis ... enough to buy plenty of food."

She turned back to Kenna and Ailis, pushing wet hair off her face, only to find them both watching her. Ailis wore a bemused expression, while Kenna's mouth curved into a knowing smile.

Her aunt cocked an eyebrow. "Kerr Mackay, aye?"

Rose feigned innocence. "Aye, what of it?"

"It must have been an invigorating ride home, lass, for yer cheeks are flushed and yer eyes bright."

"Och, stop yer teasing." Ailis dug Kenna in the ribs with a bony elbow. "Ye'll embarrass her."

Rose snorted, even as her already warm cheeks started to burn. "There's nothing to be embarrassed about," she replied crisply. "The weather was worsening … Kerr saw me with my heavy basket and offered his assistance."

"Aye, and I'm glad to see ye accepted," Kenna replied smugly. "Time was, ye would have walked home in the pouring rain just to spite the man."

21: THE LOST VALLEY

"ARE YE CERTAIN this valley exists, Mackay?"

Captain Stewart's deep voice drew Kerr's attention away from the road ahead, and he glanced at the big man riding next to him. "Aye," he replied. "It comes from a trusted source."

Fergus Stewart's mouth pursed. "Ye are cagey about where ye got this information from ... and that makes me nervous."

Kerr flashed him a hard smile. "There's no need. I'm not sending ye in there alone."

Stewart's brows knitted together under the rim of his domed helmet. He looked like he wanted to argue the point, yet he couldn't, for Kerr rode next to him at the head of the column, with Iver and Lennox just a few yards behind. In addition to the twenty soldiers who followed Stewart, ten of the Dun Ugadale Guard also rode with them.

They'd left a skeleton garrison at the broch, and Brodie now commanded them. Kyle MacAlister also remained with Brodie. The bailiff was a good fighter, and with so few men left behind to defend the walls, they'd called on his assistance. On Iver's orders, their youngest brother had lowered the portcullis and locked the gates after their departure.

No one would be getting in or out of the broch until they returned.

Glancing over his shoulder, Kerr caught Iver's eye. His brother winked at him, letting him know that his secret was safe. The eve before, Kerr had told all three of his brothers where he'd learned of this hidden valley amongst the Drum Crags. He never kept things from Iver, and he wasn't about to start now.

But Captain Stewart was another matter. Rose's father had been a cattle thief and the likes of Maisie MacDonald were just looking for a reason to condemn her. The priest was also capable of spreading lies about Rose. As such, Kerr was wary of drawing the attention of the king's men to her.

Warmth suffused Kerr's chest as thoughts of Rose fluttered up.

The day before seemed as if he'd strayed into a dream. After his rejection at Samhuinn, he'd given up hope at having a chance with Rose.

But, suddenly, he did.

The company crested the top of the last of the Red Deer Hills then, and Kerr focused once more on what lay before him. There, to the northwest, forming a jagged outline against the bright blue sky, were the Drum Crags—a succession of windswept, rocky hills.

"We must ride toward the tallest of The Crags," Kerr said, looking over at Fergus Stewart once more. "Apparently, we won't find the valley until we're virtually climbing the hill itself."

Captain Stewart nodded, although the expression on his face revealed that he thought Kerr's informant was making fools of them all.

However, Kerr was quietly confident this valley was the lair of The Black Wolves, where they'd retreated to these past months after each attack.

It made sense.

Like the rest of his kin, Kerr hadn't spent much time in this area. The Drum Crags were desolate hills, covered in dry, spindly grass. The land was poor, barely good enough for grazing sheep.

They rode into The Crags, and the men fell silent, their gazes sweeping their surroundings for any sign of an ambush.

Kerr also kept vigilant. These outlaws were all seasoned warriors and cunning too. He wouldn't be taken by surprise again.

The largest of the hills loomed above them now, and as he urged his horse toward it, Kerr's brow furrowed. For the first time since speaking to Rose, doubt crept in.

They were drawing close to their destination, and so far, there was no sign of the opening into the valley Rose had spoken of. Instead, it looked as if the hill thrust up steeply before them.

It seemed impossible that there was a valley tucked away here.

Panic fluttered up, as well as embarrassment. He couldn't think clearly when he was around Rose. What if she was wrong about the location of this valley? Maybe he should have questioned her more closely. Even worse, perhaps she had misheard her father.

However, he didn't share his worries with the man riding beside him. Instead, Kerr rode on, continuing to survey their surroundings.

Come on. Tension rippled through his stomach. *Reveal yerself.*

They were just a handful of yards from heading up the steep hillside when Kerr's gaze alighted upon a scattering of rocks, as big as bothies, to the left.

He angled his horse toward them, squeezing through a narrow gap between two of the rocks.

Kerr didn't glance behind him, although he knew the others would be following. They would have to travel in single file, which was risky if they were attacked.

The path ahead took him down a gorge so narrow that he could reach out and touch both sides as he passed through. The sides of the gorge reared up around him, and the sky narrowed to a strip of blue high above.

Kerr's pulse quickened, relief flooding through him. What a discovery this was—and yet Graham MacAlister and his forebears had managed to keep it secret. *The cunning bastard.* The outlaws had likely stumbled upon it by accident after desperation drove them up into The Crags.

He'd traveled no more than two furlongs through the gorge when it suddenly opened up, and there before him, studded with the same massive boulders that hid the entrance, stretched a wide valley.

A cluster of hide tents crouched at the heart of it, smoke rising from cookfires. Horses grazed farther away. Kerr's gaze narrowed. Even from a distance, he spotted Prionnsa. The bay gelding nipped at short grass, oblivious to their arrival.

Drawing his new dirk, Kerr pulled his mount to one side, waiting until his companions spilled out of the gorge behind him.

"God's teeth," Captain Stewart murmured, pulling up next to Kerr. "I shouldn't have doubted ye, Mackay."

Kerr's pulse quickened. No, and he shouldn't have doubted Rose either. The woman knew what she was talking about.

Flashing Stewart a hard smile, he gathered the reins. "Ready?"

Stewart grinned back. "Aye."

"Let's get the dogs then!"

They urged their horses forward, thundering down the incline onto the flat valley floor.

Moments later, the outlaws heard them coming. The men had been gathered around a fire, enjoying their noon meal. However, they now scattered, leaping for their weapons.

Kerr counted ten of them. More warriors had joined the ranks of The Black Wolves since they'd attacked him and his men, yet it mattered not, for they were outnumbered now, three to one.

But outnumbered or not, the Wolves still prepared to fight the men descending upon them, claidheamh-mòrs swinging, their shouts of rage echoing through The Lost Valley.

Kerr reined in his horse and leaped down, yanking his broadsword from the saddle. He then cut down the first warrior to come at him, a tall man with long black hair and wild peat-brown eyes.

The man fell with an agonized grunt before Kerr finished him off by driving the point of his blade into his throat. Stepping over the twitching body, Kerr went looking for his next outlaw.

However, having seen one of their number slain, while another lay groaning on the ground by Fergus Stewart's feet, the other Wolves had thrown down their weapons.

Kerr watched, bloodlust thrumming through him, as one by one, they sank to their knees in surrender.

Fury sparked in the pit of his stomach.

This wasn't what he wanted. He'd ridden into this valley looking for a fight—looking for retribution for the men he'd lost.

He didn't want them to throw down their weapons.

Heart hammering, Kerr stared them down. They were a ragged yet mean-looking band. Big, rough men who despite the fact they were beaten still managed to look threatening. He longed for one of them to lose his temper, to snatch his weapon from the ground and begin fighting once more—that way they could finish this as it had started.

"Get up and fight, ye fazarts!" he roared.

Some of the outlaws muttered under their breaths at being called cowards, yet none of them rose to the challenge.

Jaw clenched, Kerr glanced around, noting that his warriors and the king's soldiers had formed a circle around the camp, hemming the outlaws in.

There was no way out for The Black Wolves.

"Come on!" Kerr shouted once more, taking a threatening step forward. "Are any of ye man enough to fight me?"

"Leave it now, brother." Kerr cut his gaze right, to where Iver had moved close, his claidheamh-mòr blade glittering in the noon sun. "It's over."

"No," Kerr rasped. "It can't be."

Cold sweat bathed his limbs, and his pulse pounded in his ears. He couldn't believe it. Maybe this was what Rose had warned him about—this rage that devoured and destroyed. He'd never seen himself as a vengeful man, yet reckoning was all he cared about now. He craved it like air.

Iver shook his head. Casting a gaze over the outlaws, his brother then nodded to Captain Stewart. His face was hard, and his dark-blue eyes smoldered with the same anger that still fought for release inside Kerr. "Bind their wrists," he ordered.

They marched The Black Wolves back to Dun Ugadale with the warm spring sun upon their backs. The men at the rear of the company led the stolen horses behind them.

It was a silent journey. The Douglases had little to say for themselves.

Without even asking Iver, Kerr knew that his brother would behead them himself. He'd then stick their heads upon pikes outside the walls of the broch, a grisly reminder of what happened to those who killed his own.

Captain Stewart was oddly silent on the way back to the broch. He rode ahead of Kerr, Lennox, and Iver, as if deliberately keeping himself apart from them.

Kerr wondered if he too was disappointed that the skirmish had ended so quickly. His task on the Kintyre peninsula was now complete. He could return to Edinburgh and tell the king that The Black Wolves had been dealt with.

However, as they approached the crossroads between the road north and the one that would take them the last few furlongs back to Dun Ugadale, Fergus Stewart pulled up his horse. He then reined it around so that he faced the Mackay chieftain.

"We shall part ways here, Mackay," he rumbled, meeting Iver's eye. "And my men and I shall be taking the prisoners with us."

Kerr's heart thumped hard against his ribs. "What?"

Stewart ignored him, his attention never leaving Iver. "King James gave me instructions that if the Douglases were taken alive, we were to bring them back to Edinburgh with us." He paused then, noting the anger that flickered across the laird's face. "Fear not, Mackay. These turds will receive the punishment they all deserve ... but the king wants to watch their execution."

"Then invite him here," Kerr replied, his voice low and hard. "We can wait. We *all* want to witness their execution."

The captain shook his head. "Orders are orders, Mackay."

"These men killed people on my lands," Iver countered. "Isn't it up to me to deal out justice?"

"Aye ... unless the king states otherwise. And in this case, he does."

Fury twisted like a blade under Kerr's ribcage. "Why didn't ye mention this earlier?" he ground out.

Stewart did glance his way then, his mouth lifting at the corners, even as his gaze remained flinty. "It never came up," he replied lightly.

"Ye never spoke of it, for ye knew we wouldn't agree."

The captain snorted. Yet the truth of it was written over his face. "I don't know what ye are so upset about," he said, his mouth twisting. "The Black Wolves are no longer at large. Ye can sleep easy at night now."

"Aye, but it's about more than that." Kerr was aware his voice was rising, yet he didn't care. Any moment now, he was going to draw his dirk and go for smug Stewart. "They've spent months terrorizing, raping, and butchering ... the folk of these lands need to see justice done."

"Then tell them to follow us to Edinburgh," Stewart answered.

The man's flippant reply nearly undid Kerr.

He even reached for his dirk. It was only Iver's hand
fastening around his forearm, squeezing tightly, that
stopped him from drawing it. Glancing at his brother,
surprised that he hadn't even noticed Iver maneuver his
stallion close along his right flank, Kerr spied the
warning in his eyes. Lennox had also urged his horse
nearer, alongside his left flank. Lennox's face was taut,
his gaze narrowed, yet his hot-headed brother was doing
a much better job than Kerr of curbing his anger.

"Steady, Kerr," Iver murmured. "Let's keep our
blades sheathed."

"Aye, enough of this," Fergus Stewart said, his voice
cooling now as he swept his gaze over the three brothers.
"May I remind ye that to oppose the king is treason."

22: NO SMALL THING

ROSE WAS ON her hands and knees, pulling out weeds from between rows of onions, when the ground started to vibrate.

Glancing up, she caught sight of a lone rider heading down the hillside toward her. He had pale-blond hair and rode upon a leggy bay courser.

Her heart leaped, and she clambered to her feet.

Kerr.

Three days had passed since she'd seen him last, and she'd started to worry. It had been a long, warm afternoon, and she'd busied herself in weeding. She'd even told herself that if another day went by without any word from him, she'd travel to Dun Ugadale to find out what had happened. She had to know Kerr had survived the clash with The Black Wolves.

But there was no need, for here he was, his hair whipping around his face as he slowed his horse, jumped the burn at the base of the valley, and headed toward her.

Dusting dirt off her hands, Rose watched him approach.

Hades, her belly was all in knots.

What had come over her these days? Somehow, she'd developed an infatuation with the Captain of the Dun Ugadale Guard. But was that all it was? Did infatuation make her knees go weak with relief, or make her chest ache at the sight of him?

She'd told herself she'd be calm and collected when she saw Kerr again, but all composure fled now. She hurried down the path to greet him, ripping open the gate and going to him as he swung down from his courser and turned to her.

Rose had expected a wide smile, yet Kerr's face was serious, his gaze intense as it speared hers.

She halted, suddenly self-conscious. "Is something amiss?" she asked, her belly tensing as she readied herself for ill news. "Did ye find The Lost Valley?"

"Aye," he replied roughly. "We did … thanks to ye."

Rose let go of some of the tension she'd been holding in her shoulders. "And the outlaws?"

"All apprehended. They're in the custody of the king's men now … and will be executed at Edinburgh Castle."

Her gaze searched his face. "I'd have expected to see ye grinning from ear to ear at such news, yet ye are so serious, Kerr. Why?"

His mouth curved, even as his gaze remained somber. "It just wasn't the way I foresaw things going, that's all." He raked a hand through his shaggy hair before shrugging. "I thought we'd fight them, and then Iver would strike off the heads of those who survived." He pulled a face then. "I didn't get my reckoning, lass."

"Aye, ye did," Rose replied softly. "Just not in the form ye wished." She paused then, her gaze roaming over his face. "But the most important thing is that those outlaws are gone now. Travelers can pass through these lands without fear, and we can all sleep easier in our beds."

"I know." He sighed then. "I'm sorry for not coming to see ye sooner as I promised … but I was in a foul temper for a day or two after they left, and in no fit state for company."

"I was beginning to worry," she admitted shyly, shifting her gaze from his face to his chest, where the laces of his lèine had opened, revealing a triangle of lightly tanned skin.

"Ye were?"

"Aye, although don't ye go getting smug over it, Kerr Mackay," she replied, flustered now. Revealing that she'd been thinking about him over the past few days made her feel vulnerable. She didn't like the sensation and now sought to claw back a little control.

"Oh, I won't," he murmured. Suddenly, he was standing right in front of her, and his fingers slid under her chin, lifting her face so that she met his eye once more. "I'm still in awe of the fact that ye no longer snarl at the sight of me."

The teasing note in his voice was at odds with the serious look on his face, the searching expression in his eyes.

"Captain!" Kenna's voice reached them then. "It's a relief to see ye."

Kerr dropped his hand and drew back, letting Rose turn to greet her aunt. Kenna walked down the garden path behind Ailis. Both women wore aprons and were wiping their hands on damp cloths.

"Aye, and ye'll also be relieved to know that … thanks partly to Rose … the outlaws have been captured," he replied. "The king's men have taken them back to Edinburgh."

Kenna nodded, her gaze flicking from his face to Rose's. Next to her, Ailis's lean face broke into a wide smile. "That does lift a weight from our shoulders," she admitted. "The Drum Crags are far too close to us for comfort."

"They are," he said gravely. "Ye are fortunate The Wolves left ye be."

Rose suppressed a shudder at this. Indeed. Her aunt's cottage was nestled away in the fold between two hills, and most travelers west took the glen farther north rather than bother to go this way. Even so, if the outlaws had dwelled in the Drum Crags for much longer, they may have turned their focus upon this cottage.

"We're *all* grateful ye apprehended those criminals," Rose murmured.

Kerr glanced her way, a look passing between them.

Warmth crept across Rose's chest. The impact of their gazes meeting, and the warmth in his eyes, made her breathing grow shallow.

"We're making supper, Captain," Kenna announced. "It should be ready shortly. Would ye care to join us?"

Rose suppressed a wince. Supper, as always, would be plain vegetable pottage. Kenna was a good cook, but there was only so much one could do to pottage. She was sure Kerr would have preferred to return to the broch and dine on better fare.

However, before she could make an excuse for him, he flashed her aunt a warm smile and inclined his head. "Aye, thank ye, Kenna."

They ate their supper outside in the garden, at a small table, perched on stools. Bees buzzed around them, and the evening sun warmed their skin as they dipped pieces of bannock into the pottage.

Rose and Kerr sat next to each other, so close that their knees kept brushing whenever one of them leaned forward to take another wedge of bannock.

"It's a fine evening," Kerr commented as he picked up a cup of ale and took a sip. "The loveliest of the spring, so far."

"Aye, it's good to have some dry weather at last," Ailis replied. "Just in time for Beltaine."

Rose nodded. With all the excitement of late, she'd forgotten that they'd been marching through April. The first day of May and the Beltaine festivities were just a couple of days away.

Longing constricted her chest then as she recalled how much she'd enjoyed Beltaine in the past. She'd joined Eara and the other village women, ladling out caudle and giving out honey cakes before dancing around the fire.

But she was nervous to join them this year. Would she be welcome?

Of course, Eara would be happy to see her, and Rose's throat tightened as she thought of her friend. She'd missed her greatly of late.

Glancing up, Rose noted that Kerr was watching her, a groove between his eyebrows. He'd seen her gaze shadow, and she wondered if he realized the cause.

They finished supper with a small wedge of bannock smeared with heather honey each. Rose usually washed the dishes in the burn after meals, but Kenna waved her away on this occasion.

"It's too beautiful an eve for scrubbing plates," she murmured, her gaze twinkling as she nodded to Kerr. "Why don't the pair of ye take a stroll and enjoy the sunshine a little?"

Embarrassment prickled Rose's skin. God's teeth, her aunt was as subtle as a mallet to the head. However, Kerr didn't hesitate before smiling. "That's a bonnie idea, Kenna." He met Rose's eye once more. "Would ye like to?"

She nodded, deliberately not glancing her aunt's, or Ailis's, way, for she knew they'd both be wearing smug smiles. She'd been careful not to bring Kerr up in conversation over the past few days, for she was private in nature and wary of being teased, but Kenna missed little.

Wordlessly, Rose took the arm Kerr offered, and together they walked off down the path and away from the cottage.

As soon as they were out of earshot, she cast her companion a sidelong glance. "Sorry, about that."

He cocked an eyebrow. "About what?"

"My aunt's meddling."

He laughed. "She did me a favor ... for I was summoning the courage to ask ye to take a walk with me anyway."

Rose snorted. "Ye need courage to ask me such a thing?"

"Aye."

Rose shot him an arch look, not sure if he was teasing her or not. But Kerr's expression had sobered, and he was looking at her with disarming directness.

They continued down the valley, alongside the bank of the meandering burn, before stopping to watch a pair of dragonflies flitting amongst the reeds. Sunlight gilded the hills and burnished Kerr's pale hair.

The pair of them stood in silence for a few moments, watching the dragonflies, before Kerr eventually spoke. "Ye looked wistful when Beltaine was mentioned earlier ... does it remind ye of yer kin?"

"A little," she replied, "although more of my mother than my father and brothers." In truth, all she remembered of her menfolk on such occasions was them drinking too much and either getting into brawls or spewing their guts out. Like Rose, her mother had gotten involved with the festivities, preparing and handing out food and drink to revelers. She'd loved to dance.

"It's something more then?"

"Things have been ... tense ... of late. I worry how the villagers might react to me."

Kerr's brow furrowed, his jaw tightening. "Ye mustn't let those MacDonalds worry ye, Rose. Ye belong at the Beltaine fire as much as anyone." He paused then. "Would ye attend ... with me?"

Warmth kindled in her belly at the offer, her pulse quickening. "Ye're inviting me?"

He knew, as well as she did, that it was no small thing for a lad to ask a lass to attend Beltaine with him. It was as clear a show of interest as there could be. Many weddings took place during the moon following Beltaine, and plenty of bairns were born nine months after the night that represented the beginning of summer.

"I am ... will ye do me the honor?" Kerr stared down at her, hope and tenderness in his eyes. There was a hint of wariness too, as if he feared she'd refuse him.

But she wouldn't. "Aye," Rose murmured, smiling up at him. "With pleasure."

23: THE DRUMS OF BELTAINE

THE DRUMS OF Beltaine echoed over the hills surrounding Dun Ugadale. They were loud, calling the folk who lived nearby—the Mackays, the MacAlisters, and the MacDonalds—to the great bonfire that burned on a hill just outside the village.

Stomach tight with an odd blend of excitement and nervousness, Rose walked, arm-in-arm, with Kerr, up the hill toward the fire. It was so bright it lit up the sky like a beacon and was visible for miles around.

Their passage didn't go unnoticed.

Locals, women mostly, turned to watch Kerr and Rose walk by before bowing their heads together to whisper.

Rose's mouth thinned. *Foolish geese.* Who cared what they were gossiping about?

Kerr bent his head close, his breath feathering across her ear as he spoke. "Ye look even bonnier than usual this eve, Rose ... that dress suits ye well."

Rose smiled, tilting her head up to meet his gaze. "Thank ye."

This kirtle was her best, and one she only wore for special occasions. It was made of an emerald-green cloth that she and her mother had picked out at a market in Ceann Locha around five years earlier. She'd paired it with a snowy-white lèine underneath and then wound freshly picked daisies through her hair.

She paused, her cheeks warming. "And ye are handsome, indeed, Kerr."

It wasn't an exaggeration. Few women here walked with such a striking man on their arm. Clad in dark leather, his white-blond hair brushing his shoulders, Kerr was a sight to send a lass's pulse aflutter.

Kerr smiled at her compliment. Their gazes held for an instant, and Rose's belly tightened further. Things were moving swiftly now between them. She felt as if she were falling with nothing to cling to on the way down.

The sensation was both exhilarating and frightening.

Reaching the top of the hill, Kerr angled them toward where his kin had gathered, watching the revelers dance. Nearby, Rose spied Eara. Her friend walked amongst the crowd, handing out honey cakes. Catching sight of Rose, her pretty face creased into a wide smile, and she waved, hurrying up to them.

"Good eve, Rose ... Captain Mackay," Eara greeted them breathlessly, her gaze flicking between Kerr and Rose. Confusion clouded her grey eyes. Of course, she knew just how much Rose had disliked Kerr Mackay and would be wondering what she was doing on his arm.

Rose stepped forward and hugged Eara, a difficult task with the basket of honey cakes between them. "I've missed ye," she admitted, her throat constricting.

"And I've missed ye," Eara replied huskily. Her mouth curved then. "Does yer appearance here tonight mean ye are ending yer self-imposed exile?"

Rose sighed. Eara knew why she'd stayed away, yet she didn't want to sour the evening by reminding her.

"Perhaps," she murmured.

"Thank the Saints ... I could do with yer help again." Eara nodded to the fragrant basket between them. "Would ye like a honey cake?"

"Aye." Rose took two and stepped back, handing one to Kerr.

Eara's gaze shifted between them once more, and Rose could feel the questions bubbling up inside her.

"I shall find ye later," Rose promised her friend with a coy smile. "We have much to catch up on."

"Aye, we do," Eara said with a conspirator's grin. She then moved away, continuing to hand out cakes to revelers.

Meanwhile, Kerr and Rose climbed to the top of the hill.

All his family stared at the couple as they approached.

Bonnie's gaze flicked between the pair as if she was making sure she wasn't seeing things. Likewise, Davina appeared equally baffled, surprise flickering in her eyes. However, her husband, Lennox, wore a slight smirk, as did Brodie next to him, while Iver Mackay had a knowing glint in his eye. It seemed that Kerr had already confided in his brothers that he'd be bringing someone to Beltaine.

"It's lovely to see ye, Rose," Bonnie greeted her with a genuine, warm smile. "I've missed yer face around the village of late."

"As have I," Davina added, with a wide smile of her own. "How are ye faring?"

"Well enough," Rose murmured, embarrassed to be the center of attention, "thank ye."

"Ye mustn't be a stranger," Bonnie replied. "Ye are always welcome to visit me, ye know?"

Rose stiffened, surprised by the offer. "I am?"

"Aye ... with Davina ensconced in her new home, I miss the company of women my own age." She cut Davina a mock-hurt look, but her sister-by-marriage merely smiled.

Bonnie left her husband's side then and grabbed both Davina and Rose by the hands. "Come ... let us get some caudle before it's all gone." She then winked at Kerr. "Sorry, I shall have to steal Rose for a wee while."

A short while later, the three women stood by the fireside, cups of steaming caudle in their hands. The drink—made with eggs, butter, ground oats, and milk—was thick, sweet, and delicious.

"I can't believe Iver didn't tell me that Kerr is wooing ye," Bonnie grumbled.

"Or that Lennox didn't say anything to me either," Davina added archly. "They were both looking entirely too smug earlier."

"I don't think they've known for long," Rose replied, her cheeks warming. "This is still new ... for us both."

"I was under the impression that ye hated Kerr?" Davina said then. Lennox's wife had a directness that was both disarming and refreshing, although Rose had been expecting someone to bring up the subject at some point.

"I did," she replied, her fingers tightening around her cup of caudle. "Well, I *thought* I did ... but I've realized I was mistaken."

Davina smiled, her gaze softening. "It's sometimes that way," she murmured. "I couldn't stand Lennox at first. It was only when we traveled together that I saw another side to him."

Rose inclined her head, curiosity wreathing up. Whenever she spied Lennox and Davina together, they appeared madly in love. It was hard to believe things had ever been otherwise.

"My loyalty to family blinded me, I'm afraid," Rose answered after a pause. "It was easier to blame Kerr than to accept the truth about my father." Her throat tightened then. It was still hard to talk about him, to think about the way he and her brothers had thrown their lives away.

Both Davina and Bonnie's gazes clouded at this.

An awkward pause followed, and Rose glanced away. She caught a flash of black robes through the crowd then and stiffened. Father Gregor hung back from the dancers, neither eating nor drinking anything, his lean face set in censorious lines. It surprised Rose that he'd attended Beltaine since the festival had pagan roots. He was no doubt frowning at all the revelry that was taking place around him. Later, many couples would go 'green gowning', finding a quiet spot in the darkness to tumble. No doubt, he'd condemn that too.

The man's hypocrisy made the cake Rose had just eaten churn uneasily in her stomach.

Feeling the weight of her stare, Father Gregor looked her way. And when he spied Rose, his face tightened.

Glancing away from him, Rose took another sip of caudle. Hopefully, the priest would leave the Beltaine Fire soon enough and allow the villagers to enjoy the evening without his judgment.

Laughter reached her then, and she turned to watch the dancers. They moved in time to the slow, steady beat of the drums.

The bailiff, Kyle MacAlister, was among them. To Rose's surprise, he was dancing with Eara. Her friend's long tawny hair flew behind her as he swung her around, and she was smiling.

The sight took Rose aback. After her oppressive marriage, Eara was wary of men. However, this evening, she appeared almost carefree.

Rose's attention shifted to Kyle. The fire caught the golden strands in his brown hair. He wore his beard cropped short, outlining his strong jaw. The man was attractive. Unfortunately, Rose's dealings with him of late hadn't been pleasant, although that wasn't entirely his fault.

Shifting her attention back to Bonnie and Davina, Rose was surprised to find the two women watching her eagerly. She'd thought they too were observing the revelry, yet it was as if they were expecting her to elaborate.

Shyness stole over her, and she cleared her throat. As kind as they were, she didn't know either of them well.

"It's lovely weather we've been having," she murmured, searching desperately for something to say. She then kicked herself. Couldn't she have found a more interesting topic than the weather?

Nonetheless, neither woman seemed to mind.

"Finally," Davina replied with a sigh. "The garden I've been trying to establish around our broch can have a chance to dry out. At present, it looks like a bog."

"Where have ye moved to?" Rose asked. She'd heard Bonnie mention Lennox and Davina's new home earlier but didn't know any more about it.

"The laird gifted Lennox a parcel of land to the west, along the shores of Loch Lussa," Davina replied. "We have but a small broch, but it's lovely. It's a wrench to leave it."

"Aye, well, I'm glad ye did," Bonnie replied. "Dun Ugadale doesn't feel quite right with ye and Lennox now gone."

"Ye'll get used to it in time." Davina flashed her sister-by-marriage a smile then. "And ye'll have a special visitor here soon enough too."

Rose inclined her head. "A *special* visitor?"

"Aye," Davina answered, her smile widening. "Bonnie made a new friend last summer and can't stop talking about her. I was starting to feel a mite jealous."

Bonnie snorted. "When ye meet Greer Forbes, ye shall understand why I go on about her so." She paused then, excitement dancing in her blue eyes. "I received a letter from her a few days ago confirming she will be arriving at Dun Ugadale during the first week of June. She'll be staying for a while." She glanced back at Rose. "We met at Castle Varrich, and we were inseparable after the first day. Greer is the daughter of the Forbes' clan-chief, yet she has no airs about her. She has such a sunny manner, it's impossible not to like her." Bonnie paused then, her expression sobering a little. "It'll be good for Greer to get away for the summer ... she feels stifled at home at times."

"Well, I *do* look forward to meeting her," Davina replied.

Rose wished she could meet her too, although it seemed presumptuous to say so, for she wouldn't have much in common with a clan-chief's daughter.

Her silence must have indicated as such, for Bonnie turned her attention to Rose once more. "Ye shall be introduced to her too, Rose."

Rose favored her with an embarrassed smile. She knew that Bonnie wasn't like other ladies, for, before wedding Iver Mackay, she'd been a chambermaid at Stirling Castle. As such, she cared little for social boundaries.

But Bonnie's gaze didn't waver. "I'm giving out alms to the poor the day after tomorrow, would ye join me?"

The offer took Rose aback, and she stared at Lady Mackay in surprise for a moment. Warmth filtered over her then. Eara was right—maybe it was time she started spending more time in the village again. The MacDonalds couldn't go on hating her forever. Smiling, she replied, "Aye."

"Sorry to interrupt ye all." A familiar voice intruded then, and Rose turned to find Kerr standing behind them. He'd folded his arms across his chest, yet his sea-blue eyes twinkled with amusement. "But I fear if I don't, I won't see Rose again this evening."

Both Bonnie and Davina laughed at this, while Kerr met Rose's eye. "May I steal ye away for a dance?"

She smiled back, warmth curling in her belly, and handed Davina her half-finished cup of caudle. "Of course."

24: PERSISTENCE

"THE THREE OF ye appeared as thick as thieves back there," Kerr noted as he led Rose toward the dancers. "What were ye talking about?"

"Just the usual things that pass between women," Rose replied, deliberately coy.

"I suppose they asked ye about me?"

She smiled. "Why? Were yer ears burning?"

"Perhaps."

"Aye, they did ask ... although they tempered their curiosity, and I gave little away." She wasn't surprised he wanted to know what passed between women when their menfolk were absent.

His mouth quirked. "Why is that?"

Her smile faded as she held his gaze. "Because I'm not sure what *to* tell them ... I hardly understand what is happening between us myself."

"Me neither," he murmured. "But I'm glad ye are here with me tonight."

"As am I." She searched his face. "Ye look happier this eve, Kerr. Have ye let yer anger about the king robbing ye of justice go?"

He made a rueful face. "Not yet ... but I will." He shrugged then. "There's little I can do to change it ... and I'll not let bitterness cast a shadow over this eve ... not when I have such a bonnie lass at my side." He flashed her a boyish smile. "Come, Rose ... let us dance."

He took her by the hand then, drawing her into the throng moving around the edge of the bonfire.

For a few moments, Rose felt self-conscious, as if everyone was staring at them—and they likely were—but then the steady beat of the drums took over, and she forgot about everything except him.

Before she knew it, Rose was whirling around the fire, her hand clinging to Kerr's. And when she looked up into his face, his smile made a strange kind of joy thrum through her.

They danced until they were gasping for breath, until their feet ached. Afterward, they drew back a little to watch the leaping flames from a distance and enjoy cups of refreshing ale drawn from barrels men had rolled up the hill for the festival.

"I've never enjoyed a Beltaine like this one," Rose admitted as she took a sip from her cup. She then shot him a look under lowered lashes. "I had no idea ye were such a good dancer."

He grinned. "My mother insisted all her sons learned to dance ... she always said no woman likes to have her toes trampled on." He nodded to where Sheena Mackay stood on the other side of the crowd. She was a tall, elegant woman, her white hair pulled back into a severe braid. Rose had seen the woman from afar many a time over the years. She was intimidating.

"And yer Ma is right," Rose admitted.

Sheena's brow furrowed, in response to something the man standing next to her said. She then answered him, and although Rose couldn't hear the words, she knew they were sharp. Her companion, big and broad-shouldered with dark hair laced with grey, didn't seem to care.

"Whom is she talking to?" Rose asked.

"Colin Campbell," Kerr replied. "Davina's father ... the Lord of Glenorchy. He's taken to visiting us at the fire festivals of late." There was a smile in his voice as he continued. "And he usually singles out Ma for attention, although, she hardly seems happy about it."

Rose laughed. "No ... yet he persists."

"Aye, there's something to be said about persistence."

Something in his tone made her glance Kerr's way once more. He was regarding her with that intense look on his face that made her belly flutter.

"Aye," she replied softly. "Ye could have given up on me a long time ago, yet ye didn't."

Kerr's eyes darkened. "I'm not a man who changes course easily, Rose," he murmured back. "For better or for worse, once my mind is made up about something, it's hard to alter it."

Lord, he sounded as stubborn as her.

"But I've been awful to ye over the years," she pointed out.

His mouth lifted at the corners. "Aye, ye are feisty, lass … I'll give ye that."

She pulled a face. "I had to be, with three headstrong men in my family." She paused then. "Ma always let them tread over her, yet I told myself I'd never follow in her footsteps." Her voice trailed off, sadness pressing down upon her. "It's all a front ye know, Kerr … I'm not as hard as I appear."

His gaze never wavered from hers. "I know." And with that, he wrapped an arm around her shoulders and drew her close, lowering his face to hers. He then kissed her, deeply, passionately, uncaring about who looked on.

For a heartbeat, Rose froze, shock rippling through her.

She hadn't expected him to be so bold, not in front of his kin and the inhabitants of the broch and the village beyond.

Folk would gossip about this for days to come.

But then recklessness caught fire in her veins. Suddenly, she didn't care what anyone thought. The feel of his mouth on hers made her melt against him, her hand splaying across his chest, over his thundering heart.

The Virgin forgive her, she could get used to this.

Kerr Mackay tasted faintly of the ale he'd just drunk, and his mouth was hot and sensual.

Hunger tightened in her core as the kiss drew out, and she gave herself up to the moment.

Across the crowd, Father Gregor watched the couple kissing.

They stood at the back of the revelers, and most of those who danced and made merry around the bonfire hadn't noticed the embrace.

But he had—and the sight made jealousy cramp his stomach.

He started to tremble then and clenched his hands by his sides to quell it.

He'd tried to fight his desire for Rose MacAlister, had spent hours on his knees on the cold stone floor of the kirk praying for aid from God, but it was to no avail.

He still wanted her, and yet he hated her too.

She was a temptress.

From the first moment he'd laid eyes on her, on the morning he'd been greeting locals outside the kirk, lust had caught him in a chokehold. And he couldn't seem to break free.

The boldness of her gaze, the assurance with which she held herself, the imperious tilt of her chin, and that lush body of hers had become an obsession.

And to his eternal shame, he'd tried to make her his too, that day when she'd come to him to ask if her father and brothers could have a Christian burial. But she'd denied him. Her rejection had stung, and he'd nursed it like a bruise.

Pulse thundering in his ears, Gregor glared at where Kerr Mackay continued to kiss Rose.

And envy twisted like a serpent in his guts.

He'd noted that the Captain of the Guard had become protective of Rose of late, yet he hadn't realized their relationship had developed further. The gossipmongers of Dun Ugadale had whispered that the lass couldn't stand Kerr.

Things had clearly changed.

But Mackay wouldn't have her, not if Gregor couldn't. The way the man possessively mated his mouth with Rose's made Gregor want to kill him.

Bile surged, burning the back of his throat. Only a witch could seduce men so—could make *him* entertain thoughts of murder.

He knew Rose had enemies in this village. Maisie MacDonald had stirred up folk against her. Yet apart from a few taunts, they'd left her alone.

They had to be warned just how dangerous she was. Rose MacAlister was a wicked woman. He'd been in control of his desires until coming to Dun Ugadale, but the lust she provoked in him had become unbearable.

Father Gregor turned away, clutching his robes to him as he pushed through the crowd.

Something had to be done about Rose—and he would see that it was.

"Finally, I have ye to myself for a few moments." Eara caught hold of Rose's arm and drew her away from the dancers.

Kerr had gone to get them cups of ale, and her friend had seized the moment and swooped.

Eara's cheeks were flushed from the heat of the bonfire, her gaze bright with curiosity. "So, tell me … how is it ye have warmed to Kerr Mackay?"

Rose sighed. "I don't know where to start."

"But ye used to loathe him."

"I did."

"So, what happened?"

Rose squirmed under her friend's barrage of questions. "I've had a lot of upheaval in my life of late, Eara. It's altered my perspective."

Eara inclined her head, her eyes narrowing. "Who are ye?" she muttered. "And what have ye done with my friend?"

Rose laughed. "I'm no changeling, Eara … but I *have* changed."

"Well, I told ye he wasn't the devil, didn't I?"

"Ye did … yet I wasn't ready to listen." Rose paused then. "But enough about me, Eara. How have ye been of late?"

"Well enough," Eara replied airily.

"Have yer customers returned?"

Eara glanced away before nodding.

"There's no need to look so guilty about it," Rose said, stepping close and wrapping her arms about her friend. "I told ye that *I* was the problem."

"Aye," Eara muttered, returning the tight hug, "but it still makes me angry. I want ye to come back … for things to be as they were."

Drawing back, Rose met her friend's eye once more. "Do ye want to risk hiring me again?"

Eara nodded.

"But what if everyone turns their back on ye … like they did before?"

Her friend's slender jaw firmed in a stubborn expression Rose knew well. "We'll deal with that *if* it happens … but we can't let Maisie MacDonald and her friends drive a wedge between us."

Heat ignited in the pit of Rose's belly. She'd pulled away to protect the alewife yet in doing so had given the MacDonalds what they wanted. She longed to be working side by side with Eara again. "Ye are right," she said firmly. "We won't."

"Good." Eara's pewter eyes glinted. "When can ye start?"

The evening drew out, and slowly many of those who'd gathered by the bonfire drifted away from its glow. Some sought out the shadows to couple, while most merely sought their beds.

Kerr and Rose left other couples still dancing around the fire and walked down the hill together, hand in hand, back to the broch, where he collected his courser from the stables.

He then helped Rose up onto Prionnsa's back before vaulting up behind her.

Neither of them spoke as he gathered the reins in one hand. He then wrapped his other arm protectively around her midriff. They clip-clopped out of the barmkin and down the causeway before heading west, out of the village.

A full moon was out and cast a silvery veil over the land away from the ruddy glow of the Beltaine fire.

The warmth and softness of Rose's body against his was distracting, to say the least, yet Kerr managed to keep his arousal in check. He realized he could be intense at times, and he was wary of overwhelming her. This evening had been the happiest of his life. He didn't want to ruin it.

The silence between them was companionable rather than awkward, and peace wrapped itself around him in a gentle embrace.

This was what it would be like, to have Rose in his life every day. It felt right, as if everything had just clicked into place.

Rose's hand covered where his rested against her stomach then, and her fingers interlaced with his.

"I don't want this eve to end," she whispered.

"Neither do I," he murmured back.

"It feels as if I've strayed into someone else's life." He smiled. "Does it?"

"I don't ever remember feeling so carefree."

A pause followed before Kerr gathered his courage. He'd told himself he wouldn't overwhelm her, yet the longing in his gut wouldn't be silenced. He had to say this. "This could be yer life, Rose. If ye wish it." He swallowed then, attempting to loosen his throat as panic clawed its way up. What if she spurned him again?

"Kerr," she whispered. "I don't—"

"If ye were my wife, ye could live with me at Dun Ugadale. I'd cherish ye till the end of our days ... I love ye, lass." The words rushed out of him then. "I have for a long while."

Her body tensed against his, and for a long, fraught moment, he thought she might launch herself off his gelding's back and run screaming into the trees.

But she didn't.

"I know," Rose whispered huskily. "Somehow, I've always known ... I just didn't want to admit it to myself." Reaching forward, she tugged at the reins, drawing Prionnsa to a halt. They stood on a road dappled by moonlight, between sheltering pines. Rose then twisted around so she sat side-saddle next to Kerr and could see his face.

Reaching up, she tenderly cupped his cheek with her hand. In the moonlight, her green eyes were dark and limpid, her expression solemn. In that instant, Kerr dared hope that she felt the same way as he did.

"I've never been in love before, Kerr," she whispered. "But if it means that I can't bear to be parted from ye ... then it seems we are afflicted by the same thing."

25: IN THE MOONLIT GLADE

ROSE STARED UP at Kerr's face. Half of it was cast in shadow, for the moon was behind him, yet she could see his expression well enough.

A sigh slipped from his lips, the tension ebbing from the strong body that pressed against hers.

Her breathing caught, her pulse racing now.

She still couldn't believe he'd told her such a thing, or that she'd admitted she felt the same way.

But he had.

And she had.

His head lowered then, his mouth hungrily capturing hers. Back by the Beltaine fire, she'd been a little self-conscious. Desire had pulsed through her, yet she'd kept it in check. But they were alone now, and there was no need to restrain herself.

She kissed him back, sucking upon his tongue as he thrust it into her mouth. Their teeth clashed, and then when he nipped at her lower lip, a whimper escaped her.

She couldn't bear this sweet torture. It made her writhe against him. It made her *want*. A blend of tenderness and fierce longing twisted inside her.

Their kisses turned feverish. It was uncomfortable to remain seated side-saddle, and Rose longed to twist around to face Kerr properly. However, in doing so, she risked falling off his horse.

Growling a curse, Kerr ripped his mouth from hers and buried his face in her hair. "Christ's blood," he muttered. "I'd better stop kissing ye now … before I go too far."

Disappointment lanced through Rose. She might have stopped things from going further a few days earlier when they'd kissed for the first time—but, tonight, all reticence had fled.

"I don't want ye to stop," she whispered.

Kerr raised his head, drawing back and cupping her face with his hands as their gazes met. "I don't want ye to regret this, lass," he said huskily. "Or for ye to think I've taken advantage of ye."

Laughter bubbled up although she choked it down. His words weren't amusing. It was just an irony that the most noble-hearted man she'd ever met would worry about such a thing.

The tenderness welling within her overflowed then, and her throat tightened, her vision misting. "Ye can't take advantage of me, Kerr," she whispered. "For I give myself to ye freely. I want this as much as ye do."

He stared down at her, his face kissed by the moonlight.

Moments passed, and then he wordlessly swung down from the saddle before drawing her down after him.

And the instant Rose's feet touched the ground, their mouths found each other once more.

Their kisses were wild now, their hands everywhere.

Rose was untutored, yet her instincts screamed that there were far too many layers of clothing between them. She wanted to feel his skin against hers.

"Rose," Kerr rasped as he ripped his mouth from hers and kissed his way down her neck. "What are ye doing to me?"

She didn't answer. She couldn't. She was too busy sighing at the feel of his lips on her throat. She wanted to drown in him.

"Come, lass," he said then, his voice still rough with need. "We should get off the road and find somewhere private."

Kerr would have no argument from her. Clutching his hand, she let him lead her and the horse from the road. They walked through the pine thicket, weaving their way amongst the trees until they came upon a small glade where moonlight pooled upon a soft bed of pine needles.

Kerr looped his horse's reins around a tree branch before leading her into the center of the glade. And there, bathed in silver, they undressed each other.

Rose shivered as her kirtle, and then her lèine, fluttered to the ground. Not from cold, for the night was mild, but from a wanting that made her feel as if she had a fever. She had to get closer to him, feel naked skin against skin. Her fingers fumbled at the hem of Kerr's vest when she helped him strip it off.

But when she unlaced his leather trews and slid them down, her breathing caught.

His shaft sprang up to meet her.

Heat started to pulse between her thighs. Lord, his rod was much bigger and thicker than she'd imagined— and aye, she'd spent a little time over the past days thinking of such things.

However, she had little time to admire Kerr Mackay's manhood or to reach out and touch it, for he was lowering himself to his knees before her.

A heartbeat later, his mouth was on her breasts. He suckled each one in turn, gently at first, and then working himself up into a frenzy.

There was something both vulnerable and tender about this act, and emotion welled up within Rose, constricting her chest. Her gasps filtered across the glade as she threaded her fingers through his hair and urged him on.

She'd never realized her breasts could be so sensitive; his treatment of them sent darts of pleasure through her, straight to her core.

And then, after he'd spent a long while devouring her breasts, his hands slid down the curve of her naked back, squeezing her bottom, before moving around and parting her legs.

"Hold onto me, Rose," he whispered.

She obeyed, gripping his shoulders, and leaning into him as his fingers slid between her trembling thighs and stroked the sensitive flesh between them.

Rose let out a soft, choked cry, wet heat and pleasure throbbing there.

It was so intimate. She'd thought she was ready for this, but maybe she wasn't.

Whispering an endearment, Kerr pushed her legs farther apart still. Rose leaned forward, her gasps filling the clearing. He was stroking her once more, playing her as if she were a lyre, and the sensations he aroused made her push against his fingers, aching for more.

Answering her wordless plea, Kerr slid a finger gently inside her, pressing deep.

"Kerr," she gasped. The Lord help her, this man knew exactly how to touch her, and where.

"Aye, lass," he murmured. "What do ye want?"

"Ye." She couldn't believe she was behaving so lustily, yet the word burst from her before she could stop it. The emotion building inside her was too intense to hold back. She was a maid, and although she knew what couples did together, she wasn't sure what happened now. All she understood was that she was ready to give herself entirely to Kerr Mackay.

"Aye, and ye shall have me," he crooned, "but first, let me give ye this." Slowly, he slid two fingers inside her, and Rose let out a low, needy groan. He was stretching her, yet the penetration of his fingers caused pleasure to coil in her lower belly, especially when he curled them upward. She leaned into his hand, driving him deeper. And when his thumb caressed the tight nub of flesh within the petals of her sex, Rose went wild, bucking and writhing against him as she rode his hand.

Eventually, she fell against him, limp and gasping in wonder at the pleasure that still throbbed through her loins.

Wordlessly, Kerr lowered himself to the ground then, bringing her with him.

Stretched out upon his back, he pulled Rose astride him. She sat there, still struggling to catch her breath, yet aware of how his skin felt against hers. She traced her fingers over his broad chest, exploring the hard muscles there.

Kerr stared up at her, his breathing fast now. "Ye are the loveliest thing I've ever seen," he said, his voice catching.

She sighed. "I was just thinking the same thing about ye." It was true. Frosted by the moonlight, he was achingly beautiful.

Rose loved the way he watched her—with a mix of tenderness, desire, and awe. It made her feel sensual and powerful.

She leaned forward then, letting the swollen tips of her breasts graze against the rough hair on his chest before teasing his lips with hers.

A moment later, she was kissing him hungrily, exploring his mouth as boldly as he'd done hers earlier. She liked that he'd lain down upon his back and let her perch on top of him. He'd deliberately let her set the pace between them.

Their kisses drew out until Rose started to rub herself against him. The ache between her thighs grew unbearable now. She had to find a way to ease it. She had to join with him.

With one hand, Kerr gripped hold of her hip, lifting her up and shifting her backward just a little. He then reached between them and took his rod in hand, positioning its swollen tip at her entrance. "I'll go slowly," he promised her huskily.

Rose nodded. This was all so new to her, and there was a part of her that was nervous about their coupling. He was big, and she was a virgin. But she trusted him and so didn't resist as he slowly pressed down on her hips.

He worked his shaft gradually, stopping every inch to give her time to adjust.

It felt strange at first, as he stretched her in places she hadn't even realized existed, but as he sank deeper, the aching in her womb slid toward pain.

There was too much of him, and she was too tight.

Gasping, she stilled. Worry fluttered through her then. What if she wouldn't be able to do this? Disappointment arrowed through her. She wanted to lose herself in Kerr, to bond with him, but maybe it wasn't possible.

"Rose," he murmured, stroking her lower back. "All will be well ... just breathe."

She did, although she couldn't see how they could go any further.

His hand slid across her hip then between her spread thighs, his thumb finding the place that had unraveled her earlier. Gently, he began to stroke it.

Melting pleasure rippled through her loins, the sensation so intense that she cried out. Moments later, her cry died to a whimper, and she rolled her hips against him, impaling herself deeper—and before she knew it, she was sitting flush against him, with his shaft buried to the hilt inside her.

Groaning an oath, she rolled her hips once more, rounding her back as she felt him touch her deep inside. This was what she wanted, to feel him inside her, to know that she was his and he was hers.

Kerr took hold of her hips, helping her move. "Good, lass," he growled. "Like that, aye. Oh, Christ ... Rose!"

She was writhing against him, circling her hips feverishly.

They were still a tight fit, but she was so wet now he moved easily within her. And with every roll of her hips, the pleasure in her womb wound tighter, driving her faster.

Rose started to ride him then, rocking back and forth on his rod. The glide of his thick length, in and out, was exquisite, and a sob escaped her.

No one had ever told her that coupling could feel like this.

It was powerful, like being caught in the midst of a swirling tempest. It felt so good, it was almost too much—as if it could tear her heart, body, and soul to pieces. For most of her life, she'd never had anything that was truly hers, but *this* was.

It was freedom in its purest form.

"Aye!" Kerr panted, his voice hoarse, desperate. "Let yerself go. Give yerself to me! I need this. I need *ye!*"

Rose screamed, shattering. Her back arched while wave after wave of delicious pleasure broke through her body. She sobbed, the emotion of the moment overtaking her, tears trickling down her cheeks.

Her cries lifted high into the night, and she trembled and shook as Kerr gripped her hips hard and raised his own to meet her. He then found his release inside her with a hoarse cry.

26: PROMISES

HER BREATHING CAME in short, labored gasps as she lay sprawled against his chest.

Moments slid by, and Rose tried to pull herself together. However, it felt as if the earth and sky had just swapped places. Nothing would be the same after this.

"Rose?" Kerr's fingers gently stroked her cheek. "Ye are weeping."

"Aye," she whispered. It was true. The tears had started flowing shortly before he'd taken her over the edge, yet even now, she couldn't seem to stem them.

"I didn't hurt ye, did I?"

"No." She heard the worry in his voice and managed to push herself up, lifting her face so their gazes met. "Not at all … it's just" —she broke off there, struggling to articulate what she'd experienced— "I never thought coupling would be like that."

Kerr's mouth curved. "What did ye think it would be like?"

Her cheeks warmed. "I don't know," she hedged. "More perfunctory, more of a physical act rather than an emotional one … but" —she swallowed then— "being with ye like this … it turned me inside out."

Kerr stared up at her, his eyes glittering in the silvery light. "Aye, lass," he said, his voice roughening. "As it did me."

She heaved in a deep breath, her hand sliding across his sweat-slicked chest. "Is it like that for everyone?"

"I don't know," he replied softly. "But somehow ... I don't think so."

She exhaled slowly. "That makes sense ... how would anyone get anything done if it was?"

He huffed a soft laugh. "I know what ye mean. I'm tempted to steal ye away, to take ye to a place where I can swive ye for days without interruption."

Heat ignited in her lower belly at these words, her core clenching around him, for his shaft was still buried deep inside her. She wished he would. The thought of being able to focus on nothing but him for days on end filled her with a longing so fierce that an ache rose under her breastbone.

But they both had responsibilities and people who'd worry about them if they went missing.

"I don't want to be parted from ye, Kerr," she said, her voice shaking from the force of the fierce emotion that had caught her in its thrall.

He reached up, his fingers tracing the line of her jaw. "And ye won't have to be ... for I shall ask Iver to wed us."

Joy expanded like a cloudburst inside her at these words, and fresh tears spilled over. Rose then swallowed a sob. What the devil was wrong with her tonight? She wasn't usually a woman who wept over the slightest thing. However, this man—one she'd once spurned—had set something free inside her.

"Ye will?" she whispered, hardly daring to believe this was happening.

"Aye, mo chridhe," he replied, his gaze never leaving hers. "I want us to be joined as husband and wife. Nothing will prevent that."

"Where shall we live after we are wed?"

"In the broch ... my bedchamber is spacious and comfortable." Kerr lazily stroked Rose's back as they lay together upon their bed of pine needles. His limbs felt loose and relaxed after their passionate tumble. He was in no hurry to move on from here.

Rose snuggled against his chest, her breath feathering across his skin. "Yer role as Captain of the Guard keeps ye busy ... but what will be expected of me?"

Kerr's mouth curved. "Ye'll not rest idle, lass. With Davina gone, Bonnie needs assistance with sewing and spinning. In such a busy broch, there's always something to be managed."

Rose raised her head and met his gaze before giving a soft snort.

Kerr inclined his head. "What?"

"I'm no shirker, as ye well know," she pointed out archly, "but there's more to woman's work than sewing and spinning."

Kerr cocked an eyebrow. "Aye?"

Rose gave his arm a playful punch. "*Aye.*" Her expression grew serious then, and she cleared her throat. "I wish to continue working with Eara a few mornings a week ... even after we are wed." Her body tensed against his, as if she anticipated a fight on the subject. "I've already organized to start helping her again next week."

Kerr considered this news in silence for a few moments. Aye, most husbands wouldn't likely tolerate such an arrangement, yet he knew how much it meant to her. He wanted Rose to be happy, and it was but a small compromise. Reaching up, he stroked her cheek tenderly as he held her gaze. "Then ye shall."

Their gazes held for a long moment before Rose favored him with a warm smile. "I'm looking forward to spending more time with Bonnie," she admitted then. "I like her."

He grinned. "Aye, ye would have to be hard of heart indeed *not* to fall in love with her."

Rose's smile faded. "And what about yer mother?"

Kerr sobered. "Ah, well ... that's another matter." He traced his fingertips along her arm, up to the curve of her shoulder. "However, I know ye are more than capable of holding yer own against her."

He did trust Rose's ability to handle his mother. However, no doubt Sheena would have one or two things to say about him taking the daughter of a criminal as his wife. Kerr would watch their interactions carefully and wouldn't hesitate to intervene if his mother attempted to sharpen her tongue on Rose.

Dawn was nearing when Kerr finally dropped Rose off at the cottage. Helping her down from the saddle, he pulled her close and left her with a sensual, lingering kiss.

Drawing back, Kerr then brushed a lock of hair from Rose's face. "I will fetch ye as soon as I can," he promised. "Most likely tomorrow ... for I shall need a day or so to announce the news and organize the wedding. In the meantime, pack yer things and wait for me."

"I will," she whispered, smiling up at him as excitement danced in her belly. She couldn't believe this was actually happening. Soon, she'd be Kerr Mackay's wife.

Brushing her lips with his one last time, Kerr stepped back and moved to his horse. He mounted Prionnsa, his gaze finding Rose's once more.

"The next time I see ye, lass ... I shall be taking ye to our wedding," he said, his mouth quirking. With that, he turned his gelding and urged it into a canter, away from the cottage.

Rose watched Kerr go, a smile still curving her lips.

The glow of well-being and happiness that had wrapped itself around her in that pine glade had yet to lift. She felt as if she were floating.

The eastern sky was lightening now, a rosy blush announcing the dawn.

Rose placed a hand to her mouth, stifling a yawn. Neither of them had slept a wink last night. She'd be exhausted by the end of today, yet she couldn't bring herself to care.

It wouldn't take her long to pack, for there was little that she'd bring with her to Dun Ugadale, just a few keepsakes and some clothing. However, Kenna and Ailis would both want a detailed explanation of her plans.

She remembered then her promise to Bonnie to accompany her the day after this one in giving alms to the poor. She'd assured the laird's wife she'd arrive at Dun Ugadale mid-morning. She'd forgotten to say something to Kerr, although it mattered not.

Warmth suffused her chest then, her smile widening. It would just be another excuse to see him earlier in the day.

Moving down the path to the cottage, Rose quietly let herself inside.

Kenna was already awake, letting Hazel in through the window. The owl had just returned from a night hunting. There wasn't any sign of Ailis, although the gentle snoring drifting out from behind the hanging indicated she was still asleep.

"Morning," Rose's aunt greeted her with a sleepy smile as she moved across to the fire pit and put on a fresh brick of peat. "How were the festivities?"

"Bonnie indeed," Rose replied with a smile of her own. Crossing to the window, she greeted Hazel with a stroke to the back of the head. Her chest tightened just a fraction then.

"Ye'll be all right here, won't ye?" she murmured. "Kerr says I can bring ye to Dun Ugadale with me ... but it's much busier than these hills, and I wouldn't want to confine ye to the mews." The owl inclined her head, dark-golden eyes blinking. Rose smiled down at Hazel as she stroked her wing. "Watch over Kenna and Ailis for me."

"What's all this, lass?" Kenna asked from behind her. "Are ye going somewhere?"

"Aye." Rose turned to face her aunt. "Kerr and I are to be wed."

Kenna's eyes snapped wide. "He proposed last night?"

Rose nodded. *He did more than that.* Nervousness fluttered up. Would her aunt think they were taking things too fast? Would she caution her to wait?

But Kenna did no such thing. Instead, she stepped forward and took Rose by the hands, squeezing firmly. And to Rose's surprise, tears now gleamed in her eyes. "I'm overjoyed for ye, lass … for ye both," she murmured. "Happiness in this life can be a fragile and fleeting thing, and we must grab it with both hands when we find it."

"It would be an honor to wed ye both, brother."

Even though he hadn't expected Iver to deny him, Kerr exhaled sharply. The warmth in his eldest brother's eyes choked him up. "Thank ye, Iver," he said, swallowing to loosen his thickened throat.

"That is wonderful news, although not entirely unexpected," Bonnie announced, leaping up from where she was seated next to her husband in the solar. She then rushed forward and flung her arms around Kerr, squeezing tight. "Ye are both so right for each other."

Kerr went rigid with surprise at his sister-by-marriage's display of affection before he relaxed into the hug. He'd always appreciated Bonnie's warmth and kindness, yet no more than he did today.

"I appreciate that, Bonnie," he murmured, hugging her back.

"This is fine news indeed." Lennox got up from the table and slapped him on the back, while Davina rose to her feet and waited for her turn to hug Kerr. Lennox's wife was grinning broadly, and Kerr was pleased he'd been able to deliver the news to them both now, before they departed for Loch Lussa.

He drew back from hugging Davina, his gaze shifting across the table to where his mother eyed him speculatively. She then heaved a sigh. "Please tell me ye aren't speaking of Graham MacAlister's daughter, Kerr?"

Kerr held Sheena's gaze. "Aye, Ma. The very same."

Her proud face stiffened. "Could ye have chosen a more disreputable woman?"

"Rose MacAlister isn't disreputable," Bonnie replied, uncharacteristic sharpness creeping into her voice. "As ye well know, Sheena."

"Aye, she's an honest lass," Davina added.

Sheena sniffed, lifting her chin a fraction. "She carries bad blood."

"Rose can't help who her sire was," Kerr shot back, his anger quickening. He hadn't expected his mother to be thrilled by this news, yet her instant criticism rankled. Why was it so difficult for her to be supportive of her sons? "Ye sound like one of those small-minded MacDonald women."

Sheena scowled. "I'm just speaking the truth as I see it," she said, lifting her chin.

Kerr held her eye steadily. "Rose is the woman I have chosen for my wife, Ma. Ye must accept it, or make an enemy out of me."

They were strong words—the strongest he'd ever said to his mother. Nonetheless, he'd witnessed her viciousness upon Bonnie's arrival at Dun Ugadale, as well as her prickliness toward Davina initially. Only the fact that the latter was a chieftain's daughter, albeit one in disgrace, had prevented her from treating Davina as she had Bonnie.

But he wouldn't tolerate it.

Rose was about to start a new life, and he wanted it to be a happy one.

He half expected Iver to intercede, to warn him about taking such a tone with their mother. But he didn't.

A heavy silence fell in the solar. Sheena looked as if she'd just swallowed her tongue. Nonetheless, she didn't contradict him.

Satisfied, Kerr nodded to his family before stepping back from the table. "I shall let ye all return to yer bannocks," he said, a smile tugging at his lips, "while I find Brodie and tell him the news."

27: RUN, ROSE

HIS BROTHER WAS hammering a blade when Kerr entered the forge.

Stripped to the waist, sweat gleaming off his heavily muscled torso, Brodie Mackay slammed his hammer repeatedly onto the thin knife blade, sparks flying.

Folding his arms across his chest and leaning against the doorframe, Kerr cleared his throat. "Up with the lark, as usual, I see."

Brodie was usually hard at work long before anyone else in the broch sat down to their morning bannocks. By the time he joined Kerr to break their morning fast, he'd already done a few hours in the forge.

Straightening up, before wiping sweat from his brow with the back of his forearm, Brodie grunted. However, his hazel eyes glinted as his gaze swept over Kerr. "Aye, as are ye ... although I'd wager ye didn't get much sleep last night."

Kerr's mouth curved. Brodie, like everyone else, would have seen him and Rose together the eve before. It didn't take much imagination to guess where things had led.

"No, I didn't as it happens," he replied. "But I'm not here to boast about it. Rose and I are getting married."

Brodie's gaze widened. "That was fast work," he murmured. He then put down his hammer and tongs, stripped off his heavy leather gloves, and strode toward his brother, a wry smile tugging at his mouth. "And happy news."

Grinning, Kerr pushed himself off the doorframe and clasped arms with his brother before Brodie yanked him in for a crushing hug.

When Brodie drew back, his expression grew rueful. "How did yer mother take the news?"

Yer mother.

Those two words spoke volumes. There had been times over the years when he imagined Brodie brooded about his parentage or the fact that their mother had never accepted him. And knowing Sheena, she likely never would.

In contrast, Iver, Lennox, and Kerr had never treated Brodie as anything other than their brother. To them, he wasn't a bastard. He belonged here as much as they did. But Brodie's illegitimacy was a raw nerve, made worse by the fact that his mother had died when he was a bairn. Afterward, he'd been brought up in the broch by a woman who couldn't stand the sight of him.

"As well as can be expected," Kerr replied. "However, she's been warned not to make mischief."

"Aye, well, good luck with that."

Kerr shrugged before slapping his brother on the shoulder. It was best to turn the conversation away from Sheena as speaking of her tended to sour Brodie's mood. "With the rest of yer brothers spoken for ... it's now yer turn."

Brodie pulled a face. "I don't think so. I've better things to do."

"Come on, ye'll lose yer heart one day ... everyone does, eventually. How long are ye going to make us all wait?"

"A long time, brother," Brodie drawled. "Just because ye have gone daft over a lass, doesn't mean I ever will." He then waved Kerr away. "Now get out of here. I'm busy. And take those pine needles out of yer hair."

Eara Mackay towed her rickety handcart through the village. She was transporting a barrel of water she'd drawn from a spring and was heading home. She'd crushed the malted barley up the day before yet needed spring water to mash it up into a 'wort', which she would boil up in her cauldron.

She looked forward to Rose starting back with her the following week. Even though her friend didn't work with Eara every day, many of these chores were much easier with a second pair of hands.

Eara's mouth curved then into a wry smile. In truth, she wasn't sure how much longer Rose would help her—judging from the passionate embrace she'd seen her friend and the handsome Captain of the Guard locked in on Beltaine Eve, Rose was on the cusp of a new life. Surely, Rose wouldn't want to continue helping her—even a couple of days a week—not if she was a wedded woman?

Nonetheless, Eara was delighted for her, even if it meant she'd be hauling water and grain on her own again. It was a small price to pay to see her friend so happy.

As the alewife entered the village square, a strident male voice reached her.

"Evil lives amongst us ... we must strike it out!"

Squinting ahead, Eara spied a tall, robed figure standing atop a wooden box in the dirt square at the center of the village. She was surprised to see the priest out here—away from his kirk. Bathed in sunlight, Father Gregor was ranting at the crowd gathered before him.

"Beware of the Great Deceiver," he cried, shaking his fist into the air. "And those who do his bidding."

Eara frowned. The priest seemed excitable this morning. Something had clearly upset him.

"I must warn ye all," Father Gregor continued, "of the devil's handmaid in our midst. It is *Rose MacAlister*."

Eara stifled a gasp. Meanwhile, his comment brought rumbles and murmurs from the crowd. They were MacDonalds mostly, with a few Mackays scattered amongst them. And worryingly, they were all nodding their heads as if the priest talked perfect sense.

Quickening her pace, Eara decided to circuit the edge of the village square rather than cut through the heart of it.

God's blood, what was wrong with the man? Rose had done nothing to him. Eara had never seen Father Gregor so animated, so vitriolic.

"Rose MacAlister is a criminal's daughter. And I believe *she* was the one to turn her father and brothers onto the path of wickedness."

"Aye!" Maisie MacDonald shouted. "It's true, Father ... I've known it for a while now!"

Murmurs followed the woman's outburst, while Eara's heart started to thump against her ribs. This was nonsense—surely, she wasn't the only one here who thought so?

"And the outlaws that plagued our lands weren't here by accident either." Father Gregor's gaze swept the crowd of upturned faces before him. "She called them to us! Was it any coincidence the brigands were hiding in the Drum Crags ... just a short distance from where she lives with two *unnatural* women?"

"And she has an owl too!" A young man shouted. It was Keith, Duncan MacDonald's youngest son. Short and broad, the lad wore a belligerent expression. "It's her consort!"

"Aye," a woman shouted from the crowd. "A witch, for sure!"

Eara's mouth thinned. The villagers were acting like a mob of witless sheep. Would they run themselves off a cliff if the priest told them to?

"Rose MacAlister is indeed dangerous," Father Gregor intoned, his expression grave. He then motioned to where the walls of Dun Ugadale rose against a cornflower-blue sky. "She seeks to control us all. Behold, she has set upon seducing our own laird's brother ... the Captain of the Guard. Ye all saw them, yesterday eve ... I know ye did!"

This comment brought a chorus of 'aye's and fervent nods.

Disgusted, Eara tugged hard on the rope, yanking the handcart behind her. She'd not remain here and listen to another word of this.

However, Rose needed to know that Father Gregor was preaching lies about her.

Her friend had told her she was coming into the village the following morning, to help Lady Bonnie deliver bread to the poor, and Eara would ensure she sought them out. Father Gregor's days here would be numbered once Iver Mackay heard about the rot he was spreading.

Leaving the square, Eara headed down a narrow street toward her home. The roar of cheering followed her.

Rose hummed to herself as she walked east, over the hills, toward Dun Ugadale. There was a spring in her stride this morning, an eagerness to be on her way. She'd packed her things back at the cottage.

The day before had dragged on endlessly, and she was impatient to see Kerr again. All that remained now was for him to come and retrieve her. He'd said he'd likely fetch her today, yet she'd reach him first. She'd arranged to meet Lady Bonnie at the broch.

Later, Rose and Kerr could ride back to Kenna's cottage together and collect her few things.

Excitement fluttered up as she imagined sitting in front of him, pressed against the warmth and strength of his body, his arms wrapped protectively around her.

Now that she'd tasted Kerr Mackay, she was eager for more of him.

The walk to Dun Ugadale took a while, but since Rose had headed off just after dawn, it was still early when she crested the last hill. Below stretched a patchwork of fields and clusters of bothies.

Beyond the broch, the village, and the rows of run rigs, lay Kilbrannan Sound. On a bright day, the water sparkled in the sunlight, yet this morning, it resembled a beaten sheet of grey pewter, against a sky the color of pale smoke.

Rose's attention shifted to the peaked roof of the kirk. It crouched under the rocky promontory where the broch perched. Looking upward, Rose could just make out the tiny figures of men on the walls of the fortress.

Her pulse quickened. Was one of them Kerr? Her breathing grew shallow as the fluttering in her belly intensified. Of course, before she and Bonnie headed out to give alms to the poor, she'd see him.

She couldn't wait.

Descending the hill, Rose took the path past the kirk. She slowed her gait as she passed, her gaze traveling over the gravestones that studded the ground in the yard. Wistfulness wreathed up within her then, for she missed her Sunday sermons. Till now, Father Gregor had made her too uncomfortable to attend. But in the future, things would be different. When she attended services with Kerr, the priest would keep his distance.

The path continued, skirting the edge of the village. Starting to hum to herself once more, Rose tugged her shawl a little closer. The breeze gusting in from the sound had a bite to it. She glanced up at the sky and wondered if it would rain later.

Thwack.

Something hit her between the shoulder blades.

The impact made her stumble, and she was about to turn and see what had hit her when something small and sharp pinged into the back of her skull.

Dear Lord, someone was pelting her with stones.

Crying out, she raised her hand to her head and whipped around, coming face-to-face with a group of villagers.

Where the devil had they all sprung from?

Maisie MacDonald stepped out from their midst. She was smiling, although her eyes were hard. "There she is," the woman crowed. "The witch has walked into our midst." She then ruffled the hair of the lad next to her. "Thanks to my sharp-eyed nephew, who spotted yer arrival."

Rose's heart lurched.

"I'm no witch," she retorted, outrage eclipsing fear for a moment. "And shame on ye, Maisie MacDonald, for poisoning a bairn's mind against me."

"I've done no such thing," Maisie snarled, motioning to the men and women surrounding her. As Rose looked closer now, she noted they all wore hungry expressions and had wild looks in their eyes.

A stocky young man stepped forward then, his face twisted in spite. Rose's heart lurched when she recognized Keith MacDonald. He was the meanest of Duncan MacDonald's brood, the one who'd often scrapped with her brothers. "We all know what ye are ... and what must be done about ye."

Her blood started to roar in her ears.

Run, Rose. Run!

This wasn't the time to stand her ground and argue with these people. Danger crackled in the air.

Turning on her heel, she fled down the path toward the heart of the village. However, her tormentors were after her in moments, howling like hounds after a hind as they gave chase.

Rose was fast, although not as fast as some of the men, and her long skirts hampered her. She'd covered no more than a dozen yards when they caught her.

Hard fingers bit into her arms, dragging her to a halt.

Suddenly, they surrounded her on all sides. A fist caught her on the side of the head, while a boot connected with her shin.

Rose hissed in pain, struggling against them. "Let me go," she shouted. "I've done nothing wrong!"

"Witch!" A man bellowed in her face, spraying her with spittle. He was Dugan Mackay, the local tanner. Dugan had never been someone Rose had warmed to, yet she'd had no idea he had a problem with her—until today.

"Calm yerselves!" Maisie shouted over the commotion. "Remember what Father Gregor told us must be done. First, we bind her ankles and wrists ... and then we throw her into the sea. If she floats, we will have proof she is in league with the devil. We must then burn her at the stake!"

28: KILL THE WITCH

ROSE FOUGHT THEM with everything she had, terror giving her wild strength—but she couldn't tear free of the iron grip of the villagers as they towed her down the path toward the water.

Her attackers had taken a route through the apple orchard to avoid dragging her past the fields. This path was little used, and as such, there was nobody to see them.

Rose twisted and writhed against them, even as Keith tied ropes around her wrists and ankles, pulling the knots so tight it hurt.

Her screams ripped through the air—fear had turned her feral—but her attackers paid her no mind.

Chants of "Kill the witch" echoed across the sound when they carried her, hog-tied as she was, down to the water. They then picked her up, gripping her squirming body, and waded out across the slippery stones.

The cool wind caressed Rose's wet cheeks. She was sobbing now, her throat raw from screaming. Despair twisted hard in her belly. They were going to drown her, and no one was going to stop them.

Kerr!

If only he were here—but he didn't know she'd set off early for Dun Ugadale on her own this morning. He wouldn't come to her rescue. No one would.

They let go of Rose then, casting her into the water. She hit the surface with a slap, going under.

Icy water engulfed her. She sank, struggling desperately against her restraints, and then floated again, pulled to the surface by her billowing skirts.

She continued to writhe, as her lungs burned, and a high-pitched whine started in her ears. The end was close now. Yet she still fought the water, still tried to get her head up so she could take a gasp of air.

Suddenly, hands grabbed her by the shoulders and pulled her upward.

Rose came up coughing and gasping for breath. Relief washed over her. She couldn't believe it—by some miracle, someone had saved her.

But an instant later, Maisie's excited voice sliced through her relief. "She floated! I knew she would!"

"I didn't float!" Rose croaked, bile surging up her throat. "I was drowning." If she hadn't sunk like a stone, it was because air had caught in the full skirt of her kirtle.

But no one was listening to her.

"The Evil One's handmaid must burn," a woman shouted from the back of the group.

"Aye, Janet," Maisie replied. "Let us take her into the village, build a pyre, and see it done."

Eara carried a tray of soaked and drained barley outside on a tray. She was taking it to the lean-to next to her bothy, where she would lay the grain out to germinate. She walked quickly, keen to finish this last task before she set out for the broch.

The morning was still young, but she'd woken up with a sense of urgency.

After seeing Father Gregor preaching in the village square the day before, Eara was determined to tell Lady Mackay and Rose what she'd overheard.

The priest's stirring had to be dealt with.

Eara had just deposited the barley on a table in the lean-to when excited chatter on the street outside drew her attention. Intrigued, she hurried around the front of her cottage and peered over the high wattle fence.

A crowd of villagers had just passed by.

Eara's pulse quickened when she realized they were jeering and shoving someone in their midst.

An instant later, the crowd parted, and she saw whom they were manhandling.

Eara's breathing caught. *Rose!*

Drenched, her face wild with panic, her friend's hands were bound in front of her. One of the women shoved Rose hard between the shoulder blades then, and she staggered, falling onto her knees.

Two burly men, one the local tanner, and the other Duncan MacDonald's youngest son—grabbed Rose by the arms and hauled her roughly to her feet. They then herded her forward to shouts of "Burn the witch!"

"Merciful Lord," Eara gasped, watching them go.

Had she heard right?

The people of this village had lost their minds.

Heart pounding, Eara backed up, nearly tripping over a stack of peat bricks she'd just had delivered.

Someone had to stop them.

She left her garden through the narrow gate at the back, sprinting down a lane between rows of squat bothies. She wasn't sure where the villagers planned to burn Rose, but she knew she alone couldn't stop them.

She needed help.

Eara picked up her skirts, her legs flying now as she headed toward the broch.

"Captain!"

A woman's cry made Kerr glance up from where he was tightening Prionnsa's girth. It had been a busy morning, with an altercation between two of his men to deal with, and Kerr was eager to get away. He wanted to ride out to the Red Deer Hills and fetch Rose.

Iver had agreed to wed them in the hall, under the eyes of all, as soon as they arrived. Impatience thrummed through Kerr as he saddled his gelding. He couldn't wait to see Rose again.

But thoughts of her fled now as Eara Mackay, the brewer's widow, rushed at him. Her face was red, her grey eyes wild—and she was running so fast her foot caught on a cobblestone and she sprawled.

Kerr moved forward and picked the gasping woman up.

"God's blood, Eara," he muttered. "What's the matter?"

"It's Rose," Eara choked out. "They're going to burn her!"

Kerr stilled, cold washing over him. His grip on Eara's shoulders tightened. "Who?"

"The villagers ... I saw them taking her toward the center of the village. Hurry! Ye have to stop them."

Kerr didn't need to be warned twice. Letting go, he moved over to his gelding and vaulted up onto Prionnsa's back. He was just reining his horse around when Brodie emerged from the forge a few yards away.

"What's wrong?" his brother asked, scowling.

"Rose is in trouble," Kerr barked "Follow me down to the village."

And with that, not bothering to explain himself further, Kerr urged his horse into a canter, clattering out of the barmkin under the raised portcullis.

He rode as if the hounds of hell were at his heels, down the causeway and into the village. It wasn't far to the small square—a narrow patch of dirt at the heart of the village—but as he approached, Kerr could see the villagers had worked fast.

They'd built a pyre of twigs and straw around a pole, where they'd tied Rose.

She was struggling against her bindings, tears streaking her face as she shouted at them.

And a few yards away, Maisie MacDonald carried a flaming torch. The woman strode toward the pyre, a savage expression on her face.

Kerr kicked Prionnsa forward, cleaving a path through the excited crowd.

There appeared to be a scuffle going on—for some men and women were trying to break through the circle around the pyre to help Rose. Fists were flying and angry curses rang through the morning air.

None of the villagers saw Kerr. Not until he was almost upon them—and then they scattered like fowl, diving out of the way of the courser.

Maisie glanced his way then, her mouth gaping when she saw him heading straight for her.

Kerr thought she might have second thoughts about what she was about to do—that she might halt and cast aside her burning torch.

But she didn't.

Instead, the woman leaped forward, attempting to close the final gap between her and Rose.

She still intended to set fire to the twigs and straw.

Kerr ran her down.

Maisie screamed, trampled under Prionnsa's churning hooves. The torch flew from her grip, rolling away across the dirt.

Pulling up his horse, Kerr swung down from the saddle, drew his dirk, and crossed to Rose.

Tears still streaked her face, yet relief shone in her eyes.

But as he drew near, he noted that a bruise was coming up on her cheek, and there were scratches on her neck, as if someone had clawed at her.

Rage caught fire in his veins.

How dare they?

Swinging around, he swept his gaze over the men and women who'd joined Maisie. They weren't so excited now—especially since many of them were lying on the ground, held firm by the villagers who'd come to Rose's aid.

However, some, like Dugan Mackay and Keith MacDonald, hadn't been subdued. Both men approached Kerr now, their faces twisted into belligerent expressions.

"Let us have the bitch," Keith roared. "How dare ye defend Graham MacAlister's spawn?"

"Ye have let the woman bewitch ye," the tanner added, his mouth twisting. "Let us put an end to her and save yer soul."

Kerr viewed them coldly. "Touch her, and I'll carve out yer hearts."

"Aye ... get down on yer knees, Dugan," a rough voice ordered from behind. "Before I knock ye to the ground."

Brodie stepped up then, five of The Guard following close behind. All the men were out of breath from their sprint down from the broch. Fury burned in their gazes. Despite that it was a dull day, their drawn dirk blades glinted menacingly.

Dugan and Keith both hesitated. They then shared nervous looks before reluctantly doing as bid.

A heavy silence fell over the village square.

Relieved that his brother had brought help, Kerr kicked aside the twigs piled up around Rose's feet and deftly cut away the ropes tying her to the pole.

She fell against him, sobbing.

Heart pounding, Kerr scooped her up into his arms and strode away from the pyre, across the square.

Villagers drew back to let him pass. On the way, he spied Maisie lying spread-eagled on her front, beside where his gelding patiently awaited him. She was motionless, a dark stain spreading into the dirt around her head.

She was dead, and part of him thought he should be sorry. But he wasn't. Maisie had tried to burn Rose alive, even as he tried to stop her.

As he carried Rose up to Prionnsa, Kerr caught Brodie's eye. The two brothers' gazes held for a moment before Brodie asked gruffly, "What do ye want us to do with the others?"

"Bring them up to the broch," Kerr replied, battling the fury that still pummeled through him. "And fetch that damned priest too ... he's behind all of this."

29: JUSTICE IS JUSTICE

KERR STOOD AT Iver's side on the steps of the barmkin, watching as Brodie and the Guards brought in those responsible for trying to burn Rose at the stake.

Father Gregor was among them.

Brodie walked behind the priest, looming over him like an angel of death. Indeed, the glower on the blacksmith's face was dark enough that if looks could kill, Father Gregor would be writhing on the ground, gasping his last.

"I found him on his knees in the kirk, praying," Brodie announced, placing a heavy hand on the priest's shoulder so that they halted at the foot of the steps beneath the laird.

Kerr's mouth thinned, and he clenched his hands at his sides. "Of course, ye did."

"What were ye praying for, Father?" Iver asked.

Father Gregor raised his chin, his dark gaze spearing the chieftain. "For deliverance from evil, Mackay. We must cast out Satan's disciples from our midst."

"Aye, priest." Iver slowly descended the steps toward the slender figure robed in black. Even brought before the laird like this, for inciting violence and attempted murder, Father Gregor stood proud. "I agree, wholly … which is why after I have ye flogged, I shall have ye run off my lands."

One more step brought Iver up close to the priest, his fist driving hard into his guts.

Father Gregor gasped, sinking to his knees. "May the Lord forgive ye for striking a man of the cloth," he choked.

"He won't forgive me," Iver replied, meeting the priest's gaze. "But he will *thank* me for unmasking the lowliest of men. Ye aren't worthy of wearing that robe, *priest*. I invited ye into this community and trusted ye with the souls of those living here." The laird's voice sharpened further as he continued, "But in return, ye have sowed fear and hate. Ye are a corruption, and if ye don't wish me to draw my dirk and slit yer conniving throat, I suggest ye say nothing more."

Kerr watched his brother with grim satisfaction.

Father Gregor was a heartbeat away from dying—and he ached for the bastard to say something, anything, to damn himself.

But the priest realized the danger he was in, for he bent his head, breaking eye contact with Iver. His lean body trembled.

Brodie motioned to the group of men and women— ten of them—the guards had brought in with the priest. "What of the rest?"

"Their crimes cannot go unpunished either," Iver rumbled. He glanced over at Kerr then, meeting his eye. "Who is the ringleader?"

"Maisie MacDonald ... but she's dead," Kerr answered. He then nodded to the two men at the front of the group. "Dugan Mackay and Keith MacDonald were also in the thick of things. Like Maisie, they incited the others to violence."

Both men stood there, heads held high, jaws set.

Heat washed over Kerr. Their arrogance was galling. Even now, they weren't sorry—but they soon would be. Perhaps they didn't know what the punishment was for attempted murder, but Kerr did.

It was fortunate indeed for Maisie that she'd died under the hooves of his courser.

"Then they will be hung from the walls this afternoon," Iver announced after a brief pause. "And the others who took part will be left in the stocks in the village square for a week."

Both Dugan and Keith gaped at this pronouncement.

"It was the priest's fault," Dugan spluttered, recovering first from the shock of hearing his neck was about to be stretched. His eyes were now wide and frightened. "He's the one who told us to do it."

"Aye, but he didn't bind Rose MacAlister's wrists and ankles and attempt to drown her ... before dragging her to a pyre so he could set fire to her."

"But he told us she was an evil witch who fornicated with the devil!" Keith protested. The lad had turned white.

"And *ye* were the witless worm who ate up his poison," Kerr snarled, unable to keep his tongue leashed. It was up to Iver to deal out punishment, yet these two sickened him, as did the rest of the group who whimpered and trembled behind Dugan and Keith. "Ye were looking for a reason to turn on her, for ye wanted reckoning against her family, didn't ye?"

"Gregor will never don priest's robes again, I shall see to it," Iver said then, his voice growing harder still. "And before we run him out of Dun Ugadale, I shall flay the skin off his back."

The priest made a choking sound at this, yet Iver ignored him. Instead, his attention remained on Duncan MacDonald's youngest. "Justice is justice, Keith. Ye tried to murder a woman, and now ye will pay the price."

Kerr stood on the walls, watching as a naked man, blood streaming down his back from lacerations, stumbled down the causeway and into the village below.

Villagers were waiting for him, armed with rotten food and turds. As he stumbled by, weeping piteously, they pelted him.

Kerr's lip curled.

It was a nasty business, all of it. Yet it was necessary. Gregor had made it so.

Kerr turned from the wall, taking the steps down to the barmkin. A grisly sight awaited him there, for Dugan and Keith hung from the gate, their bodies swinging in the wind that barreled in from the sea this afternoon.

The clang of metal echoed through the barmkin from Brodie's forge. Now that it was all over, his brother had gone back to work.

Leaving it behind as well, Kerr mounted the steps to the broch and went inside. The hall on the bottom level was empty, for it was still too early for supper. Iver had retired to his solar with Bonnie, yet Kerr wouldn't join them.

There was someone else he needed to see.

They'd put Rose in Davina's old room in the tower, just a floor above his own bedchamber. Eara had stayed with her for a spell, although Kerr had spied the lass returning to the village a short while earlier.

Taking the winding steps up to the landing, Kerr knocked gently on the door and waited.

A moment later, a woman's voice, tired and brittle, answered. "Aye?"

"It's me, Rose. Can I come in?"

"Kerr! Aye."

He pushed the door open and stepped inside, his gaze going to where Rose sat propped up in bed. The bruise on her cheek was livid now, highlighting her pallor, but her eyes were warm as she looked upon him.

"I didn't wake ye, did I?" he asked.

She shook her head. "I was planning on rising anyway ... everyone keeps treating me like an invalid."

He huffed a soft laugh, approaching the bed and perching on the edge next to her. "That's because ye have had a terrible shock, lass."

She sighed before reaching out and taking his hand. "Bonnie told me about the punishments Iver announced earlier ... have they been carried out?"

He nodded. "Dugan and Keith are dead ... and ye won't ever set eyes on Father Gregor again."

She swallowed, nodding.

Kerr's chest constricted. "I'm so sorry, Rose," he whispered.

"It's not yer fault, my love," she replied huskily. Her grip on his hand tightened. "All that matters is that I'm alive because of ye."

My love.

His throat thickened. "I've heard rumors of people drowning or burning women they suspect of witchcraft," he murmured, clearing his throat, "but I thought that happened in far-flung places ... not *here*."

Rose sighed. "So did I."

Shifting closer to her, he placed his free hand on top of hers, clasping it tight. "I will never let anyone hurt ye again," he said, his voice low and fierce. "I swear it. On my life."

Rose stared up at him, her pine-green eyes glittering now as tears welled. "Ye are the best of men, Kerr," she whispered. "And I can't wait to be yer wife."

Kerr squeezed her hand once more. His throat was now so tight, he couldn't speak. Her words moved him deeply.

Their gazes held before a groove appeared between Rose's eyebrows. "Will we have to delay things now?"

He shook his head. "Iver told me earlier that he will wed us tomorrow afternoon in the hall ... if ye wish it," he finally managed to croak.

Indeed, his brother had insisted there was no better way to wash away the stain that Father Gregor left behind than with a wedding.

Rose's lovely face relaxed at this, her full mouth lifting at the corners.

Joy flowered in Kerr's chest at the sight. After years of longing for Rose from afar, there was a secret, insecure part of him that wondered if he'd imagined all of this. Did she really want him as much as he did her?

But this was real, and he wouldn't allow anyone to destroy the joy they'd found.

"Tomorrow it is," Rose replied. She paused then, interlacing her fingers through his. "I'd like Kenna and Ailis to be at our wedding … and Eara too."

Kerr nodded. "Of course." Rose's aunt would be worrying about what had befallen her niece. "I will send out men, first thing in the morning, to fetch them."

30: SEEKING COMFORT

NIGHT SETTLED OVER Dun Ugadale, yet Rose couldn't sleep.

She had too many thoughts churning through her mind, too many emotions that made her restless.

Time slid by, and around her, the broch quietened. However, sleep still eluded her.

Eventually, muttering a curse, she pushed back the covers and swung her legs out of bed before padding barefoot over to the window. Unlatching the shutters, she threw them open.

The moon was on the wane now, yet it hung overhead like a polished silver penny, winking down at her and frosting the walls below in silver. Its light reminded her of that magical night, just two days prior, when she and Kerr had given themselves to each other in that pine glade.

Was it only two days ago?

It felt as if a month had passed since then.

Today's events had shaken her deeply. She still couldn't believe that Father Gregor had managed to incite Maisie and her friends to do what they had. It unnerved her that folk could be so weak-minded. Nonetheless, it was worth remembering that the priest had found fertile ground here. Of course, there was an undercurrent of superstition in most communities, yet the rift between the MacDonalds and the MacAlisters made it easy to divide the village. Many of the

MacDonalds had been looking for a reason to condemn Graham MacAlister's daughter.

An owl hooted in the distance and Rose sighed, wondering where Hazel was hunting tonight. She'd miss the owl in her new life, but surely, Hazel would be happier remaining with Kenna?

Leaning against the window ledge, Rose continued to gaze out at the moonlit night. The cold wind of earlier in the day had died, and the air had a watchful stillness to it.

And all the while, the quiet just made the restlessness in her grow.

Kerr had brought a tray of supper up to her earlier, and they'd eaten together. But he'd left soon after, telling her that she should rest. He'd also reassured her that his chamber lay directly under hers, and to knock on his door if she should need anything.

Well, she did need something. *Him.*

As she'd pointed out earlier, she wasn't an invalid. Bonnie had rubbed salve on the scratches to her neck and upon the bruises to her head and shin. Fortunately, her physical wounds were all superficial.

However, today's events had bruised her in places no one could see. She longed for comfort and reassurance. For Kerr.

Pulse quickening, Rose padded toward the door. No, she didn't want to be alone. Not tonight. She wore a thin night-rail, yet before leaving her chamber, she wrapped a woolen shawl around her shoulders—just in case she met anyone on the stairwell.

Out on the landing, she was relieved to find a cresset burning on the wall, illuminating the narrow stairs that wound down beneath her. It would have been dangerous, and difficult, to descend without light as there were no windows in the stairwell to let in the moonlight.

Reaching the floor below, she knocked on Kerr's door.

Silence followed, and her heart started to race. What was she doing knocking on his door in the middle of the night? The man would be sound asleep. Just because she couldn't settle, didn't mean she had to wake him as well.

Rose took a step back and was about to turn away and climb back up the stairwell when the door creaked open.

Kerr stood there, owl-eyed and dressed in a hastily donned lèine and leather trews. Holding a flickering lantern aloft, he blinked at her, his brow furrowing. "Rose … is something wrong?"

She shook her head, warmth sweeping over her. She suddenly felt even more foolish. "No," she murmured. "I couldn't sleep … that's all."

Their gazes held before Kerr's brow smoothed and his mouth lifted into a half-smile. He then raked a hand through his already mussed hair. "Would ye like to come in, lass?"

Rose nodded, swallowing. "Can I share yer bed tonight?" Her cheeks flamed hot as his smile slowly widened. "I mean … I don't wish to be alone … not after everything that's happened."

His expression sobered at these words. He shifted back then, allowing Rose to enter, before shutting the door behind her. "I understand," he said softly.

"Thank ye," she murmured, wishing she didn't feel quite so embarrassed. This was Kerr, after all, and they'd already been intimate. Yet she didn't feel herself tonight. And although she was having difficulty holding his eye now, she could already feel the restlessness within her settle just a little.

Scooting around the edge of the bed, she cast aside her shawl and climbed in, rearranging his pillows and making herself comfortable.

Then she glanced up to find Kerr still standing there, watching her, an odd look upon his face.

Rose stilled. "What?"

Perhaps she'd overstepped, and he didn't want her in here, after all.

"Nothing," he replied, shaking his head as if to clear it. He then walked around to the opposite side of the bed, took off his lèine, and climbed in, the bed ropes creaking under his weight, pulling the blankets over them.

"Aren't ye going to undress?" Rose asked, surprised that he was still wearing his trews.

"Best I don't, lass," he replied, a strained edge to his voice now. "Ye are still upset from today … it wouldn't be right."

Rose stiffened. She wanted to tell him that he didn't have to worry about such things. Nonetheless, he was being considerate, and she didn't want to embarrass him.

Moments passed before she asked. "Will ye still hold me though? I might be able to sleep then."

Kerr cleared his throat, "Of course."

Rose wriggled close, a sigh escaping her as she found him. She then snuggled against his chest, nestling her cheek into the hollow of his shoulder. In response, Kerr wrapped his arms around her.

They lay like that for a while as Rose slowly relaxed.

The smell of him, the heat and strength of his body against hers, was a balm. When Kerr held her in his arms, she felt as if nothing could touch her, as if everything was well and always would be.

But, after a while, as drowsiness started to tug her eyelids downward, she realized his body was tense. She might be about to drop off to sleep, yet he wasn't. His breathing had grown shallow.

"Kerr?" Rose murmured, running her hand over his chest to where his heart now thumped against her palm. "Is something amiss?"

He huffed a soft laugh. "Don't worry about me, lass … just get some sleep."

"Are ye not comfortable lying like this? Maybe we should roll on our sides and ye can put yer arms around me from behind."

He made a strangled noise at this.

Rose tensed. "What?"

"I think that'll make it worse."

"What worse?"

"This." Gently, he took her hand that lay upon his chest and moved it down, over his belly, to the hard bulge straining against his leather trews.

Rose gasped, excitement quickening in the cradle of her hips. "Oh," she said quietly. "I didn't realize."

He shifted her hand back to his chest. "Just ignore it ... it'll go away ... eventually."

Rose didn't reply. It was noble of him to suffer in silence, yet she didn't *want* to ignore it. Now that he'd made her aware of his arousal, the drowsiness disappeared, and in its place rose a keen awareness and hunger.

Wordlessly, she slid her hand back down the bed, trailing her fingers up the length of his erection, from the base to the tip.

"Rose," Kerr gasped, grabbing hold of her wrist. "What are ye doing?"

"What we both want," she replied firmly. "Can we have some light in here?"

Moments passed, and then Kerr murmured an oath under his breath. He released her wrist and rolled sideways. He then climbed out of bed and fumbled with the shuttered window. An instant later, he'd opened it, and silvery moonlight flooded the bedchamber.

It was surprisingly bright and frosted Kerr as he stood before the bed.

Rose rolled onto her knees and drew back the covers.

Her breathing quickened as her gaze feasted on the outline of his swollen member against the tight leather of his trews.

Then, without second-guessing her instinct, she reached down, grabbed the hem of her night-rail, and pulled it over her head so that she crouched naked before him.

Kerr's breathing hitched.

Rose scooted across the bed and perched on the edge, before reaching out and unlacing his trews, releasing his shaft from its leather prison.

A sigh gusted out of her at the sight of it, thick and proud, and bone hard. Its tip was swollen and wet, and need twisted low in her belly.

Lord, how she wanted him.

"Teach me how to touch ye," she whispered, tearing her gaze from his groin to his face.

Kerr was watching her with a sensual, hooded gaze, his chest rising and falling sharply now. "Are ye sure?"

"Aye."

"Then wrap yer fingers firmly around the base of my rod."

Swallowing, her mouth dry now, Rose did as bid. Hades, it was hot and hard, the skin silky.

"Now, slide yer hand up toward the tip, keeping yer grip firm."

Rose eagerly followed his instructions and was rewarded by a low groan. "Aye, good lass."

Wetness flooded between her thighs at the gravelly edge to his voice. She loved listening to him slowly unraveling, hearing him encourage her. He'd done the same when they'd lain together at Beltaine.

She continued to slide her hand up and down his shaft, feeling it grow larger and harder still under her grip.

"What else?" she breathed.

"Ye can kiss it, if ye like?"

Excitement twisted inside her. She'd been hoping he'd make such a suggestion. She slid from the bed to the floor, kneeling there before him. She then leaned down and brushed her lips over the slick crown of his shaft. And then, with a sigh, she took him into her mouth, letting him slide in deep until the tip hit the back of her throat.

Kerr's ragged groan rumbled through the chamber. "Sweet Jesu, Rose!"

His hands tangled in her hair then, holding her firm as she dragged her mouth up and down the length of him. He was too big to take in completely, and so she continued to work the base of his rod with her hand.

The sensitive flesh between her thighs ached now, desire twisting tighter with every groan she dragged from him, every gasp.

She was intent on bringing him over the edge, on making him spill in her mouth. However, Kerr prevented her. He pulled her up and lifted her onto the bed. Then, he spread her legs wide and shifted between them.

Panting, Rose gazed up at his face. His cheeks were flushed, his gaze hot. "It's my turn now," he growled.

31: A ROSE FOR A ROSE

KERR WAS FINDING it hard to keep himself leashed.

After Rose had just sucked his rod like that, he could barely think straight. All he knew was that he had to give her the same pleasure.

He ached for her.

Spread out naked underneath him, she was the most beautiful thing he'd ever seen—all soft curves and smooth skin in the moonlight. She watched him now, her gaze fever-bright with need, her magnificent breasts heaving.

Kerr would get to those breasts later, but first, he would taste something else.

Spreading her wider still, he slid his hands under her backside. He then lifted her hips. And when his mouth found her, he was rewarded by a soft, keening cry. Rose trembled against him as he stroked her with his tongue.

Reaching down, she tangled her fingers in his hair, as he'd done with her, urging him on. Her lustiness inflamed him, as did her scent, her taste. He devoured her, holding her fast until she shattered against his tongue.

Breathing hard, he lowered her to the bed, crawling up over her trembling body so he could capture her lips with his.

He'd known from the moment she'd slipped into his bed that he'd get no rest tonight. He hadn't planned on touching her, and indeed had decided he'd lie awake all night so long as she managed to get some sleep.

But then one thing had led to another—and now, here they were.

Mating her mouth with his, he stroked her breasts before cupping them in his hands and bringing them up so that he could lavish attention on each swollen tip.

She groaned his name softly as he tended her, her fingernails raking his back.

"Please, Kerr," she gasped finally. "I need ye … inside me … now!"

"Aye, lass," he replied, positioning his rod at her slick entrance. "I'll not make ye beg twice."

And with that, he slid deep into her, in one powerful thrust.

Rose's cry echoed through the chamber. They were making too much noise, and although this broch had thick walls, someone was sure to hear. Yet Kerr didn't care.

Let them hear. All that mattered to him right now was being buried to the hilt in this woman, losing himself in her. Bracing himself above her, and watching Rose's face all the while, Kerr rode her in deep, slow thrusts.

Sweat coated his skin now, his breathing ragged. It was almost too much for him. Her tightness and heat, and the fluttering against his rod as she reached her peak, almost undid him.

Gasping his name, Rose arched up against him, her body shuddering. He felt a gush of wetness inside her and pushed himself up, parting her thighs wider so he could plow her deeper still.

It was too much. His self-control snapped, and his release barreled into him.

Kerr's back snapped rigid, his head falling back as pleasure pulsed up through his body from his groin, and the world went dark for a few moments.

"Do ye think ye shall be able to sleep now?" The question was a cheeky one, yet Rose hadn't been able to resist it. In the aftermath of their loving, she and Kerr lay spooned together, her bottom nestled into his groin.

Kerr's laugh rumbled against her back. "Aye … like a bairn."

Rose smiled, her throat thickening at the depth of emotion she felt for this man. His touch. The sound of his voice. The way he made her feel both free and protected. He was all she needed in this world.

"Thank ye, Kerr," she whispered.

"What for?"

"For being *ye*." She swallowed as a lump lodged in her throat. What was wrong with her these days? She could hardly get through a sentence without wanting to weep. "I'm lucky indeed."

And she was, for she'd found a man who loved and protected her yet allowed her the freedom to be herself. They were sure to have their disagreements—for they could both be bullheaded at times—but she felt safe with him. Even after they were wed, she'd continue her work with Eara. Unlike her poor, downtrodden mother—who'd run after her menfolk until she was too ill to leave her bed—Rose would have a life of her own.

Kerr's hold on her tightened. His lips brushed against her ear as he whispered, "Ye are all I've ever wanted, Rose. I love ye with a fierceness that scares me."

"And I love ye," she whispered back. "I didn't think it was possible to feel so at one with the world."

It was true. Even though there were many things that gave her satisfaction, especially her work with Eara, she sometimes felt as if she was fighting with life. Yet, there wasn't any struggle now.

"Neither did I," he admitted, his mouth curving. "I thought I was destined to pine for ye for the rest of my days."

A soft hoot intruded then, and Rose twisted around to see a familiar outline sitting on the window ledge illuminated by the hoary light of the moon.

"Hazel," she gasped. "How did ye find me?"

The owl made a soft cooing noise in response.

"Well, that's settled then," Kerr said, amusement lacing his voice. "The owl has also come to live here along with its mistress."

Rose shifted, meeting Kerr's gaze. "Really? Ye won't confine her to the mews?"

He snorted. "Of course not ... Hazel is welcome to roost in here during the day."

A wry smile tugged at Rose's lips. "I warn ye, she makes a mess ... what with her feathers and the pellets she spits up."

Kerr winced. "Och, lass, don't make me regret it already."

"Ye won't," she assured him, leaning down and brushing her lips over his.

"Here, see if ye can slide this into her hair ... I've snipped off the thorns so it shouldn't draw blood."

Eara handed Bonnie the velvety red rose, one of a bunch she'd brought from her garden, before meeting Rose's eye. Her friend then winked. "A rose for a rose."

"Aye," Bonnie replied, threading the stalk into the elaborate coil of hair she'd piled onto the crown of Rose's head. "It's perfect ... look."

Smiling, Rose shifted her gaze right to where Bonnie now held up a looking glass. They sat in her wardrobe, a small chamber where Lady Mackay kept her clothing and jewelry.

The reflection that greeted Rose made her breathing catch.

She hardly recognized herself.

For years, she'd dressed in plain kirtles and pulled her hair back from her face so that it wouldn't annoy her while she worked. But this afternoon, she wore one of Bonnie's surcotes. They were of a similar build, although

Rose was a bit taller than the laird's wife, so they'd let down the gown's hem.

The surcote was a deep red, the same color as the rose in her hair, while underneath, she wore a sea-blue kirtle. She'd never realized she had a heart-shaped face before or that her skin was unblemished. Her eyes were large and the color of pine, fringed with dark lashes.

"I can't believe it," she breathed. "I look ..." Her voice trailed off as she struggled to find the right words.

"Beautiful," Eara finished the sentence for her. "Ye always have been ... it's just that ye haven't had a looking glass to view yerself in before."

Rose's throat thickened at these words, her vision misting. She'd never been pampered like this before or been the center of attention. It was almost overwhelming.

"Eara's right," Bonnie murmured. "Ye are lovely, and Kerr will swallow his tongue when he sees ye." Lady Mackay then moved over to a shelf, where she picked up a small clay bottle. "Now all that's needed is the right scent." She unstoppered the bottle and waved it under Rose's nose. "What do ye think?"

Rose inhaled the sweet, musky scent, sighing in pleasure. "It's wonderful ... what is it?"

"Damascus Rose," Bonnie replied with a grin. "Iver gave it to me for my birthday. Will ye wear it?"

Rose nodded, touched that Bonnie was being so generous with her clothing and perfume. "This is very kind of ye, My Lady," she murmured.

"Please, call me Bonnie ... it's only fitting since we are soon to be sisters."

Rose's pulse quickened. Downstairs in the hall, the others would be readying themselves for the wedding ceremony. True to his word, Kerr had sent out riders to pick up Kenna and Ailis, and they'd fetched Eara from the village.

Everyone Rose cared for would be present.

Favoring Bonnie with a warm smile in response, Rose then turned to Eara. Her friend watched her with bright eyes.

"I will never forget what ye did, Eara," she murmured. She hadn't thanked Eara properly the day before, yet she was determined to let her friend know just how much she appreciated her quick response. "Ever."

Eara snorted, even as her cheeks reddened. "Well, I could hardly stand by and let the rabble kill ye, could I?" Her face tightened then, and she swallowed convulsively. "In truth, I feel a terrible guilt, Rose, for I heard Father Gregor preaching to them all in the village square the day before. I told myself I'd go up to the broch in the morning and tell Lady Bonnie and ye about it … and I intended to." Her voice turned husky then, as she concluded. "But I was too late."

Rose stepped forward, taking her friend by the hands. "No, ye weren't."

Eara shook her head. "I should have rushed up to the broch, the moment I heard him speaking ill of ye … but instead, I was more concerned with getting my work done." Her friend's voice wobbled then. "I'm sorry."

"Don't apologize," Rose replied, squeezing Eara's hands tightly. "It changes nothing. Ye still saved my life."

"Aye, lass," Bonnie said, moving close and placing a reassuring hand on Eara's shoulder. "Don't take responsibility for the wrongdoings of others."

A soft knock on the door to the wardrobe intruded then. "Come in," Bonnie called.

The door cracked open, and a tall, broad-shouldered figure stood there. Rose was used to seeing Brodie Mackay dusted in soot, wearing his smith's apron and a sweat-soaked lèine. However, he'd clearly bathed and changed into his best clothing for this afternoon's ceremony.

His hair still curled against his scalp from his recent bath, and he wore a crisp white lèine and chamois braies tucked into polished boots.

His hazel gaze swept over the women before a smile tugged at the corners of his mouth. "Kerr's starting to get a little twitchy, Rose," he greeted her. "Ye had better present yerself downstairs before he thinks ye've changed yer mind."

Rose smiled back at him, even as nervousness tightened her stomach. This was real. She was about to become Kerr's wife.

"Aye, Brodie," she said, releasing Eara's hand and moving forward, taking the arm he offered. "Let's not keep him waiting any longer."

Rose's breathing caught as she stepped into the hall.

She'd been here a few times over the years, for audiences with the laird and the odd Yuletide celebration. Nonetheless, she'd never seen the hall look like this.

Despite the short notice, the women of Dun Ugadale had worked miracles, festooning the walls and rafters with garlands of roses. Banks of candles flickered along the walls, and the tables had been cleared away so that a crowd could gather.

All gazes swiveled to Rose. Among the crowd, she spied Kenna and Ailis. They both grinned at her. Rose tried to smile back, yet she suddenly felt uncertain under so many stares. Memories of what she'd suffered the day before resurfaced, and her step faltered.

"I have ye, lass," Brodie murmured. "Just keep walking."

The smith's solid presence at her side settled Rose's nerves, and she nodded. She appreciated that, without her needing to explain anything, he understood. His perception surprised her.

"Just keep yer eyes on Kerr," Brodie advised her then. "He's all that matters now."

Rose nodded once more, her gaze sliding past where Iver Mackay stood resplendent in his clan sash upon the dais as he waited to perform the ceremony, to where Kerr waited at the foot of the platform.

The breath she hadn't even realized she'd been holding rushed out of her.

Dressed in a black velvet lèine and leather trews, his white-blond hair brushing his collar, he was so handsome it made her chest ache.

And he was hers.

Their gazes fused, the stare drawing out as, around them, the hall hushed.

Suddenly, the busy hall disappeared, along with Rose's nerves. Brodie was right. This was their day. Nothing else mattered.

He favored her with a slow smile then, one that made her heart start to kick against her ribs. Moving forward at Brodie's side, she started across the floor, through the crowd that parted for her, toward her husband-to-be.

Toward her future.

EPILOGUE: EVERYTHING I'VE EVER WANTED

A month later ...

"I'M WITH BAIRN."

Bonnie's announcement brought Rose to her feet with a shriek. "I knew it!"

For the past couple of weeks, Bonnie had been complaining of feeling a little off-color, and when she'd thrown up her bannock the morning before, Iver insisted they paid the healer in Ceann Locha a visit.

The laird and his wife set off early that morning and had only just returned.

It was now mid-afternoon, and Rose had been ensconced in the ladies' solar with her mother-by-marriage, working her way through a pile of mending, when Bonnie rushed in. As usual, she'd worked alongside the alewife in the morning, yet there was always plenty in the broch to keep her occupied later in the day.

Bonnie's cheeks were flushed, her blue eyes bright with joy.

Rose knew how much this meant to her. Iver and Bonnie had been wed a year and a half now, and her womb hadn't quickened. Bonnie had confided in her that she worried there was something amiss.

But now, her fears had been allayed.

"How far along are ye?" Sheena asked, rising to her feet. Unlike Bonnie, their mother-by-marriage managed to contain her excitement.

"The healer thinks at least two moons."

"Didn't ye notice yer courses had stopped?"

"Aye, but they have never been regular … and so I thought little of it."

"What wonderful news," Rose said, approaching Bonnie and enfolding her in a hug. "I'm so happy for ye both."

"Iver is overjoyed," Bonnie admitted, her eyes shining. "We both are."

"He'll be eager for a son," Sheena replied, moving forward, and favoring Bonnie with the stiffest hug Rose had ever seen.

"He'll be equally happy with a daughter too," Bonnie corrected her gently.

Rose's mouth quirked. Sheena Mackay was as prickly as a thistle, yet Bonnie handled her with grace.

Rose wished she had the same patience. However, there had been a few times over the past weeks when she'd 'had words' with her mother-by-marriage. Sheena didn't dare make comments about Rose's father and brothers. Instead, she found fault with most things Rose did. Her stitches weren't neat enough, she didn't pour wine properly, or speak to the servants with the right gravitas.

Finally, Rose had lost her patience and told the woman that she didn't need her opinion or advice on such things. Sheena hadn't appreciated her response, yet Rose's tone had been sharp enough to warn her from continuing. Ever since then, relations between them had been cool, yet much politer.

"I must tell Davina!" Bonnie exclaimed, running her hands over her midriff, which still bore no sign of the bairn she carried.

"Aye, and ye'll get the chance," Sheena replied, her mouth lifting at the corners just a fraction. "Have ye forgotten she and Lennox arrive tomorrow?"

"Of course ... with all the excitement of getting things ready for Greer's arrival, I forgot," Bonnie replied, shaking her head. "I must calm myself or Davina will start fussing over me the moment she arrives." She then glanced over at Rose, smiling. "I don't know what I'd have done without yer help."

"Aye, well, the broch has never looked finer," Rose replied. Indeed, they'd scrubbed the floors and walls, put down fresh rushes in the hall, and redecorated Davina's old chamber for their guest.

"It doesn't matter how ye dress this place up," Sheena said, returning to her window seat and picking up her sewing. "A clan-chief's daughter will find this broch shabby indeed compared to the finery of Druminnor Castle."

That was the wrong thing to say, for Bonnie's face fell, her gaze shadowing. "Do ye think so?" she asked, her voice faltering.

Sheena's reaction reminded Rose that, like her, Bonnie didn't hail from this world. It didn't matter much to Rose, for she was wedded to the third-born Mackay son. It was unlikely that Kerr would ever rule the Mackays of Dun Ugadale. But Bonnie's position as the laird's wife meant that she was constantly navigating uncharted waters.

Rose didn't miss the gleam of satisfaction in Sheena's eyes now. Bonnie's insecurity gave her back the reins of control.

"That's not to say she won't find it charming," Sheena said lightly, making a deft, neat stitch with her needle and thread, "I, for one, can't understand why she even agreed to spend the summer here."

"Greer was fascinated by my tales of Dun Ugadale," Bonnie answered. Her smile was gone now. She appeared a little subdued. "And she was delighted when I suggested she stay with us."

Sheena pulled a face, while Rose frowned. She wasn't about to let their mother-by-marriage ruin this for Bonnie.

"Ye read out her last letter to me, Bonnie, if ye recall?" she said, stepping forward and placing a hand on her sister-by-marriage's arm. "She seemed beside herself with excitement to be spending the summer on the Kintyre Peninsula. Her missive was warm ... she doesn't appear to be the sort to pass judgment." Rose paused then. "Besides, Dun Ugadale is an impressive broch ... and now that the south walls are mended, ye should be proud to show it off."

She could almost feel Sheena's glower upon her, yet she ignored it.

Let the woman skewer her with her stare. She wouldn't allow her to upset Bonnie. Their special guest was due to arrive either late that afternoon or the following morning at the latest.

"Greer will be pleased to hear yer news too," Rose added. She cut a glance at Sheena, who was viewing her, mouth pursed. "We shall *all* start sewing clothes for the bairn."

The afternoon was drawing out, the shadows lengthening and the sunlight turning golden, when Rose made her way out to the barmkin. Kerr would soon be finishing for the day, and she was eager to see him.

"Go on, Brodie. Let's see if ye can hit the bullseye!"

Emerging from the broch, her gaze alighted upon the group of men gathered at one end of the space. Kerr was among them, and they were watching Brodie throw knives at a board a few yards distant.

Rose halted on the steps a moment, watching as her brother-by-marriage launched knife after knife from the belt at his waist.

Thud. Thud. Thud.

They hit the target's inner ring—but not dead-center.

Brodie halted then, arching a dark eyebrow at his brother. "Yer turn."

Kerr nodded. He stepped up, taking the knife belt from Brodie and strapping it around his hips. He then walked forward and pulled the five knives his brother had thrown free of the wooden target.

"Two silver pennies if ye hit the bullseye, Captain!" One of the men called out.

"Aye, Brodie didn't quite manage it … but can ye?" another quipped.

Brodie cast a dark look at the warrior, who abruptly stopped sniggering.

"Two pennies it is," Kerr replied, his expression inscrutable. "That should buy my fair wife some more of that rose-scented soap she loves so much."

Rose smiled. Aye, the soap had been quite a discovery—quite unlike the coarse blocks she'd used all her life. She was fortunate indeed, for Kerr often surprised her with gifts.

"Go on then," Brodie said grumpily, folding his brawny arms across his chest, his dark brows drawing together. "Show us all how it's done."

Kerr stepped up to the spot where his brother had thrown his knives, his gaze narrowing as he focused on the target.

Rose continued to watch with interest. The throwing knives looked deadly: twelve-inch blades with slender wooden handles.

Kerr positioned himself carefully, with one leg before the other, his weight resting on the leg opposite his throwing arm. Sighting the target, he then brought the blade back behind his shoulder. Rose held her breath as he swung his arm in an arc and let the knife fly easily from his hand. It completed two full spins before thudding into the target.

He threw each of the five knives in quick succession, each landing on the inner ring of the target. And the last one he threw hit dead-center.

Rose's breath gusted out of her, a grin flowering across her face. She'd had no idea Kerr was so good at knife throwing, although after watching Brodie, *he* wasn't lacking in skill either.

"Well done," she called out, clapping.

All the men turned, surprise rippling across their faces. They hadn't realized they had an audience.

Kerr smiled back, his eyes crinkling at the corners. He then bowed to her. "Thank ye, my love." Straightening up, her husband held out his hand to the warrior he'd made the bet with. "That'll be two silver pennies, Ceard."

"I didn't think ye'd be as good at that as Brodie, Captain," the man muttered as he dug into the coin purse on his belt. "Have ye been practicing in secret?"

Kerr's smile widened. It warmed Rose to see the expression. In the past, he'd always been so serious—a man who seemed to carry the weight of the world upon his shoulders—but since they'd been together, Kerr smiled far more readily. "No, it was just a timely shot." He then winked at Brodie, who snorted.

"Aye, just timely," the smith replied.

"Well ... that's it for the day, lads," Kerr said then, retrieving the knives and sliding them back into the belt. He then unbuckled it, handing the belt to Ceard. "Ye'd all better wash up for supper."

The warriors moved to comply, and Brodie walked back to his forge. Meanwhile, Kerr approached Rose.

"Did ye hear the news about Bonnie?" she greeted him.

"Aye," he replied, stopping before her, and leaning in for a soft yet lingering kiss. When he drew back, he was smiling. "Iver has been grinning like a fool all afternoon."

"I hope that I too will soon make ye that happy," she murmured, placing her hands upon his chest. He wore a sleeveless leather vest, although she could feel the warmth of his skin through it. The day had been still and hot, the warmest of summer so far.

"Ye already do," he replied, his gaze softening. "Bairns would be nice, aye ... but I already have everything I've ever wanted."

Rose leaned into him, favoring him with a lingering kiss, before she whispered. "Tha gaol agam ort, Kerr."

And she did love him. Wholeheartedly. Passionately. Life at Dun Ugadale hadn't been without its challenges. She missed her aunt and Ailis's company at times, and Sheena could be wearying, but she wouldn't give this up for anything.

Every morning when she woke up in Kerr's arms, she felt blessed.

He smiled down at her. "I never tire of hearing ye say that, mo chridhe," he murmured.

"Captain!" A shout from above interrupted them. "We've got visitors!"

Rose stepped back from her husband, her gaze traveling across to the open gate and raised portcullis. Moments later, she heard the clatter of approaching hoofbeats. "It must be Greer Forbes," she said. "Bonnie said she was due here at any time."

"Can ye see their plaid?" Kerr called up to the guard.

"Aye, dark green and black."

Kerr turned back to Rose. "Sounds like the Forbeses to me." He reached out and put his arm around her shoulders then, and they moved out into the center of the barmkin. "Come, wife ... let's give them a warm Mackay welcome."

The End

HISTORICAL NOTES

This story was set almost exclusively around Dun Ugadale—but that doesn't mean I didn't need to do a lot of research for it. I went down quite a few research rabbit holes for this one. My recent trip to Scotland gave me so many juicy ideas I just had to include in this book. Get ready for details about brigands, cattle rustlers, and witches!

Of course, the novel's location is a real one. The stronghold of Dun Ugadale is an iron age fort on the promontory near Ugadale on the Kintyre peninsula. Although it's now a ruin, the fort was owned by the Mackays from the 14th century and was passed through marriage in the 17th century to the MacNiels.

The conflict with the Douglas outlaws is a continuation of the real historical incident when King James II murdered William Douglas. During a meeting at Stirling castle, the earl refused to break his alliance with two powerful Highland clan-chiefs. An argument ensued, which ended with the king stabbing him to death and throwing his body out the window. Afterward, the Douglas clan marched on Stirling with the letters of safe conduct pinned to a horse's tail and disavowed their oath to James.

The months of conflict that followed (the time in which this novel takes place) were tantamount to civil war. James II kept hold of the crown and the Stewart dynasty would continue. In the aftermath of William's murder, James set out to remove the Douglas's power from Scotland, resulting in the family's ultimate destruction in 1455.

The Black Wolves are entirely fictional, although there would likely have been a number of displaced Douglases in Scotland at this time. What's to say that some of them didn't turn rogue?

This novel deals with the persecution of witches (or more appropriately, of women suspected of being witches).

Unfortunately, many of the things I described weren't just creative license on my part. Scotland has a bloody history when it comes to witch hunts. From the mid-16th to the early 18th century, nearly 4,000 people in Scotland—most of them women—were tried for witchcraft. Up to two-thirds of this number may have been executed. Per capita, during the period between the 16th and 18th centuries, the Scots executed five times as many people as elsewhere in Europe.

The Scottish witch craze began in earnest in 1590, with the trial of a group of people, mainly women, from East Lothian. They were accused of meeting with the Devil and conjuring up storms to destroy James VI on his return from Denmark with his bride, Anne.

My novel takes place over a century earlier. However, there would have been a steady increase in incidents before the craze kicked off, and a growing intolerance for women who were different.

It was no coincidence either that I have Rose's friend Eara as a brewer of ale in this novel. Did you know that broomsticks, cauldrons, black cats, and pointed black hats were often associated with 'alewives'? This was the name for women who brewed weak beer to combat poor water quality. The broomstick sign was to let people know beer was on sale, the cauldron to brew it, the cat to keep mice down, and the hat to distinguish them at market. Women were ejected from brewing and replaced by men once it became a profitable industry.

Women like Eara would have likely been targeted by witch hunters later in history. However, in my story, the craze hadn't yet started.

Father Gregor's preaching wasn't unusual in those times. Indeed, people were told to look out for women with red hair and green eyes, and if they had a 'consort' (a pet cat or bird was enough) they fell under even greater suspicion. Inquisition usually consisted of tying the woman's wrists and ankles together and throwing her into water. If she floated (which she often did thanks to the voluminous skirts women wore in those days) rather than sank, she was taken from the water and burned at the stake.

It was a grim chapter of Scottish history, yet one that's important never to forget.

The 'Lost Valley' I included in this novel comes from history as well. The real Lost Valley (Coire Gabhail) I was inspired by is in Glencoe. Coire Gabhail is the hidden valley where the MacDonalds of Glencoe hid their rustled cattle. It's also where the few who survived the brutal massacre in 1692 managed to hide.

Cattle rustling also features in this novel—a real problem at the time. I discovered Rob Roy MacGregor used to steal cattle from farmers taking their herds to market before selling them off at another market a day or two later. This gave me the idea for Rose's father's plan. Unfortunately for Graham MacAlister, everything goes awry.

I was inspired for both the cattle rustling and the outlaw problems in my novel by the 'Wild MacGregors'. For centuries, these cattle rustlers and brigands were the plague of the Trossachs in Scotland. The Wild MacGregors earned their name and living through 'cattle lifting' and extracting money from people in exchange for offering them protection from thieves.

I mention Goatweed as a remedy in the novel. This was an old name for St John's Wort.

Hazel the eagle owl is real too. I met her in Edinburgh on the Royal Mile just a month before writing this novel. She was a magnificent bird, and I had to include her in this story (thanks to reader Kathy Tatum, for suggesting I did!).

Due to its large eyes and plumes that look like horns, there are many old legends and myths in which the eagle owl has been described as 'demonic', or 'the devil's helper'—a fact which is very apt for the book!

So, there you have it—a tapestry of inspirations and historical details that I have woven into this book. I hope you enjoyed it!

REBELLIOUS HIGHLAND HEARTS CHARACTER GLOSSARY

Main characters

Kerr Mackay (Captain of the Dun Ugadale Guard)
Rose MacAlister (A farmer's daughter)

Other characters

Bonnie Mackay (Iver's wife)
Brodie Mackay (blacksmith at Dun Ugadale)
Captain Fergus Stewart (Captain of the king's men)
Clyde and Knox MacAlister (Graham MacAllister's sons)
Colin Campbell (the Lord of Glenorchy)
Cory (cook at Dun Ugadale)
Davina Campbell (Lennox's wife)
Duncan MacDonald (farmer)
Eara Mackay (brewer of ale)
Evan, Athol, Rae, Lorcan, Ronan, Tavish, Murtagh, and Coby (Dun Ugadale guards)
Father Gregor (priest at Dun Ugadale)
Graham MacAlister (farmer at Dun Ugadale)
Iver Mackay (Mackay chieftain—laird of Dun Ugadale)
Kyle MacAlister (bailiff at Dun Ugadale)
Lennox Mackay (guard at Dun Ugadale)
Sheena Mackay (mother to Iver, Lennox, and Kerr)

DIVE INTO MY BACKLIST!

Check out my printable reading order list on my website: https://www.jaynecastel.com/printable-reading-list

ABOUT THE AUTHOR

Multi-award-winning author Jayne Castel writes epic Historical and Fantasy Romance. Her vibrant characters, richly researched historical settings, and action-packed adventure romance transport readers to forgotten times and imaginary worlds.

Jayne is the author of a number of best-selling series. In love with all things Scottish, she writes romances set in both Dark Ages and Medieval Scotland.

When she's not writing, Jayne is reading (and re-reading) her favorite authors, cooking Italian feasts, and going on long walks with her husband. She lives in New Zealand's beautiful South Island.

Connect with Jayne online:
www.jaynecastel.com
www.facebook.com/JayneCastelRomance
https://www.instagram.com/jaynecastelauthor/
Email: contact@jaynecastel.com